Praise for

HIDDEN
PICTURES

**The International Bestseller Translated into
Twenty-Five Languages**

Winner of a 2022 Goodreads Choice Award

"Part ghost story, part social-inequality satire [with] genuine
paper jump scares."
—*The Guardian*

"I read *Hidden Pictures* and loved it. The language is straightforward,
the surprises really surprise, and it has that hard-to-achieve
propulsiveness that won't let you put it down. And the pictures are
terrific!"
—**Stephen King**

"Truly fantastic."
—*The Times*

"Mr. Rekulak has a freakishly fertile imagination."
—*The New York Times*

"Memorable [and] twisty . . . A novel that seems designed to be
read at the side of a pool with a drink in your hand and a smile
on your face."
—*Esquire*

"A gripping supernatural thriller . . . Rekulak [holds] a mirror
up to white, affluent Gen X and [asks] pointed questions about
class, trauma, and horror conventions."
—*Publishers Weekly*

"The explosive third act gives this story a nail-biting ending
sure to thrill. Paranormal perfection."
—*Booklist*

**This paperback edition includes "The Art of Hidden Pictures," an
interview featuring twenty never-before-published illustrations!**

ALSO BY JASON REKULAK

The Impossible Fortress

HIDDEN PICTURES

JASON REKULAK

Illustrations by Will Staehle and Doogie Horner

SPHERE

SPHERE

First published in the US in 2022 by Flatiron Books,
an imprint of Macmillan Publishers
This edition published in Great Britain in 2023 by Sphere

1 3 5 7 9 10 8 6 4 2

A CIP catalogue record for this book
is available from the British Library.

ISBN 978-0-7515-8370-0

Printed and bound in Great Britain by
Clays Ltd, Elcograf S.p.A.

Papers used by Sphere are from well-managed forests
and other responsible sources.

Sphere
An imprint of
Little, Brown Book Group
Carmelite House
50 Victoria Embankment
London EC4Y 0DZ

An Hachette UK Company
www.hachette.co.uk

www.littlebrown.co.uk

FOR JULIE

HIDDEN PICTURES

1

A few years back I was running out of money so I volunteered for a research study at the University of Pennsylvania. The directions brought me to the campus medical center in West Philly and a large auditorium filled with women, all between eighteen and thirty-five years old. There weren't enough chairs and I was among the last to arrive so I had to sit shivering on the floor. They had free coffee and chocolate donuts and a big TV playing *The Price Is Right*, but most everyone was looking at their phones. The vibe was a lot like the DMV except we were all getting paid by the hour so people seemed happy to wait all day.

A doctor in a white lab coat got up and introduced herself. She said her name was Susan or Stacey or Samantha and she was a fellow in the Clinical Research program. She read all the usual disclaimers and warnings, and reminded us that compensation would be issued in the form of Amazon gift cards, not checks or cash. A couple people grumbled, but I didn't care; I had a boyfriend who bought gift cards off me for eighty cents on the dollar, so I was all set.

Every few minutes, Susan (I think it was Susan?) called a name from her clipboard and one of us would leave the room. No one ever came back. Pretty soon there were plenty of open seats, but I stayed on the floor because I didn't think I could move without throwing up. My body ached and I had the chills. But eventually word got around that they weren't prescreening people—which is to say, no one was going to test my urine or take my pulse or do anything that might disqualify me—so I popped a 40 in my mouth and sucked until the waxy yellow coating came off. Then I spat it back in my palm, crushed it between my thumbs, and snuffed like maybe a third of it. Just enough to get me back on. The rest went into a tiny piece of foil for later. And after that I stopped shaking, and waiting on the floor wasn't so bad.

Some two hours later the doctor finally called "Quinn? Mallory Quinn?" and I walked down the aisle to meet her, dragging my heavy winter parka on the floor behind me. If she noticed I was high, she didn't say anything. She just asked for my age (nineteen) and my date of birth (March 3), and then she compared my answers to the information on her clipboard. And I guess she decided I was sober enough, because she led me through a maze of hallways until we arrived at a small windowless room.

There were five young men seated in a row of folding chairs; they were all staring at the floor, so I couldn't see their faces. But I decided they were med students or residents—they all wore hospital scrubs, still creased and bright navy blue, like they were fresh off the rack.

"All right, Mallory, we'd like you to stand at the front of the room, facing the guys. Right here on the X, that's perfect. Now let me tell you what's going to happen, before we put on your blindfold." And I realized she was holding a black eye mask—the sort of soft cotton visor that my mother used to wear at bedtime.

She explained that all the men were currently looking at the floor—but sometime in the next few minutes, they were going to look at my body. My job was to raise my hand if I felt "the male gaze" on my person. She told me to keep my hand suspended for as long as the feeling lasted, and lower it whenever the feeling went away.

"We'll do it for five minutes, but after we finish we might want you to repeat the experiment. Do you have any questions before we start?"

I started laughing. "Yeah, have you guys read *Fifty Shades of Grey*? Because I'm pretty sure this is chapter twelve."

This was my attempt at a little light humor, and Susan smiled to be polite but none of the guys were paying attention. They were futzing with their clipboards and synchronizing their stopwatches. The mood in the classroom was all business. Susan fitted the mask over my eyes, then adjusted the strap so it wasn't too tight. "All right, Mallory, does that feel okay?"

"Sure."

"And you're ready to begin?"

"Yes."

"Then we'll start on my count of three. Gentlemen, get your watches ready. That's one, two, three."

It's very weird, standing still for five minutes, blindfolded, in a perfectly silent room, knowing that guys might be looking at your boobs or your butt or whatever. There were no sounds or clues to help me guess what was happening. But I definitely felt them watching. I raised and lowered my hand several times, and the five minutes seemed to last an hour. After we finished, Susan asked me to repeat the experiment, and we did it all over again. Then she asked me to repeat the experiment a third time! And when she finally pulled off the blindfold, all the guys stood up and started clapping, like I'd just won an Academy Award.

Susan explained that they'd been performing the experiment all week on hundreds of women—but I was the first person to deliver a near-perfect score, to report the gaze three times with 97 percent accuracy.

She told the guys to take a break and then ushered me into her office and started asking questions. Namely, how did I know the men were staring at me? And I didn't have the words to explain—I just knew. It was like a fluttery feeling on the periphery of my attention—a kind of spidey sense. I bet there's a good chance you've felt it yourself, that you know exactly what I'm talking about.

"Plus, there's a kind of sound."

Her eyes went wide. "Really? You *hear* something?"

"Sometimes. It's very high-pitched. Like when a mosquito buzzes too close to your ear."

She reached for her laptop so fast she nearly dropped it. She typed a bunch of notes, then asked if I'd be willing to come back in a week for more tests. I said for twenty bucks an hour, I would come back as much as she wanted. I gave her my cell phone number and she promised to call me to set up an appointment—but that very night, I traded my iPhone for five Oxy-80s, so she had no way of tracking me down, and I never heard from her again.

Now that I'm clean, I have a million regrets—and trading away my iPhone is the least of them. But sometimes I'll remember the experiment and I'll start to wonder. I've tried to find the doctor online but obviously I don't even remember her name. One morning I took the bus to the university medical center and tried to find the auditorium, but the campus is all different now; there are a bunch of new buildings and everything's scrambled. I've tried googling phrases like "gaze detection" and "gaze perception" but every result says these aren't real phenomena—there's no evidence that anyone has "eyes in the back of their head."

And I guess I've resigned myself to the fact that the experiment didn't actually happen, that it's one of the many false memories I acquired while abusing oxycodone, heroin, and other drugs. My sponsor, Russell, says false memories are common among addicts. He says an addict's brain will "remember" happy fantasies so we can avoid dwelling on real memories—all the shameful things we did to get high, all the shitty ways we hurt good people who loved us.

"Just listen to the details of your story," Russell points out. "You arrive on the campus of a prestigious Ivy League university. You're strung out on kickers and no one cares. You enter a room full of handsome young doctors. Then they stare at your body for fifteen minutes and erupt in a standing ovation! I mean, come on, Quinn! You don't have to be Sigmund Freud to figure this out!"

And he's right, obviously. One of the hardest things about recovery is coming to terms with the fact that you can't trust your brain anymore. In fact, you need to understand that your brain has become your own worst enemy. It will steer you toward bad choices, override logic and common sense, and warp your most cherished memories into impossible fantasies.

But here are some absolute truths:

My name is Mallory Quinn and I am twenty-one years old.

I've been in recovery for eighteen months, and I can honestly say I have no desire to use alcohol or drugs.

I have worked the Twelve Steps and I have surrendered my life to my lord and savior Jesus Christ. You won't see me on street corners handing out Bibles, but I do pray every day that He will help me stay sober, and so far it's working.

I live in northeast Philadelphia at Safe Harbor, a city-sponsored home for women in advanced stages of recovery. We call it a "three-quarters house" instead of a halfway house because we've all proven our sobriety and earned a lot of personal freedoms. We buy our own groceries, cook our own meals, and don't have a lot of annoying rules.

Mondays through Fridays, I'm a teacher's aide at Aunt Becky's Childcare Academy, a mouse-infested rowhome with sixty young scholars ages two to five. I spend a good part of my life changing diapers, dishing out Goldfish crackers, and playing *Sesame Street* DVDs.

After work I'll go for a run and then attend a meeting, or I'll just stay in Safe Harbor with my housemates and we'll all watch Hallmark Channel movies like *Sailing into Love* or *Forever in My Heart*. Laugh if you want, but I guarantee you will never turn on a Hallmark Channel movie and see a prostitute snorting lines of white powder. Because I don't need those images taking up space in my brain.

Russell agreed to sponsor me because I used to be a distance runner and he has a long history of training sprinters. Russell was an assistant coach on Team USA at the 1988 Summer Olympics. Later he led teams at Arkansas and Stanford to NCAA track and field championships. And later still he drove over his next-door neighbor while blitzed on methamphetamine. Russell served five years for involuntary manslaughter and later became an ordained minister. Now he sponsors five or six addicts at a time, most of them washed-up athletes like myself.

Russell inspired me to start training again (he calls it "running to recovery") and every week he drafts customized workouts for me, alternating long runs and wind sprints along the Schuylkill River with weights and conditioning at the YMCA. Russell is sixty-eight years old with an artificial hip but he still benches two hundred pounds and on weekends he'll show up to train alongside me, offering pointers and cheering me on. He's forever reminding me that women runners don't peak until age thirty-five, that my best years are way ahead of me.

He also encourages me to plan for my future—to make a fresh start in a new environment, far away from old friends and old habits. Which is why he's arranged a job interview for me with Ted and Caroline Maxwell—friends of his sister who have recently moved to Spring Brook, New Jersey. They're looking for a nanny to watch their five-year-old son, Teddy.

"They just moved back from Barcelona. The dad works in computers. Or business? Something that pays good, I forget the details. Anyhow, they moved here so Teddy—the kid, not the dad—can start school in the fall. Kindergarten. So they want you to stay through September. But if things work out? Who knows? Maybe they keep you around."

Russell insists on driving me to the interview. He's one of these guys who's always dressed for the gym, even when he's not working out. Today he's wearing a black Adidas tracksuit with white racing stripes. We're in his SUV, driving over the Ben Franklin Bridge in the left lane, passing traffic, and I'm clutching the oh-shit handle and staring at my lap, trying not to freak out. I'm not very good in cars. I travel everywhere by bus and subway, and this is my first time leaving Philadelphia in nearly a year. We're traveling only ten miles into the suburbs but it feels like I'm blasting off to Mars.

"What's wrong?" Russell asks.

"Nothing."

"You're tense, Quinn. Relax."

But how can I relax when there's this enormous BoltBus passing us on the right? It's like the *Titanic* on wheels, so close I could reach out my window and touch it. I wait until the bus passes and I can talk without shouting.

"What about the mom?"

"Caroline Maxwell. She's a doctor at the VA hospital. Where my sister Jeannie works. That's how I got her name."

"How much does she know about me?"

He shrugs. "She knows you've been clean for eighteen months. She knows you have my highest professional recommendation."

"That's not what I mean."

"Don't worry. I told her your whole story and she's excited to meet you." I must look skeptical because Russell keeps pushing: "This woman works with addicts for a living. And her patients are military veterans, I'm talking Navy SEALs, real f'd-up Afghan war trauma. Don't take this the wrong way, Quinn, but compared to them your history ain't that scary."

Some asshole in a Jeep throws a plastic bag out his window and there's no room to swerve so we hit the bag at sixty miles an hour and there's a loud *POP!* of breaking glass. It sounds like a bomb exploding. Russell just reaches for the AC and pushes it two clicks cooler. I stare down at my lap until I hear the engine slowing down, until I feel the gentle curve of the exit ramp.

Spring Brook is one of these small South Jersey hamlets that have been around since the American Revolution. It's full of old Colonial- and Victorian-style houses with U.S. flags hanging from the front porches. The streets are paved smooth and the sidewalks are immaculate. There's not a speck of trash anywhere.

We stop at a traffic light and Russell lowers our windows.

"You hear that?" he asks.

"I don't hear anything."

"Exactly. It's peaceful. This is perfect for you."

The light turns green and we enter a three-block stretch of shops and restaurants—a Thai place, a smoothie shop, a vegan bakery, a doggie day care, and a yoga studio. There's an after-school "Math Gymnasium" and a small bookstore/café. And of course there's a Starbucks with a hundred teens and tweens out front, all of them pecking at their iPhones. They look like the kids in a Target commercial; their clothes are colorful and their footwear is brand-new.

Then Russell turns onto a side street and we pass one perfect suburban house after another. There are tall, stately trees that shade the sidewalks and fill the block with color. There are signs with big letters saying CHILDREN LIVE HERE—SLOW DOWN! and when we arrive at a four-way intersection, there's a smiling crossing guard in a neon safety vest, waving us through. Everything is so perfectly detailed, it feels like we're driving through a movie set.

At last Russell pulls over to the side of the road, stopping in the shade of a weeping willow. "All right, Quinn, are you ready?"

"I don't know."

I pull down the visor and check my reflection. At Russell's suggestion, I've dressed like a summer camp counselor, with a green crewneck, khaki shorts, and immaculate white Keds. I used to have long hair that fell to my waist but yesterday I lopped off my ponytail and donated it to a cancer charity. All that's left is a sporty black bob, and I don't recognize myself anymore.

"Here's two pieces of free advice," Russell says. "First, make sure you say the kid is gifted."

"How can I tell?"

"It doesn't matter. In this town, all the kids are gifted. Just find some way to work it into the conversation."

"All right. What's the other advice?"

"Well, if the interview's going badly? Or if you think they're on the fence? You can always offer this."

He opens his glove box and shows me something that I really don't want to carry inside their house.

"Oh, Russell, I don't know."

"Take it, Quinn. Think of it like a trump card. You don't have to play it, but you might need to."

And I've heard enough horror stories in rehab to know he's probably right. I take the stupid thing and shove it deep down into my bag.

"Fine," I tell him. "Thanks for driving me over."

"Listen, I'll go wait at the Starbucks. Give me a call when you're done, and I'll drive you back."

I insist that I'm fine, I tell him I can take the train back to Philly, and I urge Russell to drive home now before the traffic gets any worse.

"All right, but call me when you're finished," he says. "I want to hear all the details, okay?"

2

Outside the car, it's a hot muggy June afternoon. Russell toots the horn as he drives away and I guess there's no turning back now. The Maxwell house is a big classic Victorian, three stories high, with yellow wood siding and white gingerbread trim. There's a big wraparound porch with wicker furniture and planters full of yellow flowers—daisies and begonias. The property backs up to a large forest—or maybe some kind of park?—so the street is full of birdsongs, and I can hear the insects buzzing and chirping and trilling.

I walk up the flagstone path and climb the steps to the front porch. I ring the doorbell, and a little boy answers. He has orange-reddish hair that's sticking straight up. He reminds me of a Troll doll.

I squat down so we're seeing eye to eye.

"I bet your name is Teddy."

The boy gives me a shy smile.

"I'm Mallory Quinn. Is your—"

He turns and sprints up the stairs to the second floor, vanishing from sight.

"Teddy?"

I'm not sure what to do. Ahead of me is a small foyer and a passage leading back to a kitchen. I see a dining room (to the left) and a living room (to the right) and gorgeous hard pine floors (everywhere). I'm struck by the fresh clean scent of central air-conditioning—mixed with a hint of Murphy Oil, as if someone has just given the floors a good scrubbing. All the furniture looks modern and brand-new, like it's just arrived from the Crate and Barrel showroom.

I press the doorbell but it doesn't make a sound. I press it three more times—nothing.

"Hello?"

At the far end of the house, in the kitchen, I see the silhouette of a woman turning to notice me.

"Mallory? Is that you?"

"Yes! Hi! I tried your doorbell but—"

"I know, sorry. We're getting it fixed."

Before I can even wonder how Teddy knew I'd arrived, she's stepping forward to welcome me. She has the most graceful walk I've ever seen—she moves soundlessly, like her feet are barely touching the floor. She's tall, thin, and blond, with fair skin and soft features that seem too delicate for this world.

"I'm Caroline."

I put out my hand but she greets me with a hug. She's one of those people who radiate warmth and compassion, and she holds me an extra moment longer than necessary.

"I'm so glad you're here. Russell's told us so many wonderful things. Are you really eighteen months clean?"

"Eighteen and a half."

"Incredible. After everything you've been through? That is just extraordinary. You should be really proud of yourself."

And I worry I might start to cry because I wasn't expecting her to ask about recovery right away, first thing, before I've even stepped inside her house. But it's a relief to get it over with, to just put all my worst cards on the table.

"It wasn't easy, but it's easier every day."

"That's exactly what I tell my patients." She steps back, reviews me from head to toe, and smiles. "And look at you now! You're so healthy, you're glowing!"

Inside the house, it's a crisp pleasant sixty-eight degrees—a welcome retreat from the muggy weather. I follow Caroline past the staircase and underneath the second-floor landing. Her kitchen is full of natural light and looks like a cooking show set on the Food Network. There's a large refrigerator and a small refrigerator and the gas range has eight burners. The sink is a kind of trough, wide enough to require two separate faucets. And there are dozens of drawers and cabinets, all different shapes and sizes.

Caroline opens a tiny door and I realize this is a third refrigerator, a miniature one, stocked with cold drinks. "Let's see, we've got seltzer, coconut water, iced tea . . ."

"I'd love a seltzer." I turn to marvel at the wall of windows facing the backyard. "This is a beautiful kitchen."

"It's huge, isn't it? Way too big for three people. But we fell in love with the rest of the house, so we went for it. There's a park right behind us, did you notice? Teddy loves to go stomping through the woods."

"That sounds like fun."

"But we're constantly checking him for ticks. I'm thinking of buying him a flea collar."

She holds a glass to the ice dispenser and it makes a gentle tinkling sound—like the wind chimes on her front porch—and out fall dozens of tiny crystalline ice pearls. I feel like I've just witnessed a magic trick. She fills the glass with fizzy seltzer water and hands it to me. "How about a sandwich? Can I make you something?"

I shake my head no but Caroline opens the big refrigerator anyway, revealing a smorgasbord of groceries. There are jugs of whole milk and soy milk, cartons of brown eggs from cage-free hens, one-pint tubs of pesto and hummus and pico de gallo. There are wedges of cheese and bottles of kefir and white mesh bags exploding with leafy green vegetables. And the fruit! Giant clamshells of strawberries and blueberries, raspberries and blackberries, cantaloupe and honey-dew. Caroline reaches for a bag of baby carrots and a pint of hummus and then uses her elbow to close the fridge. I notice there's a child's drawing on the door, a crude and unskilled portrait of a bunny rabbit. I ask if Teddy is responsible, and Caroline nods. "Six weeks in this house and already he's hinting for pets. I told him we have to finish unpacking."

"He seems gifted," I tell her, and I worry the words sound forced, that I've gone too far too soon.

But Caroline agrees with me!

"Oh, definitely. He's really advanced for his peer group. Everyone says so."

We settle at a small dining table in the breakfast nook and she hands me a sheet of paper. "My husband typed up some guidelines. Nothing too crazy but we might as well get them out of the way."

HOUSE RULES

1. No drugs
2. No drinking
3. No smoking
4. No profanity
5. No screens
6. No red meat
7. No junk food
8. No visitors without permission.
9. No photos of Teddy on social media.
10. No religion or superstition. Teach science.

Underneath the typed list, there's an eleventh rule, handwritten in delicate feminine script:

Have fun! ☺

Caroline starts apologizing for the rules before I've even finished reading them. "We don't really enforce number seven. If you want to make cupcakes, or buy Teddy an ice cream, that's fine. Just no soda. And my husband insisted on number ten. He's an engineer. He works in technology. So science is very important to our family. We don't say prayers and we don't celebrate Christmas. If a person sneezes, we won't even say God Bless You."

"What *do* you say?"

"Gesundheit. Or 'to your health.' It means the same thing."

There's an apologetic tone in her voice and I see her glance at the tiny gold cross that hangs from my neck—a gift from my mother on my first Holy Communion. I assure Caroline that her House Rules won't be a problem. "Teddy's religion is your business, not mine. I'm just here to provide a safe, caring, and nurturing environment."

She seems relieved. "And have fun, right? That's rule eleven. So if you ever want to plan a special trip? To a museum or a zoo? I'm happy to pay for everything."

We talk for a while about the job and its responsibilities, but Caroline doesn't ask a lot of personal questions. I tell her that I grew up in South Philly, on Shunk Street, just north of the stadiums. I lived with my mother and younger sister, and I used to babysit for all the families on my block. I attended Central High School and I had just received a full athletic scholarship to Penn State when my life ran off the rails. And Russell must have told Caroline the rest, because she doesn't make me rehash the ugly stuff.

Instead she just says, "Should we go find Teddy? See how you two get along?"

The den is just off the kitchen—a cozy, informal family room with a sectional sofa, a chest full of toys, and a fluffy shag rug. The walls are lined with bookshelves and framed posters of the New York Metropolitan Opera—*Rigoletto*, *Pagliacci*, and *La Traviata*. Caroline explains that these are her husband's three favorite productions, that they used to visit Lincoln Center all the time before Teddy came along.

The child himself is sprawled on the rug with a spiral-bound pad and some yellow number two pencils. At my arrival, he looks up and flashes a mischievous smile—then immediately returns to his artwork.

"Well, hello again. Are you drawing a picture?"

He gives his shoulders a big, exaggerated shrug. Still too shy to answer me.

"Honey, sweetheart," Caroline interjects. "Mallory just asked you a question."

He shrugs again, then moves his face closer to the paper until his nose is practically touching the drawing, like he's trying to disappear inside it. Then he reaches for a pencil with his left hand.

"Oh, I see you're a leftie!" I tell him. "Me, too!"

"It's a common trait in world leaders," Caroline says. "Barack Obama, Bill Clinton, Ronald Reagan—they're all lefties."

Teddy maneuvers his body so I can't see over his shoulders, I can't see what he's working on.

"You remind me of my little sister," I tell him. "When she was your age, she loved to draw. She had a giant Tupperware bin full of crayons."

Caroline reaches under the sofa and pulls out a giant Tupperware bin full of crayons. "Like this?"

"Exactly!"

She has a light, pleasant laugh. "I'll tell you a funny story: The whole time we lived in Barcelona, we couldn't get Teddy to pick up a pencil. We bought him markers, finger paints, watercolors—he showed no interest in art. But the moment we move back to the States? And move into this house? Suddenly, he's Pablo Picasso. Now, he draws like crazy."

Caroline lifts the top of the coffee table and I see it doubles as some kind of storage chest. She removes a sheaf of paper that's an inch thick. "My husband teases me for saving everything, but I can't help myself. Would you like to see?"

"Definitely."

Down on the floor, Teddy's pencil has stopped moving. His entire body has tensed up. I can tell that he's listening carefully, that he's focusing all his attention on my reaction.

"Oooh, this first one is really nice," I tell Caroline. "Is this a horse?"

"Yes, I think so."

"No, no, no," Teddy says, springing off the floor and moving to my side. "That's a goat, because he has horns on his head, see? And a beard. Horses don't have beards." Then he leans into my lap and turns the page, directing my attention to the next drawing.

"Is that the weeping willow out front?"

"Yes, exactly. If you climb it, you can see a bird's nest."

I keep turning pages and it isn't long before Teddy relaxes in my arms, resting his head against my chest. I feel like I'm cradling a large puppy. His body is warm and he smells like laundry that's fresh out of the dryer. Caroline sits off to the side, watching our interaction, and she seems pleased.

The drawings are all pretty standard kid stuff—lots of animals, lots of smiley-faced people on sunny days. Teddy studies my reaction to every drawing and he soaks up my praise like a sponge.

Caroline seems surprised to find this last picture in the stack. "I meant to set this one aside," she says, but now she has no choice but to explain it. "This is Teddy and his, um, special friend."

"Anya," Teddy says. "Her name is Anya."

"Right, Anya," Caroline says, winking at me, encouraging me to play along. "We all love Anya because she plays with Teddy while Mommy and Daddy are working."

I realize Anya must be some kind of weird imaginary playmate so I try to say something nice. "I bet it's great having Anya around. Especially if you're a little boy in a new town, and you haven't met the other children yet."

"Exactly!" Caroline is relieved that I've grasped the situation so quickly. "That's exactly right."

"Is Anya here now? Is she in the room with us?"

Teddy glances around the den. "No."

"Where is she?"

"I don't know."

"Will you see her later tonight?"

"I see her every night," Teddy says. "She sleeps under my bed so I can hear her singing."

Then there's a chime in the foyer and I hear the front door open and close. A man's voice calls out, "Hello?"

"In the den!" Caroline calls back, and she looks to Teddy. "Daddy's home!"

Teddy springs from my lap and runs to greet his father, and I return the drawings to Caroline. "These are . . . interesting."

She shakes her head and laughs. "He's not possessed, I swear. It's just a really weird phase. And lots of children have imaginary friends. My colleagues in pediatrics say it's extremely common."

She sounds embarrassed and I'm quick to assure her that of course it's perfectly normal. "I bet it's because of the move. He's invented her so he has someone to play with."

"I just wish she wasn't so weird-looking. How am I supposed to hang this on the refrigerator?" Caroline turns the picture facedown, then buries it in the stack of other drawings. "But here's the thing, Mallory: Once you start working here, I bet he forgets all about her. He'll be having too much fun with his new babysitter!"

And I love how she's talking—like the interview's over and I've already got the job, and now we're just problem-solving. "I'm sure the playgrounds here are crawling with kids," I tell her. "I'll make sure Teddy has tons of real friends before school starts."

"Perfect," Caroline says. Out in the hallway, there are footsteps approaching, and she leans closer. "Also, I meant to warn you about my husband? He's not really comfortable with your history. Because of the drugs? So he's going to look for reasons to say no. But don't worry."

"So what should—"

"Also, call him Mr. Maxwell. Not Ted. He'll like that."

Before I can ask what any of this means, Caroline backs away and her husband enters, carrying a grinning Teddy on his hip. Ted Maxwell is older than I'm expecting, a good ten or fifteen years older than Caroline, tall and trim with gray hair, dark-framed glasses, and a beard. He's dressed in designer jeans, scuffed Oxfords, and a sports coat over a V-neck T-shirt—the sort of outfit that looks casual but costs ten times more than you'd ever imagine.

Caroline greets him with a kiss.

"Honey, this is Mallory."

I stand and shake his hand. "Hello, Mr. Maxwell."

"Sorry I'm late. Something came up at work." He and Caroline exchange a look, and I wonder if something comes up a lot. "How's the interview going?"

"Very well," Caroline says.

"Very *very* well!" Teddy exclaims. He wriggles out of his father's arms and jumps back into my lap, like I'm Santa Claus and he wants to tell me everything on his Christmas list. "Mallory, do you like hide-and-seek?"

"I *love* hide-and-seek," I tell him. "Especially in big old houses with lots of rooms."

"That's us!" Teddy looks around the den in wide-eyed astonishment. "We have a big old house! With lots of rooms!"

I give him a little squeeze. "Perfect!"

Ted seems uncomfortable with the direction of the conversation. He takes his son by the hand and coaxes him out of my lap. "Listen, buddy, this is a job interview. A very serious grown-up conversation. Mommy and Daddy need to ask Mallory some important questions. So you need to go upstairs now, okay? Go play LEGOs or—"

Caroline interrupts him. "Honey, we already went over everything. I want to take Mallory outside and show her the guest cottage."

"I have my own questions. Give me five minutes."

Ted gives his son a little push, sending him on his way. Then he unbuttons his coat and sits across from me. I realize he's not quite as trim as I thought—he has a bit of a paunch—but the extra weight suits him. He looks well fed, well cared for.

"Did you bring an extra copy of your résumé?"

I shake my head no. "Sorry."

"No problem. I've got it somewhere."

He unbuckles his briefcase and removes a manila folder stuffed with documents. As he flips through the file, I see that it's full of letters and résumés from other applicants. There must be fifty of them. "Here it is, Mallory Quinn." And as he extracts my résumé from the pile, I see it's covered with handwritten annotations.

"Central High School but no college, right?"

"Not yet," I tell him.

"Are you enrolling in the fall?"

"No."

"Spring?"

"No, but hopefully someday soon."

Ted looks at my résumé, then squints and cocks his head, like he can't quite make sense of it. "This doesn't say if you speak a foreign language."

"No, sorry. I mean unless you count South Philly. 'Do youse guys wanna jawn of that wooder-ice?'"

Caroline laughs. "Oh, that's funny!"

Ted just marks his notes with a small black X.

"How about musical instruments? Any piano or violin?"

"No."

"Visual arts? Painting, drawing, sculpture?"

"No."

"Have you traveled much? Gone abroad?"

"We went to Disney when I was ten."

He marks my résumé with another X.

"And now you work for your aunt Becky?"

"She's not my aunt. It's just the name of the day care: Aunt Becky's Childcare. Because ABC, get it?"

He sifts through his notes. "Right, right, I remember now. They're a recovery-friendly workplace. Do you know how much the state pays them to employ you?"

Caroline frowns. "Honey, is that relevant?"

"I'm just curious."

"I don't mind answering," I tell her. "The state of Pennsylvania pays one-third of my salary."

"But we would pay all of it," Ted says, and he starts scribbling figures in the margins of my résumé, doing some kind of elaborate calculation.

"Ted, do you have other questions?" Caroline asks. "Because Mallory's been here a long time. And I still need to show her out back."

"That's fine. I've got everything I need." I can't help but notice that he moves my résumé to the very bottom of the stack. "It was nice to meet you, Mallory. Thanks for coming by."

"Don't mind Ted," Caroline tells me just a few moments later as we exit the kitchen through sliding glass patio doors. "My husband's very smart. With computers, he's a wizard. But socially, he's awkward, and he doesn't understand recovery at all. He thinks you're too high-risk. He wants to hire a student from Penn, some whiz-kid with sixteen hundred SAT scores. But I'll convince him you deserve a chance. Don't worry."

The Maxwells have a big backyard with a lush green lawn, surrounded by tall trees and shrubs and flower beds popping with color. The centerpiece of the yard is a gorgeous swimming pool ringed with patio chairs and umbrellas, like something you'd see in a Las Vegas casino.

"This is beautiful!"

"Our private oasis," Caroline says. "Teddy loves playing out here."

We walk across the lawn, and the grass feels taut and springy, like the surface of a trampoline. Caroline points to a tiny path at the edge of the yard and tells me it descends into Hayden's Glen—a three-hundred-acre nature preserve crisscrossed with trails and streams. "We won't let Teddy go alone, because of the creeks. But you're welcome to take him as much as you want. Just watch out for poison ivy."

We've nearly crossed the yard before I finally glimpse the guest cottage—it's half-hidden behind the trees, as if the forest were in the process of consuming it. The house reminds me of the candy cottage in the Hansel and Gretel story—it's a miniature Swiss chalet with rustic wood siding and an A-frame roof. We climb three steps to a tiny porch, and Caroline unlocks the front door. "The previous owner kept his lawn mower in here. Used it like a garden shed. But I've fixed it up for you."

Inside, the cottage is just one room, small but spotlessly clean. The walls are white and the roof rafters exposed, thick brown beams criss-crossing the ceiling. The wood floors are so pristine, I'm compelled to kick off my sneakers. To the right is a small kitchenette; to the left is the most comfortable-looking bed I've ever seen, with a fluffy white comforter and four enormous pillows.

"Caroline, this is amazing."

"Well, I know it's a little tight, but after being with Teddy all day, I figured you'd appreciate the privacy. And the bed's brand-new. You should give it a try."

I sit on the edge of the mattress and lie back, and it's like falling into a cloud. "Oh my God."

"That's a Brentwood pillowtop. With three thousand coils supporting your body. Ted and I have the same one in our bedroom."

On the far side of the cottage, there are two doors. One opens to a shallow closet lined with shelves; the other is the world's smallest bathroom, complete with shower, toilet, and pedestal sink. I step inside and discover I'm just short enough to pass beneath the shower-head without ducking.

The entire tour doesn't take more than a minute, but I feel obligated to spend a little more time inspecting everything. Caroline has outfitted the cottage with dozens of small, thoughtful design touches: a bedside reading lamp, a foldaway ironing board, a USB charger for cell phones, and a ceiling fan to keep the air circulating. The kitchen cabinets are stocked with basic amenities: plates and glasses, mugs and silverware, all the same high-end stuff they use in the main house. Plus a few simple provisions for cooking: olive oil, flour, baking soda, salt and pepper. Caroline asks if I like to cook and I tell her I'm still learning. "Me, too," she says with a laugh. "We can figure it out together."

Then I hear heavy footsteps on the porch and Ted Maxwell opens the door. He's traded his sports coat for an aquamarine polo shirt, but even in casual clothes he still cuts an intimidating figure. I'd hoped I would finish the interview without seeing him again.

"Teddy needs you for something," he tells Caroline. "I can finish showing her around."

And it's awkward because I've already seen everything there is to see, but Caroline's out the door before I can say anything. Ted just stands there, watching me, like he thinks I'm going to steal the sheets and towels.

I smile. "This is really nice."

"It's a single-occupancy apartment. No guests without permission. And definitely no sleepovers. It's too confusing for Teddy. Will that be a problem?"

"No, I'm not seeing anyone."

He shakes his head, annoyed that I've missed his point. "We can't forbid you from seeing anyone, legally. I just don't want strangers sleeping in my yard."

"I understand. That's fine." And I want to believe this is progress, like we've taken a tiny step closer to a working relationship. "Do you have other concerns?"

He smirks. "How much time do you have?"

"All the time that's necessary. I really want this job."

He moves over to the window and points outside to a small pine tree. "Let me tell you a story. The day we moved into this house, Caroline and Teddy found a baby bird under that tree. It must have fallen out of its nest. Maybe it was pushed, who knows? Anyway, my wife has a big, big heart so she found a shoebox and filled it with shredded paper and she started feeding the baby bird with sugar water, from an eyedropper. Meanwhile I've got movers in the driveway, I'm trying to unpack the whole house so we can start a life together, and Caroline's telling Teddy how they're going to nurse this baby bird back to health, and one day it's going to soar high over the treetops. And of course Teddy loves this idea. He names the bird Robert and he checks on

Robert every hour, he treats the bird like a baby brother. But within forty-eight hours, Robert is dead. And I swear to you, Mallory, Teddy cried for a week. He was devastated. Over a baby bird. So the point is, we need to be extra careful about the person we invite to live with us. And given your history, I worry you're too much of a gamble."

And how can I argue with him? The job pays good money and Ted has a folder stuffed with applications from women who have never been addicted to drugs. He could hire a fresh-faced nursing school student who's trained in CPR or a five-time grandmother from Honduras who gives Spanish lessons while preparing homemade *enchiladas verdes*. With options like these, why take a chance on me? I realize my best hope now is to play my trump card—my last-minute gift from Russell, before I got out of his car.

"I think I have a solution." I reach in my bag and remove something that looks like a paper credit card with five cotton tabs on the bottom. "This is a drug test dip card. They're a buck a piece on Amazon, and I will happily pay for them out of my own wages. They test for meth, opiates, amphetamines, cocaine, and THC. Results take five minutes and I will voluntarily submit to testing every week, on random days of your choosing, so you never have to worry. Would that put your mind at ease?"

I offer the card to Ted and he holds it at a distance, like he's disgusted by it, like somehow it's already dripping with warm yellow urine. "No, see, this is the problem," he says. "You seem like a nice person. I wish you all the best, I really do. But I want a nanny who doesn't have to pee in a cup every week. You can understand that, right?"

I wait in the foyer of the main house while Ted and Caroline squabble in the kitchen. I can't hear the specifics of the conversation but it's pretty clear who's arguing what. Caroline's voice is patient and pleading; Ted's responses are short, harsh, and staccato. It's like listening to a violin and a jackhammer.

When they finally return to the foyer, their faces are flushed, and Caroline forces a smile. "We feel bad keeping you waiting," she says. "We're gonna talk more and be in touch, okay?"

And we all know what that means, right?

Ted opens the door and practically shoves me outside into the sweltering summer heat. The front of the house is so much warmer than the backyard. I feel like I'm standing on the border of paradise and the real world. I put on a brave face and thank them for the interview. I tell them I'd love to be considered for the job, that I would really enjoy working with their family. "If I can do anything to make you feel more comfortable, I hope you'll ask me."

And they're about to close the door when little Teddy squeezes between his parents' legs and hands me a sheet of paper. "Mallory, I drew you a picture. As a present. You can take it home with you."

Caroline looks over my shoulder and sharply draws in her breath. "Oh my gosh, Teddy, it's beautiful!"

And I know it's just a couple of stick figures but there's a sweetness to the drawing that really gets me. I crouch down so I am staring eye to eye with Teddy, and this time he doesn't flinch or run away. "I love this drawing, Teddy. As soon as I get home, I'm going to hang it on my wall. Thank you so much." I open my arms for a quick hug and he gives me a big one, wrapping his short arms around my neck and burying his face into my shoulder. It's the most physical contact I've had in months and I feel myself getting emotional; a tear squeezes out the corner of my eye and I wipe it away, laughing. Maybe Teddy's father doesn't believe in me, maybe he thinks I'm just another burnout doomed to relapse, but his adorable little boy thinks I'm an angel. "Thank you, Teddy. Thank you, thank you, thank you."

I take my time going to the train station. I stroll along the shady sidewalks, past little girls making chalk drawings and teenage boys shooting baskets in driveways and lawn sprinklers going *fitz!-fitz!-fitz!-fitz!* I walk through the little shopping district, past the smoothie shop and the mob of teenagers standing outside the Starbucks. I imagine how nice it must be to grow up in Spring Brook—in a town where everyone has enough money to pay their bills and nothing bad ever happens. And I wish I didn't have to leave.

I go inside the Starbucks and order a strawberry lemonade. As a recovering addict, I've decided to avoid every kind of psychoactive stimulant, including caffeine (but I'm not totally crazy; I'll still make an exception for chocolate, since it only has a couple milligrams). I'm spearing my straw through the lid when I recognize Russell on the far side of the dining room, drinking black coffee and reading the sports pages of the *Philadelphia Inquirer*. He's probably the last man in America who still buys a print newspaper.

"You shouldn't have waited," I tell him.

He closes the paper and smiles. "I had a hunch you'd stop here. And I want to know how it went. Tell me everything."

"It was horrible."

"What happened?"

"Your trump card was a disaster. It didn't work."

Russell starts laughing. "Quinn, the mother already called me. Ten minutes ago. As soon as you left her house."

"She did?"

"She's afraid some other family is going to steal you. She wants you to start as soon as possible."

3

Packing my stuff takes ten minutes. I don't have a ton of belong-
ings, just some clothes and toiletries and a Bible. Russell gives
me a secondhand suitcase so I won't have to carry everything in
a plastic garbage bag. My housemates at Safe Harbor throw me a
sad little going-away party with take-out Chinese and a ShopRite
sheet cake. And just three nights after my job interview, I leave
Philadelphia and return to Fantasyland, ready to start my new life
as a nanny.

If Ted Maxwell still has concerns about hiring me, he does a great
job of hiding them. He and Teddy meet me at the train station and
Teddy is carrying a bouquet of yellow daisies. "I picked these out," he
says, "but Daddy bought them."

His father insists on carrying my suitcase to the car—and on the
drive to the house, they give me a short tour of the neighborhood,
pointing out the pizza shop and the bookstore and an old rail trail
that's popular with runners and cyclists. There's no trace of the old
Ted Maxwell—the unsmiling engineer who grilled me on foreign languages and international travel. The New Ted Maxwell is jovial and
informal ("Please, call me Ted!") and even his clothes appear more

relaxed. He's wearing a Barcelona soccer jersey, dad jeans, and pristine New Balance 995s.

Later that afternoon, Caroline helps me unpack and settle into the cottage. I ask about Ted's abrupt transformation, and she laughs. "I told you he'd come around. He sees how much Teddy likes you. More than anyone else we interviewed. It was the easiest decision we've ever made."

We all eat dinner on the flagstone patio in the backyard. Ted grills his signature shrimp-and-scallop kabobs and Caroline serves home-brewed iced tea and Teddy runs around the grass like a whirling dervish, still astonished that I've come to live with them full-time, every day, all summer long. "I can't believe it, I can't believe it!" he exclaims, and then he falls back onto the lawn, deliriously happy.

"I can't believe it, either," I tell him. "I'm so glad to be here."

And before we've even had dessert, they've already made me feel like a member of the family. Caroline and Ted share a gentle and relaxed affection. They finish each other's sentences and pick food from each other's plates, and together they tell me the charming fairy-tale story of how they met at the Lincoln Center Barnes and Noble some fifteen years ago. Midway through the story, Ted's hand reflexively drifts to his wife's knee, and she rests her hand on top, weaving their fingers together.

Even their disagreements are kind of funny and charming. At one point in the meal, Teddy announces he has to go to the bathroom. I stand to go with him, but Teddy waves me off. "I'm five years old," he reminds me. "The bathroom is a private place."

"Attaboy," Ted says. "Don't forget to wash your hands."

I return to my seat, feeling foolish, but Caroline tells me not to worry. "This is a new phase for Teddy. He's exerting his independence."

"And staying out of prison," Ted adds.

Caroline seems irked by the wisecrack. I don't understand what it means, so she explains.

"A few months ago, we had an incident. Teddy was showing off to a couple children. I mean, he was exposing himself. Typical little boy behavior but it was new to me so I may have had an overreaction."

Ted laughs. "You may have called it sexual assault."

"If he were an adult male, it would be sexual assault. That was my point, Ted." Caroline turns to me. "But I agree I could have chosen my words a little more carefully."

"The boy can't even tie his own shoes," Ted says, "and already he's a sexual predator."

Caroline makes an exaggerated show of removing her husband's hand from her knee. "The point is, Teddy learned his lesson. Private parts are private. We don't show them to strangers. And next we're going to teach him about consent and inappropriate touching because it's important for him to learn these things."

"I agree one hundred percent," Ted says. "I promise you, Caroline, he'll be the most enlightened boy in his class. You don't have to worry."

"He's really sweet," I assure her. "With you guys raising him, I'm sure he's going to be fine."

Caroline takes her husband's hand and returns it to her knee. "I know you're right. I just worry about him anyway. I can't help it!"

And before the conversation can go any further, Teddy comes hurrying back to the table, breathless and wild-eyed and ready to play.

"Speak of the devil!" Ted says, laughing.

Once we've finished dessert and it's time to go in the pool, I'm forced to admit that I don't actually own a swimsuit—that I haven't been swimming since high school. So the very next day, Ted gives me an advance of $500 against future wages, and Caroline drives me to the mall to shop for a one-piece. And later that afternoon she stops by my cottage with a dozen outfits on hangers, really nice dresses and tops from Burberry and Dior and DKNY, all new or barely worn. She says she's already grown out of them, that she's ballooned to a size eight, and I'm welcome to the clothes before she turns them over to Goodwill.

"Also, you're going to think I'm paranoid, but I bought you one of these." She hands me a tiny pink flashlight with two metal prongs sticking out the top. "In case you go running at night."

I switch it on and there's a loud crackle of electricity; I'm so startled I immediately drop it, and the device clatters to the floor.

"I'm sorry! I thought it was—"

"No, no, I should have warned you. It's a Vipertek Mini. You clip it on your key chain." She retrieves the stun gun from the floor and then demonstrates its features. There are buttons labeled LIGHT and STUN, plus a safety switch that toggles on and off. "It fires ten thousand volts. I tested mine on Ted? Just to see if it worked? He said it felt like he'd been struck by lightning."

I'm not surprised to learn that Caroline carries a weapon for self-defense. She's mentioned that many of her patients at the VA hospital have mental health issues. But I can't imagine why I'd need a stun gun for jogging around Spring Brook.

"Is there a lot of crime here?"

"Hardly ever. But two weeks ago? A girl your age was carjacked. Right in the Wegmans parking lot. Some guy made her drive to an ATM and take out three hundred dollars. So I figure better safe than sorry, you know?"

She's waiting expectantly, and I realize she won't be satisfied until

I get out my keyring and attach the device, and it feels like my mother's looking after me again.

"I love it," I tell Caroline. "Thank you."

The job itself is pretty easy and I adjust to my new routine quickly. A typical workday goes something like this:

6:30—I wake up early, no alarm needed, because the forest is alive with birdsongs. I pull on a robe and make myself hot tea and oatmeal, and then I'll sit on my porch and watch the sun rise over the swimming pool. I'll see all kinds of wildlife grazing on the edge of the yard: squirrels and foxes, rabbits and raccoons, an occasional deer. I feel like Snow White in the old animated cartoon. I start leaving out platters of blueberries and sunflower seeds, encouraging the animals to join me for breakfast.

7:30—I walk across the yard and enter the big house through the sliding patio doors. Ted leaves early for work, so he's already gone. But Caroline insists on serving a hot breakfast to her son. Teddy is partial to home-made waffles, and she cooks them in a special gadget that's shaped like Mickey Mouse. I'll clean up the kitchen while Caroline gets ready for work, and when it's finally time for Mommy to leave, Teddy and I follow her outside to the driveway and wave goodbye.

8:00—Before Teddy and I can start the day in earnest, we have to complete a couple minor chores. First I need to lay out Teddy's clothes, but this is easy because he always wears the same thing. The kid has a vast wardrobe of adorable outfits from Gap Kids but he always insists on wearing the same striped purple shirt. Caroline has grown tired of washing it so she went back to The Gap and bought five more of the same top. She's willing to indulge him, but she's asked me to "gently encourage" other choices. When I lay out his clothes, I'm supposed to offer a couple different options, but he always lands on the same purple stripes. Afterward, I'll help him brush his teeth and I'll wait outside the bathroom while he uses the potty, and then we're ready to start our day.

8:30—I try to structure every morning around a big activity or outing. We'll walk to the library to attend a Storytime Hour, or we'll go to the supermarket and buy ingredients to make cookies. Teddy is easy to please and never balks at my suggestions. When I tell him I have to go into town to buy toothpaste, he reacts like we're going to Six Flags. He's a joy to be around—smart, affectionate, and full of mind-boggling questions: What is the opposite of square? Why do girls have such long hair? Is everything in the world "real"? I never get tired of listening to him. He is like the little brother I never had.

12:00—After our morning activity, I'll prepare a simple lunch—mac and cheese or pizza bagels or chicken nuggets. Teddy will go into his bedroom for Quiet Time, and I'll take an hour for myself. I'll read a book, or I'll listen to a podcast on my headphones. Or sometimes I'll just lie on the couch and catch a twenty-minute catnap. Eventually Teddy will come downstairs and shake me awake and he'll have one or two new drawings to share. Often he illustrates our favorite activities—he'll show us walking through the forest or playing in the backyard or hanging around my cottage. I keep these drawings on the door of my refrigerator—a gallery of his artistic progress.

2:00—This is usually the hottest part of the day, so we'll stay inside playing Chutes and Ladders or Mouse Trap, and then we'll slather on sunscreen and go out to the pool. Teddy doesn't know how to swim (and I'm not very good myself), so I make sure he puts on floaties before we get in the water. Then we'll play tag or have a swordfight with the pool noodles.

Or we'll climb atop the large inflatable raft and play make-believe games like Castaway or Titanic.

5:00—Caroline gets home and I'll recap my day with Teddy while she starts preparing dinner. Then I'll go out for a run, anywhere from three to eight miles, depending on what Russell recommends. I'll pass all kinds of people out on their sidewalks or watering their lawns, and everyone assumes I'm a resident of Spring Brook. Some of the neighbors will even wave and call out hello, like I've been living here all my life, like I must be someone's daughter home from college on summer break. And I love the way it makes me feel—the sense of community—like I've finally arrived in the place where I belong.

7:00—After running I'll take a quick shower in the world's smallest bathroom, and I'll fix myself a simple meal in the cottage's tiny kitchen. Once or twice a week, I'll walk downtown to browse the local shops and restaurants. Or I'll attend an open meeting in the church basement of Our Lady the Redeemer. The discussion leaders are very good and the participants are friendly but I'm always the youngest person in the circle by at least ten years, so I'm not expecting to make a ton of new friends. I certainly don't stick around for "the meeting after the meeting," when everyone walks down the block to Panera Bread to complain about their kids, their mortgages, their jobs, etc. After just two weeks of living with the Maxwells, safely cocooned from all temptations, I'm not even sure I need meetings anymore. I think I can handle things on my own.

9:00—By this time I'm usually in bed, reading a library book or watching a movie on my phone. As a gift to myself, I open a subscription to the Hallmark Channel so I can stream unlimited romances for $5.99 a month, and they're the perfect way to unwind at the end of the night. As I turn out the light and rest my head on my pillow, I revel in the comfort of happily ever after—of families reunited and scoundrels sent packing, of treasures recovered and honor restored.

Maybe this all sounds boring. I know it's not rocket science. I realize I'm not changing the world or curing cancer. But after all my troubles, I feel like I've taken a huge step forward, and I'm proud of myself. I have my own place to live and a steady paycheck. I'm cooking nutritious meals and setting aside two hundred a week for savings. I feel like my work with Teddy is important. And I feel validated by Ted and Caroline's absolute faith in me.

Especially Ted's. I don't see much of him during the day, because he leaves for his office at six thirty every morning. But sometimes I'll see him at night, after I'm back from a run. He'll be sitting on the patio with his laptop and a glass of wine, or he'll be out in the swimming pool doing laps, and he'll wave me over and ask about my run. Or he'll ask about my day with Teddy. Or he'll ask my opinion of some random consumer brand—Nike, PetSmart, Gillette, L.L.Bean, and so on. Ted explains that his company designs "back-end software" for big corporations all over the world, and he's constantly seeking out new partnerships. "What do you think of Urban Outfitters?" he'll ask me, or "Have you ever eaten dinner at a Cracker Barrel?" And then he'll really *listen* to my answers, as if my opinions might actually shape his business decisions. And it's flattering, to be honest. Apart from Russell, I haven't met a ton of people who care what I think. So I'm always happy to see Ted, and I always feel a little charge when he invites me over to talk.

Ironically, the only person at my new job who gives me any trouble is the one person who doesn't exist: Anya. Teddy's imaginary BFF has an annoying habit of undermining my instructions. For example, one day I ask Teddy to pick up his dirty clothes and put them in his laundry hamper. Two hours later, I'm back in his bedroom, and the clothes are still scattered across the floor. "Anya says Mommy should do that," he tells me. "Anya says that's *her* job."

Another time I'm frying crispy tofu squares for lunch and Teddy asks me for a hamburger. I tell him he can't have one. I remind him that his family doesn't eat red meat because it's bad for the environment, because cattle are one of the largest sources of greenhouse gases. I serve him a plate of tofu and white rice and Teddy just pushes the food around with his fork. "Anya thinks I would really like meat," he says. "Anya thinks tofu is garbage."

Now I'm no expert in child psychology but I understand what Teddy is doing: using Anya as an excuse to get his way. I ask Caroline for advice and she says we just need to be patient, that the problem will eventually take care of itself. "He's already getting better," she insists. "Whenever I come home from work, it's always 'Mallory this' and 'Mallory that.' I haven't heard Anya's name in a week."

But Ted urges me to take a stronger stance. "Anya is a pain in the ass. She doesn't make the rules around here. We do. Next time she shares her opinions, just remind Teddy that Anya isn't real."

I decide on an approach that's somewhere between these two extremes. One afternoon while Teddy is upstairs in Quiet Time, I bake a tray of his favorite snickerdoodle cookies. And when he comes downstairs with a new drawing, I invite him to sit at the table. I bring over the cookies and two glasses of cold milk, and I casually ask him to tell me more about Anya.

"How do you mean?" He's instantly suspicious.

"Where did you meet? What's her favorite color? How old is she?"

Teddy shrugs, like all these questions are impossible to answer. His gaze moves around the kitchen, like he's suddenly reluctant to make eye contact.

"Does she have a job?"

"I don't know."

"What does she do all day?"

"I'm not sure."

"Does she ever come out of your bedroom?"

Teddy glances across the table to an empty chair.

"Sometimes."

I look at the chair.

"Is Anya here now? Sitting with us?"

He shakes his head. "No."

"Would she like a cookie?"

"She's not here, Mallory."

"What do you and Anya talk about?"

Teddy lowers his nose to his plate until his face is just inches above his cookies. "I know she's not real," he whispers. "You don't have to prove it."

He sounds sad and disappointed and suddenly I feel guilty—like I've just bullied a five-year-old boy into admitting there isn't any Santa Claus.

"Listen, Teddy, my little sister, Beth, had a friend like Anya. Her friend was Cassiopeia, isn't that a beautiful name? During the day, Cassiopeia worked for a Disney on Ice show that traveled all over the world. But every night she came back to our rowhouse in South Philly and she slept on the floor in our bedroom. I had to be careful I didn't step on her, because she was invisible."

"Did Beth think Cassiopeia was real?"

"We *pretended* Cassiopeia was real. And it worked out fine, because Beth never used Cassiopeia as an excuse to break rules. Does that make sense?"

"I guess," Teddy says, and then he shifts in his chair, like he has a sudden pain in his side. "I have to go to the bathroom. I have to make number two." Then he climbs down from his chair and hurries out of the kitchen.

He hasn't touched any of his snack. I cover the cookies with Saran

Wrap and put his glass of milk in the refrigerator for later. Then I go over to the sink and wash all the dishes. When I'm finally finished, Teddy is still in the bathroom. I sit at the table and realize I've yet to admire his latest drawing, so I reach for the sheet of paper and turn it right-side-up.

4

Teddy's parents have strict rules about screen time, so he has never seen *Star Wars* or *Toy Story* or any of the movies that other kids love. He's not even allowed to watch *Sesame Street*. But once a week the Maxwells gather in the den for Family Movie Night. Caroline will make popcorn and Ted will stream a film with "genuine artistic merit," which usually means old or tagged with foreign language subtitles, and I promise the only one you've ever heard of is *The Wizard of Oz*. Teddy loves the story and he claims it is his favorite movie of all time.

So when we're outside in the swimming pool we'll often play a make-believe game called Land of Oz. We'll cling to the inflatable life raft and Teddy will play Dorothy, and I'll play everyone else in the movie—Toto, the Scarecrow, the Wicked Witch, and all the Munchkins. And not to brag but I pull out all the stops, I sing and dance and flap my Flying Monkey wings and carry on like it's Opening Night on Broadway. It takes us nearly an hour to reach the end of the story, when the raft turns into a hot-air balloon that carries Teddy-Dorothy back to Kansas. And by the time we finish and take our bows, I'm so cold my teeth are chattering. I have to get out of the water.

"No!" Teddy exclaims.

"Sorry, T-Bear, I'm freezing."

I spread a towel on the concrete deck at the edge of the pool, then lay out to dry in the sun. Temperatures have soared into the low nineties—the sun is strong and quickly bakes away my chills. Teddy keeps splashing nearby. His new game is filling his mouth with water and then spitting it out, like he's a winged cherub in a fountain.

"You shouldn't do that," I tell him. "There's chlorine."

"Will it make me sick?"

"If you swallow enough, yes."

"And would I die?"

Suddenly he is very concerned. I shake my head.

"If you drank the whole swimming pool, yes, you would probably die. But don't drink even a little, okay?"

Teddy climbs onto the raft and paddles to the edge of the water, so we're both lying parallel—Teddy on the raft and me on the deck.

"Mallory?"

"Yeah?"

"What happens when people die?"

I look over. He's staring down into the water.

"How do you mean?"

"I mean, what happens to the person *inside* the body?"

Now obviously I have strong opinions on this subject. I believe in God's gift of eternal life. I draw a lot of strength from knowing that my little sister, Beth, is surrounded by angels. And I know that someday, if I'm lucky, we'll be reunited in heaven. But I don't share any of this with Teddy. I still remember my job interview and rule number ten: no religion or superstition. Teach science.

"I think you should ask your parents."

"Why can't you tell me?"

"I'm not sure I know the answer."

"Is it possible some people die but stay alive?"

"Like ghosts?"

"No, not scary." He's struggling to express himself—the way we all struggle, I guess, when discussing these things. "Does *any* part of the person stay alive?"

"That is a big, complicated question, Teddy. I really think you should ask your parents."

He's frustrated by my nonanswer, but he seems resigned to the fact that I'm not going to help him. "Well then can we play Land of Oz again?"

"We just finished!"

"Only the melting scene," he says. "Just the ending."

"Fine. But I'm not getting back in water."

I stand up and wrap my towel around my shoulders, holding it like a witch's cloak. I curl my fingers into claws and cackle maniacally. "I'll get you, my pretty, and your little dog, too!" Teddy splashes me with water and I scream loud enough to scare the birds from the trees. "Oh, you cursed rat! Oh, look what you've done!" With incredible dramatic flair I sink to the patio, waving my arms and writhing in agony. "I'm melting! I'm melting! Oh, what a world, what a world!" Teddy laughs and applauds as I collapse onto my back, close my eyes, and stick out my tongue. I give my legs a few final twitches and then I'm still.

"Uh, miss?"

I open my eyes.

There's a young man not five feet away, standing on the far side of the pool fence. He's wiry but well built, dressed in grass-stained khakis, a Rutgers T-shirt, and work gloves. "I'm with Lawn King? The landscapers?"

"*Hola*, Adrian!" Teddy exclaims.

Adrian winks at him. "*Hola*, Teddy. *¿Cómo estás?*"

I try to pull my towel over my body, only I'm already lying on top of it, so I end up thrashing and flailing like a beetle flipped onto its back.

"I'm gonna bring the big mower around, if that's okay. I just wanted to give you a heads-up. It's pretty loud."

"Sure," I tell him. "We can go inside."

"No, we have to watch!" Teddy says.

Adrian leaves to get the mower and I look at Teddy. "Why do we have to watch?"

"Because I love the big mower! It's amazing!"

I hear the mower coming before I see it, the loud gasoline engine ripping through the silence of our backyard sanctuary. And then Adrian comes tearing around the side of the house, riding atop a machine that's somewhere between a tractor and a go-kart. He's standing in the back and leaning over the steering wheel, like he's racing an ATV, leaving stripes of fresh-cut grass in his wake. Teddy climbs out of the pool and runs to the fence so he can see better. The landscaper is showing off, taking turns way too fast, driving in reverse, even pulling his hat down over his eyes so he's driving blind. It's not the best example to set for a little kid, but Teddy is riveted; he watches in openmouthed astonishment like it's a performance of Cirque du Soleil. For his Grand Finale, Adrian speeds up in reverse, slams the gearshift into drive, and then hurtles toward us, popping a wheelie, keeping the mower aloft for three terrifying seconds so we can see its furiously spinning blades. And then with a loud crash the whole machine comes down, stopping inches shy of the pool fence.

Adrian hops off the side and offers the keys to Teddy. "You want to take her for a spin?"

"Really?" Teddy asks.

"No!" I tell them. "That is definitely not happening."

"Maybe when you turn six," Adrian says, winking at him. "Are you going to introduce me to your new friend?"

Teddy shrugs. "This is my babysitter."

"Mallory Quinn."

"It's great to meet you, Mallory."

He pulls off his work glove and sticks out his hand and there's something oddly formal about the gesture—especially since I'm in a one-piece and he's covered in mud stains and grass clippings. It's my first hint there might be more to him than meets the eye. The inside of his palm feels hardened, like leather.

Suddenly Teddy remembers something and he starts fumbling to open the pool's child-proof gate.

"Where are you going?"

"I made Adrian a picture," he says. "It's inside. Up in my bedroom."

I lift the latch so he can get out, and Teddy sprints across the lawn. "Your feet are still wet!" I call after him. "Be careful on the stairs!"

"Okay!" he shouts back.

Adrian and I are forced to make awkward conversation until Teddy returns. It's really hard to pinpoint his age. His body is all adult—tall, lean, tanned, muscular—but his face is still boyish and a little shy. He could be anywhere from seventeen to twenty-five.

"I love this kid," Adrian says. "He learned some Spanish in Barcelona so I've been teaching him new phrases. Do you watch him full-time?"

"Just for the summer. He starts school in September."

"How about you? Where do you go?"

And I realize he's mistaken me for a fellow student. He must think I'm a neighbor, that I live here in Spring Brook, where all the young women attend four-year colleges and universities. I start to correct him but I don't know how to say "I don't go anywhere" without sounding like a failure. I know I could share my whole awful backstory, but for the sake of small talk I just go along with his assumption. I pretend that my life hadn't gone off the rails and everything had happened according to plan.

"Penn State. I'm on the women's cross-country team."

"No kidding! You're a Big Ten athlete?"

"Technically, yes. But the football team gets all the glory. You're never gonna see us on ESPN."

I know it's wrong to lie. A big part of recovery—probably the most important part—is owning your past and acknowledging all the mistakes you've made. But I have to say it feels pretty nice to embrace the fantasy, to pretend I'm still a normal teenager with normal teenage dreams.

Adrian snaps his fingers, like he's suddenly made a connection. "Do you go running at night? Around the neighborhood?"

"That's me."

"I've seen you training! You're really fast!"

And I'm wondering why the landscapers might be working in the neighborhood after dark but there's no time to ask because Teddy's already running back across the yard, clutching a sheet of paper. "Here it is," he says, winded and out of breath. "I saved it for you."

"Oh, buddy, this is amazing!" Adrian says. "Check out those sunglasses! I look pretty good, right?" He shows me the picture and I have to laugh. He looks like the stick figure from Hangman.

"Very handsome," I agree.

"*Muy guapo*," Adrian says to Teddy. "That's your new word for the week. It means super-good-looking."

"*Muy guapo*?"

"*Bueno*! That's perfect!"

Across the yard, an old man walks around the side of the Maxwells' house. He's short, with wrinkled brown skin and close-cropped gray hair. He shouts Adrian's name and it's clear he's not happy. "*¿Qué demonos estás haciendo?*"

Adrian waves to him, then shoots an amused look in our direction. "It's El Jefe. I gotta go. But I'll be back in two weeks, Teddy. Thank you for the picture. And good luck with your training, Mallory. I'm gonna watch for you on ESPN, all right?"

"*Prisa!*" the old man yells. "*Ven aqui!*"

"Okay, okay!" Adrian shouts back. He jumps onto the mower, starts it up, and crosses the yard in seconds. I can hear him apologizing in Spanish but the old man just yells over him, and they continue arguing as they disappear around the side of the house. I have a rudimentary grasp of Spanish from high school—I still remember *el jefe* means "the boss"—but they're talking too fast for me to keep up.

Teddy seems concerned. "Is Adrian in trouble?"

"I hope not." Then I look around the yard and marvel at the fact that—for all Adrian's high-speed daredevil antics—the newly cut grass looks fantastic.

The Maxwells have a small outdoor shower on the back of their house so they can rinse off after swimming. It's a tiny wooden stall about the size of an old-fashioned phone booth, and Caroline stocks it with absurdly expensive shampoos and body washes. Teddy goes first and I shout instructions through the door, reminding him to rinse his hair and shake out his bathing suit. When he's finished, he shuffles outside with a beach towel wrapped around his body. "I'm a veggie burrito!"

"You're adorable," I tell him. "Go get dressed and I'll meet you upstairs."

I'm hanging my towel and getting ready to enter the stall when I hear a woman calling my name. "It's Mallory, right? The new sitter?"

I turn and see the Maxwells' next-door neighbor hurrying across the lawn, a short old woman with wide hips and a wobbly gait. Caroline has warned me that she's very flaky and rarely leaves her house and yet here she is, dressed in an aquamarine muumuu and covered in jewelry: gold necklaces with crystal charms, big hoop earrings, jangly bracelets, and gemstone rings on her fingers and toes. "I'm Mitzi, honey, I live next door? And since you're new to the neighborhood I want to give a bit of friendly advice: When those landscapers come around? You shouldn't sit out by the pool. With everything on display." She gestures at the full length of my torso. "This is what we used to call a provocation."

She steps closer and I'm hit by the skunky smell of burnt rope. Either she needs a bath or she's very high, or possibly both. "Excuse me?"

"You got a nice figure and I understand you want to show it off. And it's a free country, I'm Libertarian, I say do what makes you feel good. But when these Mexicans come through, you need to show a little discretion. A little common sense. For your personal safety. Are you following?" I start to answer but she keeps talking: "This might sound racist, but it's true. These men—they've already broken the law once, when they crossed the border. So if a criminal sees a pretty girl all alone in a backyard, what's stopping him?"

"Are you serious?"

She grabs my wrist to underscore her remarks, and her hand is trembling. "Princess, I am serious as a heart attack. You need to cover your fanny."

Above us, Teddy calls through the screen of his open bedroom window, "Mallory, can we have Popsicles?"

"After my shower," I tell him. "Five minutes."

Mitzi waves to Teddy and he ducks out of sight. "He's a cute kid. Such a sweet face. Not a big fan of the parents, though. A bit uppity for my taste. Do you get that sense?"

"Well—"

"The day they moved in, I baked a lasagna. To be neighborly, okay? I bring it to their front door and do you know what she says to me? 'I'm sorry but we can't accept your gift.' Because of the chopped meat!"

"Maybe—"

"I'm sorry, honey, but that is *not* how you handle that situation. You smile, you say thank you, you take it inside, and *you throw it away*. Don't fling it back in my face. That's rude. And the father's even worse! He must drive you crazy."

"Actually—"

"Ecch, you're still a child. You can't read people yet. I'm a warm person, very empathetic, I read auras for a living. You'll see clients knocking on my door all day long but don't worry, there's nothing shady going on. I lost all interest after my hysterectomy." She winks at me. "But how do you like the guest cottage? Do you ever get nervous? Sleeping out there all alone?"

"Why should I be nervous?"

"Because of the history."

"What history?"

And for the first time in our conversation, Mitzi finds herself at a loss for words. She reaches for a lock of her hair, twisting it in her fingers until she's isolated a single strand. Then she yanks it from its root and tosses it over her shoulder. "You should ask the parents."

"They just moved here. They don't know anything. What are you talking about?"

"When I was a kid, we called your cottage the Devil House. We'd dare each other to peek through the windows. My brother offered me quarters if I would stand on the porch and count to a hundred, but I'd always chicken out."

"Why?"

"A woman was murdered. Annie Barrett. She was an artist, a painter, and she used your house as her studio."

"She was murdered in the cottage?"

"Well, they never actually found her body. This was a long time ago, right after World War Two."

Teddy's face reappears in the second-floor window. "Has it been five minutes yet?"

"Almost," I tell him.

When I look back at Mitzi, she's already backing across the yard. "Don't keep the little angel waiting. Go enjoy your ice creams."

"Wait, what's the rest of the story?"

"There is no rest of the story. After Annie died—or went missing, who knows—her family turned the cottage into a garden shed. Wouldn't let anyone stay out there. And it's been that way ever since, seventy-some years. Until this month."

Caroline comes home with a minivan full of groceries, so I help her unload and unpack all the bags. Teddy is upstairs in his bedroom, drawing pictures, so I use the opportunity to ask about Mitzi's story.

"I told you she was cuckoo," Caroline says. "She thinks the mailman steams open her Visa bills so he can learn her credit scores. She's paranoid."

"She said a woman was murdered."

"Eighty years ago. This is a very old neighborhood, Mallory. All these

houses have some kind of horror story." Caroline opens her refrigerator and loads the crisper drawer with spinach, kale, and a bundle of
radishes with soil still clinging to their roots. "Plus the previous owners
lived here forty years, so obviously they didn't have any problems."

"Right, that's true." I reach into a canvas grocery bag and pull out a
six-pack of coconut water. "Except they used the cottage as a toolshed,
right? No one was sleeping out there."

Caroline looks exasperated. I sense she's had a long day at the VA
clinic, that she doesn't appreciate being ambushed with questions the
minute she walks through the door. "Mallory, that woman has probably done more drugs than all my patients combined. I don't know how
she's still alive, but her mind is definitely not right. She is a nervous,
twitchy, paranoid mess. And as someone who cares about your sobriety, I'm going to strongly suggest you limit contact with her, okay?"

"No, I know," I tell her, and I feel bad, because this is the closest
Caroline has ever come to yelling at me. I don't say anything else after
that, I just open the pantry and unpack boxes of arborio rice, couscous,
and whole grain crackers. I put away bags and bags of rolled oats, raw
almonds, Turkish dates, and weird shriveled-up mushrooms. After
everything is unpacked, I tell Caroline I'm heading out. And she must
sense that I'm still upset because she comes over and rests a hand on
my shoulder.

"Listen, we have a terrific guest bedroom on the second floor. If
you want to move over here, we'd be thrilled to have you. Teddy would
go bananas. What do you think?"

And somehow, since she already has one arm around me, it turns
into a kind of hug. "I'm fine out there," I tell her. "I like having my
own space. It's good practice for the real world."

"If you change your mind just say the word. You are *always* welcome in this house."

That night I put on my good sneakers and go out for a run. I wait until after dark but the weather is still muggy and gross. It feels good to push myself, to run through the pain. Russell has a saying that I love—he says we don't know how much our bodies can endure until we make cruel demands of them. Well, that night I demand a lot of myself. I do wind sprints up and down the neighborhood sidewalks, running through shadows of streetlamps and clusters of fireflies, past the ever-present hum of central air conditioners. I finish 5.2 miles in thirty-eight minutes and walk home feeling deliriously spent.

I take another shower—this time, in the small, cramped bathroom of the cottage—and then fix myself a simple supper: a frozen pizza heated in the toaster oven and a half-pint of Ben & Jerry's for dessert. I feel like I deserve it.

By the time I'm finished with everything, it's after nine o'clock. I turn out all the lights except for the lamp on my nightstand. I get into the big white bed with my phone and put on a Hallmark movie called *Winter Love*. I have a hard time focusing, though. I can't tell if maybe I've seen it before, or maybe the story is just identical to a dozen other Hallmark movies. Also, it's a little stuffy inside the cottage, so I stand up and open the curtains.

There's a large window next to the front door, and a smaller window over my bed, and at night I keep them open to generate a cross-breeze. The ceiling fan spins in slow, lazy circles. Outside in the woods, the crickets are chirping, and sometimes I'll hear small animals pacing through the forest, soft footsteps padding over dead leaves.

I get back into bed and start the movie again. Every minute or so, a moth smacks against my window screens, drawn to the light. There's a *tap-tap-tapping* on the wall behind my bed but I know it's just a branch; there are trees growing close on three sides of the cottage and they scrape at the walls every time the wind picks up. I glance at the door and make sure it's locked, and it is, but it's a very flimsy lock, nothing that would stop a determined intruder.

And then I hear the sound, a sort of high-frequency humming, like a mosquito flying too close to my ear. I wave it off, but after a few seconds it's back again, a gray speck flitting around my peripheral vision, always just out of reach. And I think back to the doctor from the University of Pennsylvania and the research experiment that didn't actually happen.

And it's the first night I feel like someone might be watching me.

5

My weekends are pretty quiet. Caroline and Ted will often plan a family activity—they'll drive to the shore for a Beach Day, or they'll take Teddy to a museum in the city. And they always invite me along but I never go, because I don't want to intrude on their family time. Instead I'll just putter around my cottage, trying to keep busy, because idle hands invite temptation, etc. On Saturday night, while millions of young people across America are drinking and flirting and laughing and making love, I'm kneeling in front of my toilet with a spray bottle of Clorox bleach, scrubbing the grout on my bathroom floor. Sundays aren't much better. I've sampled all the local churches, but so far nothing's clicking. I'm always the youngest person by twenty years, and I hate the way the other parishioners stare at me, like I'm some kind of zoological oddity.

Sometimes I'm tempted to go back on social media, to reactivate my accounts with Instagram and Facebook, but all my NA counselors have warned me to steer clear. They say these sites carry addiction risks of their own, that they wreak havoc on a young person's self-esteem. So I try to keep busy with simple, real-world pleasures: running, cooking, taking a walk.

But I'm always happiest when the weekend is over and I can finally go back to work. Monday morning, I arrive at the main house and find Teddy down under the kitchen table, playing with plastic farm animals.

"Hey there, Teddy Bear! How are you?"

He holds up a plastic cow and mooooos.

"No kidding, you turned into a cow? Well, I guess I'm cow-sitting today! How exciting!"

Caroline darts through the kitchen, clutching her car keys and cell phone and several folders stuffed with papers. She asks if I can join her in the foyer for a minute. Once we're a safe distance from Teddy she explains that he wet his bed and his sheets are in the washing machine. "Would you mind moving them into the dryer when they're done? I already put new ones on his bed."

"Sure. Is he all right?"

"He's fine. Just embarrassed. It's been happening a lot lately. The stress of the move." She grabs her satchel from the hall closet and slings it over her shoulder. "Just don't mention that I said anything. He doesn't want you to know."

"I won't say a word."

"Thank you, Mallory. You're a lifesaver!"

Teddy's favorite morning activity is exploring the "Enchanted Forest" at the edge of his family's property. The trees form a dense canopy over our heads, so even on the warmest days it's cooler in the woods. The trails are unmarked and unlabeled so we've invented our own names for them. Yellow Brick Road is the flat, hard-packed route that starts behind my cottage and runs parallel to all the houses on Edgewood Street. We follow it to a large gray boulder called Dragon's Egg and then veer off onto Dragon's Pass, a smaller trail that twists through a dense thicket of sticker bushes. We have to walk single file, with our hands outstretched, to keep from getting scratched. This path brings us down a valley to the Royal River (a fetid and slow-moving creek, barely waist deep) and Mossy Bridge, a long rotting tree trunk spanning the banks, covered with algae and weird mushrooms. We tiptoe across the log and follow the trail to the Giant Beanstalk—the tallest tree in the forest, with branches that touch the sky.

Or so Teddy likes to say. He spins elaborate stories as we hike along, narrating the adventures of Prince Teddy and Princess Mallory, brave siblings separated from the Royal Family and trying to find their way back home. Sometimes we'll walk all morning without seeing a single person. Occasionally a dog walker or two. But rarely any kids, and I wonder if this is why Teddy likes it so much.

I don't mention this theory to Caroline, however.

After two hours of stumbling around the woods, we've worked up an appetite for lunch, so we go back to the house and I make some grilled cheeses. Then Teddy goes upstairs for Quiet Time, and I remember that his bedsheets are still in the dryer, so I head upstairs to the laundry room.

On my way past Teddy's room, I overhear him talking to himself. I stop and press my ear to his door, but I can only make out words and fragments. It's like listening to one side of a telephone conversation where the other person is doing most of the talking. There are pauses between all his statements—some longer than others.

"Maybe? But I—"

". . . . ."

"I don't know."

". . . . ."

"Clouds? Like big? Puffy?"

". . . . ."

"I'm sorry. I don't under—"

". . . . ."

"Stars? Okay, stars!"

"...
........................."

"Lots of stars, I got it."

"...
...."

And I'm so curious, I'm tempted to knock—but then the house phone starts ringing, so I leave his door and hurry downstairs.

Ted and Caroline both have cell phones but they insist on keeping a landline for Teddy so he can dial 911 in case of an emergency. I answer, and the caller identifies herself as the principal of Spring Brook Elementary. "Is this Caroline Maxwell?"

I tell her I'm the babysitter and she stresses that it's nothing urgent. She says she's calling to personally welcome the Maxwells to the school system. "I like to talk with all the parents before opening day. They tend to have a lot of concerns."

I take her name and number and promise to deliver the message to Caroline. A little while later, Teddy wanders into the kitchen with a new drawing. He places it facedown on the table and climbs up into a chair. "Can I have a green pepper?"

"Of course."

Green bell peppers are Teddy's favorite snack so Caroline purchases them by the dozen. I grab one from the refrigerator, rinse it under cold water, and carve out the stem. Next I slice off the top, creating a sort of ring, and slice the rest of the bell into bite-size strips.

We're sitting at the table and he's happily munching on his pepper when I turn my attention to his latest illustration. It's a picture of a man walking backward through a dense and tangled forest. He's dragging a woman by the ankles, pulling her lifeless body across the ground. In the background, between the trees, there's a crescent moon and many small twinkling stars.

"Teddy? What is this?"

He shrugs. "A game."

"What kind of game?"

He bites into a strip of pepper and answers while chewing. "Anya acts out a story and I draw it."

"Like Pictionary?"

Teddy snorts and sprays little flecks of green pepper all over the table. "Pictionary?!?" He flops back in his chair, laughing hysterically, and I grab a paper towel to wipe up the mess. "Anya can't play *Pictionary*!"

I gently coax him to calm down and take a sip of water.

"Start over from the beginning," I tell him, and I try to keep my tone light. I don't want to sound like I'm freaking out. "Explain to me how the game works."

"I told you, Mallory. Anya acts out the story and I have to draw it. That's it. That's the whole game."

"So who is the man?"

"I don't know."

"Did the man hurt Anya?"

"How should I know? But it's not Pictionary! Anya can't play board games!"

And then he flops back in his chair again, caught up in another giggle fit, the kind of blissfully carefree laughter that only children can produce. It's so joyous and genuine, I suppose it outweighs any concerns I might have. Clearly there's nothing bothering Teddy. He seems as happy as any kid I've ever met. So he's created a weird imaginary friend and they play weird imaginary games together—so what?

He's still flailing around in his chair as I stand and carry the drawing across the kitchen. Caroline keeps a file folder in the bills drawer where she's asked me to place Teddy's artwork, so she can scan all the pictures into her computer.

But Teddy sees what I'm doing.

He stops giggling and shakes his head.

"That one's not for Mommy or Daddy. Anya says she wants *you* to have it."

I haven't owned a computer since high school. For the past few years, I've been getting by with just a phone. But that night, I walk a mile to a shopping plaza and spend some of my paycheck on a new Android tablet. I'm back at the cottage by eight o'clock. I lock the door and change into my pajamas and then get into bed with my new toy. It only takes a few minutes to set up the tablet and connect to the Maxwells' Wi-Fi network.

My search for "Annie Barrett" generates sixteen million results: wedding registries, architecture firms, Etsy shops, yoga tutorials, and dozens of LinkedIn profiles. I search again for "Annie Barrett + Spring Brook" and "Annie Barrett + Artist" and "Annie Barrett + dead + murdered" but none of these yield anything helpful. The internet has no record of her existence.

Outside, just over my head, something smacks against the window screen. I know it's one of the fat brown moths that are all over the forest. They have the color and texture of tree bark, so they can easily camouflage themselves—but from my side of the window screen, all I see are their slimy segmented underbellies, three pairs of legs and two twitchy antennae. I rattle the screen and shake them loose, but they just fly around for a few seconds and come back. I worry they'll find some gap in the screen and wriggle through, that they'll migrate to my bedside lamp and swarm it.

Next to the lamp is my drawing of Anya being dragged through the forest. I wonder if I was wrong to keep it. Maybe I should have passed it to Caroline as soon as she walked through the door. Or better yet, I could have crumpled it into a ball and stuffed it into the recycling bin. I hate the way Teddy has drawn her hair, the obscene length of her long black tresses, dragged behind her body like entrails. Something on my nightstand shrieks and I spring out of bed before realizing it's just my phone—an incoming call with my ringtone set to high.

"Quinn!" Russell says. "Am I calling too late?"

This is such a typical Russell question. It's only eight forty-five, but he advocates that anyone serious about fitness should be in bed with the lights out by nine thirty.

"It's fine," I tell him. "What's up?"

"I'm calling about your hamstring. The other day, you said you were tight."

"It's better now."

"How far'd you go tonight?"

"Four miles. Thirty-one minutes."

"You tired?"

"No, I'm fine."

"You ready to push a little harder?"

I can't stop staring at the drawing, at the tangle of black hair trailing behind the woman's body.

What kind of kid draws this?

"Quinn?"

"Yeah—sorry."

"Everything okay?"

I hear a mosquito whine and I slap the right side of my face, hard. Then I look at my palm, hoping to see mangled black ash, but my skin is clean.

"I'm fine. A little tired."

"You just said you *weren't* tired."

And his voice shifts gears a tiny bit, like he's suddenly aware there's something going on.

"How's the family treating you?"

"They're fantastic."

"And the kid? Tommy? Tony? Toby?"

"Teddy. He's sweet. We're having fun."

For just a moment, I consider telling Russell about the situation with Anya, but I don't know where to begin. If I come right out and tell him the truth, he'll probably think I'm using again.

"Are you having glitches?" he asks.

"What kind of glitches?"

"Lapses in memory? Forgetfulness?"

"No, not that I can recall."

"I'm serious, Quinn. It would be normal, under the circumstances. The stress of a new job, a new living situation."

"My memory's fine. I haven't had those problems in a long time."

"Good, good, good." Now I hear him typing on his computer, keying in adjustments to my workout spreadsheet. "And the Maxwells have a swimming pool, right? You're allowed to use it?"

"Of course."

"Do you know the length? Ballpark?"

"Maybe thirty feet?"

"I'm emailing you some YouTube videos. They're swimming exercises. Easy low-impact cross-training. Two or three times a week, all right?"

"Sure."

There's still something in my voice he doesn't quite like. "And call me if you need anything, okay? I'm not in Canada. I'm forty minutes away."

"Don't worry, coach. I'm fine."

6

I'm a pretty lousy swimmer. Growing up, we had a public pool in our neighborhood, but during the summer it was always a zoo, hundreds of shrieking screaming kids standing body-to-body in three feet of greasy water. You couldn't do any laps; there was barely room to float on your back. My mother warned me and my sister not to put our heads underwater because she was afraid we would get pinkeye.

So I'm not looking forward to Russell's new exercises. It's after ten o'clock the following night when I finally head out to the pool. The Maxwells' backyard is a strange place after dark. We're just a stone's throw from Philadelphia, but at this time of night it feels like we're miles deep into the rural countryside. The only light comes from the moon and the stars and the glowing halogen lamps at the bottom of the pool. The water is an eerie neon blue, like radioactive plasma, casting strange shadows on the rear of the house.

It's a warm evening and it feels good to plunge into the deep end. But when I surface for air and open my eyes, I could swear the forest has moved forward, like somehow all the trees have crept closer. Even the chorus of crickets seems louder. I know it's just an illusion, that the new angle has flattened my depth perception, erasing the twenty feet of grass between the pool fence and the tree line. But it weirds me out, anyway.

I grab the edge of the pool and warm up with five minutes of leg kicks. Over at the big house, all the downstairs lights are on and I can see into the kitchen, but there's no trace of Ted or Caroline. They're probably sitting in the den, drinking wine and reading books, which is how they spend most evenings.

After I'm warmed up, I kick off the wall and start with a sloppy freestyle stroke. I'm aiming for ten laps, out and back, across the length of the pool. But by the middle of the third, I know I'm not going to finish. My deltoids and triceps are burning; my entire upper body is woefully out of shape. Even my calves are tightening up. I dig deep to finish the fourth lap, and halfway through my fifth I have to stop. I cling to the side of the pool, struggling to catch my breath.

And then—from the forest—I hear a soft *crack*.

It's the sound of a person putting all their weight on a dry branch, pressing down hard until the wood splits. I turn toward the trees and squint into the shadows and I can't see anything. But I hear something, or someone—soft footsteps padding across dry leaves, walking in the direction of my cottage. . . .

"How's the water?"

I turn around and it's Ted, opening the gate to the pool, shirtless and dressed in swim trunks with a towel slung over his shoulder. He exercises in the pool several nights a week but I've never seen him out this late. I paddle over to the ladder and say, "I was just getting out."

"No need. There's plenty of room. You start down there and I'll start here."

He throws his towel on a chair and then steps off the edge of the pool—dropping into the water without flinching. And then on his signal we start swimming in parallel lines from opposite ends of the pool. In theory we should only pass each other once, in the center of the lanes, but Ted is crazy-fast and after a minute he laps me. His form is excellent. He keeps his face submerged for nearly the entire length of the pool, so I'm not even sure how he's breathing. He moves like a shark, barely making a sound, while I thrash and flail like a drunk cruise ship passenger who's fallen overboard. I eke out another three laps before quitting. Ted keeps going, another six laps, and finishes beside me.

"You're really good," I tell him.

"I was better in high school. We had a terrific coach."

"I'm jealous. I'm learning on YouTube."

"Then can I offer some unsolicited advice? You're breathing too much. You want to breathe every other stroke. Always on the left or right, whatever feels more natural."

He encourages me to try it, so I kick off the edge and cross the pool using his suggestions. The results are instantaneous. I'm breathing half as much and moving twice as fast.

"Better, right?"

"Much better. Any other tips?"

"No, I just gave you my best advice. Swimming is the only sport where coaches yell at you for breathing. But if you practice, you'll get better."

"Thanks."

I grab the pool ladder and climb out, ready to call it a night. My swimsuit is riding up and I reach down to tug it back into place, but apparently I'm not fast enough.

"Hey, go Flyers," he says.

He's referring to the small tattoo at the base of my hip. It's the wild-eyed face of Gritty, the furry orange mascot of Philadelphia's NHL team. I've been careful to keep it concealed from the Maxwells, and I'm angry at myself for slipping up.

"It's a mistake," I tell him. "As soon as I save the money, I'm getting it lasered off."

"But you like hockey?"

I shake my head. I've never played. I've never even watched a game. But two years ago I became friendly with an older man who had an abiding love of the sport and ready access to prescription pharmaceuticals. Isaac was thirty-eight years old, and his father played for the Flyers back in the 1970s. He'd earned a lot of money and died young and Isaac was slowly squandering his fortune. There were a couple of us living in Isaac's condo and crashing on his floor and occasionally sharing his bed and basically I got the tattoo to impress him, with the hope that he'd think I was cool and he'd let me keep hanging around. But the plan was a bust. I had to wait five days to remove the bandage, and in that time Isaac was arrested for possession, and his landlord chased all of us back into the streets.

Ted's still waiting for me to explain.

"It was stupid," I tell him. "I wasn't thinking clearly."

"Well, you're not alone. Caroline has a tattoo she wants to get rid of. She went through an artsy phase in college."

This is a nice thing to say, but it doesn't make me feel any better. I'm sure Caroline's tattoo is extremely tasteful. It's probably a rose, or a crescent moon, or a meaningful Chinese character—not some freakish googly-eyed monster. I ask Ted where she's hiding it but I'm interrupted by another loud *crack*.

We both turn toward the forest.

"Someone's out there," I tell him. "I heard them walking around earlier."

"Probably a rabbit," he says.

There's another crack and then a quick panicked thrashing, the sound of a small animal darting across a forest.

"*That* was a rabbit. But earlier, before you came out, the noise was louder. It sounded like a person."

"Maybe it was teenagers. I'm sure these woods are popular with high school kids."

"It's worse at night. Sometimes I'm lying in my bed and it sounds like they're right outside my window."

"Probably doesn't help for Mitzi to fill your head with strange stories." He winks. "Caroline told me about your encounter."

"She's an interesting person."

"I'd steer clear of her, Mallory. All this business about so-called energy readings? Strangers parking in her driveway, knocking on her back door? Paying in cash? It feels shady to me. I don't trust her."

I sense that Ted hasn't spent much time in the company of psychics. Growing up, I had a neighbor, Mrs. Guber, who read tarot cards in the back of the local pizzeria. She was legendary for predicting that one of the waitresses would win $100,000 on a scratch-off ticket. She also consulted on marriage proposals, adulterous boyfriends, and other affairs of the heart. My friends and I called her The Oracle, and we trusted her more than the front page of the *Inquirer*.

But I don't expect Ted to understand any of this. The guy won't even acknowledge the existence of the tooth fairy. A few nights ago, Teddy spat up a loose molar, and Ted just reached into his billfold and pulled out a dollar—no mystery, no fanfare, no late-night tiptoeing into the bedroom to avoid detection.

"She's harmless."

"I think she's dealing," Ted says. "I can't prove it, but I'm watching her. You need to be careful around her, okay?"

I raise my right hand. "Scout's honor."

"I'm serious, Mallory."

"I know. And I appreciate it. I'll be careful."

I'm opening the gate to the pool, ready to leave, when I realize Caroline is walking across the yard, still dressed in her work clothes, carrying her notebook and a pencil. "Mallory, wait. Did you get a phone call yesterday? From Teddy's school?"

Immediately, I realize I've messed up. I remember the call, and I remember writing the principal's number on a slip of paper. But then Teddy walked into the kitchen with his weird drawing, and I must have been distracted.

"Yes—the principal," I tell her. "I have the message in my cottage. It's probably still in my shorts. I'll go get it—"

Caroline shakes her head. "It's fine. She just emailed me. But I could have used the message yesterday."

"I know. I'm sorry."

"If we miss a single deadline, Teddy will lose his spot. The kindergarten class has a waitlist with thirty names on it."

"I know, I know—"

She cuts me off. "Stop saying 'I know.' If you *really* knew, you would have given me the message. Next time be more careful."

She turns and walks back to the house, and I'm shocked. It's the first time she's really yelled at me. Ted hurries out of the pool and rests a hand on my shoulder. "Listen, don't worry about it."

"I'm sorry, Ted, I feel awful."

"She's mad at the school, not you. They're drowning us in paperwork. Vaccines, allergies, behavioral profiles—this stupid kindergarten application has more pages than my tax return."

"It was an honest mistake," I tell him. "I wrote down the phone number, but I was distracted by something Teddy gave me." I'm so desperate to make things right, I start describing the drawing to him, but Ted just talks over me. He seems anxious to get back to the house. I can see Caroline's silhouette in the sliding glass door, watching us.

"She'll cool off, don't worry," he says. "Tomorrow she won't even remember."

His voice is relaxed but he walks away in a hurry. As he crosses the yard, his form flattens into a silhouette—and when he reaches Caroline, he puts his arms around her. She reaches for the light switch, and after that I can't see anything else.

A little breeze kicks up and I start to shiver. I wrap my towel around my waist and walk back to my cottage. I lock the door and I'm changing into my pajamas when I hear the footfalls again, light steps treading on soft grass—only this time, they're right outside my window. I pull back the curtains and try to peek outside but all I see through the screen are the slimy wriggling moths.

A deer, I tell myself. It's just a deer.

I close the curtains and turn off the lights and get into bed, pulling the blankets up to my chin. Outside, the thing moves right behind my bed—I can hear it moving on the other side of the wall, inspecting the cottage, circling the perimeter, like it's searching for a way inside. I curl my fingers into a fist and bang on the wall, hoping a good loud noise will spook it away.

Instead, it ducks under the cottage, scratching at the dirt, squeezing itself beneath the floorboards. I don't know how anything can fit down there. The building can't be more than eighteen inches off the ground. There's no way it's a deer but it sounds big, like it's the size of a deer. I sit up in bed and stomp on the floor to no avail.

The thing just burrows deeper and deeper, wriggling itself into the center of the room. I stand up and turn on the lights. Then I climb down on all fours and listen, trying to follow the noise. I pull back the rug and discover a square outline cut into the floorboards—an access panel large enough for a person to crawl through. There are no hinges or handles, just two oval-shaped slots allowing someone to grab hold of the panel and lift.

I guess if it were earlier in the evening—and if Caroline wasn't already mad at me—I might call the Maxwells and ask for help. But I'm determined to fix the problem on my own. I go to the kitchen and fill a plastic pitcher with water. This thing, whatever it is, can't be as big as it sounds. I know noises can be deceiving, especially in the dark, especially late at night. I kneel on the floor and try to lift the panel, but it won't budge. All the summer humidity has expanded the wood, locking it into place. So I apply all my force to one side, pulling with both hands, ignoring the pain in my fingers, the sharp dry wood cutting into tender skin. Finally, with a loud pop and a cloud of gray dust, the panel springs out of the floor, like a cork exploding from a champagne bottle. I grab it and hold it close to my chest, using the panel like a shield. Then I lean forward and peer down into the hole.

It's too dark to see anything. The earth below is arid and lifeless, like ash left after a campfire. The cottage is silent. The creature, whatever it is, has vanished. There's nothing to see down there, just mounds of gray dust speckled with black spots. I realize I've been holding my breath, and I exhale with relief. All the noise from yanking open the hatch must have frightened the thing away.

But then the ash moves and the black spots blink and I realize I'm staring at the thing itself—rearing up on its legs to meet me, baring ugly pink claws and long sharp teeth. I scream, a full-bodied shriek that pierces the night. Then I slam down the panel and throw myself on top of it, using all my body weight to barricade the hatch. I hammer the edges with my fists, trying to force the warped wood back into place, but it no longer fits. Caroline is at my cottage within a minute, unlocking the door with her key. She's dressed in a nightgown and Ted is right behind her, shirtless, wearing pajama bottoms. They hear the noises under my cottage, the thrashing beneath the floorboards.

"It's a rat," I tell them, and I am so freaking relieved they're here, that I'm not alone anymore. "It's the biggest rat I've ever seen."

Ted takes the plastic pitcher of water and carries it outside while Caroline puts a hand on my shoulder, calming me, assuring me everything is going to be okay. Together we turn the panel ninety degrees so it fits back into the hatch, and then I hold it steady while she stomps the corners back into place. Even after she's finished, I'm afraid to move from the spot, afraid the panel will fly out of the floor. She stands beside me, holding me, until we hear a splash of water through the open window.

A moment later, Ted returns with an empty pitcher. "Possum," he says, grinning. "Not a rat. He moved pretty fast but I got him."

"Why was it under her cottage?"

"There's a hole in the lattice. On the west wall. Looks like a tiny section rotted off." Caroline frowns and starts to say something but Ted is way ahead of her. "I know, I know. I'll fix it tomorrow. I'll go to Home Depot."

"First thing tomorrow, Ted. This thing scared Mallory to death! What if she was bitten? What if it had rabies?"

"I'm fine," I tell her.

"She's fine," Ted says, but Caroline is unconvinced. She stares down at the hatch in the floor. "What if it comes back?"

Even though it's nearly midnight, Caroline insists that Ted go get his tool kit from the big house. She insists that he drive nails through the hatch into the floorboards so that nothing can ever force its way into my cottage. While we wait for him to finish, she boils water on my stove and makes chamomile tea for all three of us, and afterward the Maxwells stay a few minutes longer than necessary, just to make sure I feel calm and relaxed and safe. The three of us sit on the edge of my bed, talking and telling stories and eventually laughing, and it's like the scolding about the phone call never happened.

7

The next day is a hot and muggy Fourth of July and I force myself to go for a long run, eight miles in seventy-one minutes. On the walk home, I pass a house that Teddy and I have started calling the Flower Castle. It's three blocks from the Maxwells, a giant white mansion with a U-shaped driveway and a yard exploding with colorful flowers: chrysanthemums, geraniums, daylilies, and many others. I notice some new orange blossoms climbing a trellis in the front yard, so I take a few steps up the driveway to get a closer look. The flowers are so odd and peculiar—they look like tiny traffic cones—and I snap a few pictures with my cell phone. But then the front door opens, and a man steps outside. In my peripheral vision I see that he's wearing a suit and I sense he's come to chase me off his property, to yell at me for trespassing.

"Hey!"

I walk back to the sidewalk and wave a lame apology but it's too late. The guy is already out the door, coming after me.

"Mallory!" he calls. "How are you doing?"

And only then do I realize I've seen him before. It's well over ninety degrees but Adrian looks perfectly comfortable in his light gray suit, like all those guys in the Ocean's 11 movies. Under the jacket he wears a crisp white shirt and a royal blue tie. Without his cap on, I see he's got a mop of thick dark hair.

"I'm sorry," I tell him. "I didn't recognize you."

He glances down at his outfit, as if he's forgotten he's wearing it. "Oh, right! We have a thing tonight. At the golf club. My dad—he's getting an award."

"You live here?"

"My parents do. I'm home for the summer."

The front door opens and out walk his parents—his mother tall and elegant in a royal blue dress, his father in a classic black tuxedo with silver cuff links. "Is that El Jefe?"

"He's the Lawn King. We do half the lawns in South Jersey. In the summers he has a crew of eighty guys, but I swear to you, Mallory, I'm the only one he yells at."

His parents approach a black BMW that's parked in the driveway but Adrian waves them over to join us, and I really wish he hadn't. You know all those runners in Tampax ads who finish their workouts with glowing complexions and runway-ready hair? After eight miles in ninety-degree weather, I don't look anything like them. My shirt is soaked with sweat, my hair is a stringy, greasy mess, and there are dead gnats speckled all over my forehead.

"Mallory, this is my mother, Sofia, and my father, Ignacio." I dry my palm on my shorts before shaking their hands. "Mallory babysits for the Maxwells. The new family on Edgewood. They have a little boy named Teddy."

Sofia looks at me suspiciously. She's so well dressed and perfectly coiffed, I can't imagine she's broken a sweat in thirty years. But Ignacio greets me with a friendly smile. "You must be a very dedicated athlete, running in all this humidity!"

"Mallory's a distance runner at Penn State," Adrian explains. "She's on the cross-country team."

And I cringe at the lie because I've already forgotten about it. If

Adrian and I were alone, I'd come clean and fess up—but I can't say anything now, not with both his parents staring at me.

"I'm sure you're faster than my son," Ignacio says. "It takes him all day to mow two backyards!" Then he laughs uproariously at his own joke while Adrian shifts his feet, embarrassed.

"That's landscaping humor. My father thinks he's a stand-up comic."

Ignacio grins. "It's funny because it's true!"

Sofia studies my appearance and I'm convinced she sees right through me. "What year are you in?"

"Senior. Almost finished."

"Me, too!" Adrian says. "I go to Rutgers, in New Brunswick, for engineering. What's your major?"

And I have no idea how to answer this question. All my college planning focused exclusively on coaches, scouts, and Title IX funding. I never reached the point of considering what I might actually study. Business? Law? Biology? None of these answers seem credible—but now I'm taking too long to respond and they're all staring at me and I need to say something, anything—

"Teaching," I tell them.

Sofia looks skeptical. "You mean education?"

She pronounces the word slowly—*ed-u-ca-tion*—like she suspects I'm hearing it for the first time.

"Right. For little kids."

"Elementary education?"

"Exactly."

Adrian is delighted. "My mom teaches fourth grade! She was an education major, too!"

"No kidding!" And it's a good thing I'm flush from my run, because I'm sure my face is burning.

"It's the most noble profession," Ignacio says. "You've made a wonderful choice, Mallory."

At this point I'm desperate to change the subject, to say something—*anything*—that's not a lie. "Your flowers are beautiful," I tell them. "I run past your house every day to look at them."

"Then here's the million-dollar question," Ignacio says. "Which is your favorite?"

Adrian explains this is a game that his parents play with visitors. "The idea is that your favorite flower says something about your personality. Like a horoscope."

"They're all so beautiful," I tell them.

Sofia refuses to let me off the hook. "You have to pick one. Whatever you like best."

So I point to the orange flowers that just came up, the ones that are growing on the trellis. "I don't know the name, but they remind me of little orange traffic cones."

"Trumpet vines," Adrian says.

Ignacio seems delighted. "No one ever picks the trumpet vine! She's a beautiful flower, very versatile and low-maintenance. You give her a little sun and water—not too much attention—and she takes care of herself. Very independent."

"But also kind of a weed," Sofia adds. "A little hard to control."

"That's called vitality!" Ignacio says. "It's good!"

Adrian shoots an exasperated look in my direction—see what I have to put up with?—and his mother reminds them that they're very late, that they need to get going. So we all say hasty goodbyes and nice-to-meet-yous and I resume walking home.

A few seconds later, the black BMW drives past and Ignacio toots the horn while Sofia stares straight ahead. Adrian waves to me through the rear window and I catch a glimpse of the little boy he used to be—traveling with his parents in the backseat of their car, riding his bike on these shady sidewalks, accepting these beautiful tree-lined streets as a kind of birthright. I have the sense his childhood was perfect, that he has lived life with absolutely zero regrets.

Somehow I've made it to twenty-one without ever having had a real boyfriend. I mean, I've been with men—when you are a reasonably normal-looking woman addicted to drugs, there is always one surefire way to acquire more drugs—but I've never had anything resembling a traditional relationship.

But in the Hallmark Channel movie version of my life—in an alternate reality where I'm raised in Spring Brook by kind, affluent, well-educated parents like Ted and Caroline—my ideal boyfriend would be someone a lot like Adrian. He's cute, he's funny, he works hard. And as I walk along I start doing the arithmetic in my head, trying to calculate when two full weeks will elapse and he'll be back to work on the Maxwells' yard.

Spring Brook is full of small children but I've had no luck introducing Teddy to anyone. At the end of our block is a big playground full of swings, spinners, and shrieking, screaming five-year-olds—but Teddy wants nothing to do with them.

One Monday morning we find ourselves sitting on a park bench, watching a group of little boys "drive" their Hot Wheels down a sliding board. I urge Teddy to go over and play with them and he says, "I don't have a Hot Wheels."

"Ask them to share."

"I don't want to share."

He slouches next to me on the bench, pissed off.

"Teddy, please."

"I'll play with you. Not them."

"You need friends your own age. You start school in two months."

But there's no convincing him. We spend the rest of the morning playing LEGOS in the house, and then he eats lunch and goes upstairs for Quiet Time. I know I should use my downtime to clean the kitchen but it's hard to muster the energy. I didn't sleep well the night before—

the Fourth of July fireworks went pretty late—and arguing with Teddy has left me feeling defeated.

I decide to lie down on the sofa for a few minutes and the next thing I know Teddy is standing over me, shaking me awake.

"Can we go swimming now?"

I sit up and notice the light in the room has changed. It's almost three o'clock. "Yes, of course, get your swimsuit."

He hands me a drawing and runs out of the room. It's the same dark and tangled forest from the previous picture—only this time, the man is shoveling dirt into a large hole, and Anya's body lies crumpled at the bottom.

Teddy returns to the den, wearing his swimsuit. "Ready?"

"Hang on, Teddy. What is this?"

"What is what?"

"Who is this person? In the hole?"

"Anya."

"And who's the man?"

"I don't know."

"Is he burying her?"

"In a forest."

"Why?"

"Because he stole Anya's little girl," Teddy says. "Also can I have some watermelon before swimming?"

"Sure, Teddy, but why—"

It's too late. He's already skipping into the kitchen and pulling open the refrigerator. I follow and find him standing on tiptoes, reaching for the top shelf and a slab of ripe red melon. I help him carry it over to the butcher block and then I use a chef's knife to carve off a slice. Teddy doesn't wait for a plate; he just grabs it and starts eating.

"T-Bear, listen to me, what else did Anya say to you? About the drawing?"

His mouth is full of melon and red juice dribbles down his chin. "The man dug a hole so no one would find her," he says with a shrug. "But I guess she got out."

8

That night the whole family goes out for dinner. Caroline invites me to join in, but I tell her I need to run, and then I putter around the cottage until I hear her car backing out of the driveway.

Then I walk across the lawn to the house next door.

Mitzi has one of the smallest houses on the block, a redbrick ranch with a metal roof and roller shades drawn tight over every window. Her place would look right at home in my old neighborhood of South Philly, but here in well-to-do Spring Brook it's a bit of an eyesore. The rusty rain gutters are sagging, weeds have sprouted in the sidewalk cracks, and the mottled yard could use some help from Lawn King. Caroline has commented more than once that she can't wait for Mitzi to move away, so a developer will bulldoze the house and start over.

There's a small handwritten note taped to the front door: WELCOME CLIENTS. PLEASE USE BACK ENTRANCE. I have to knock three times before Mitzi finally answers. She keeps the chain latched and peers out through the one-inch gap. "Yes?"

"It's Mallory. From next door?"

She unlatches the chain and opens the door. "Jesus, Mary, and Joseph, you scared the heck out of me!" She's wearing a purple kimono and clutching a canister of pepper spray. "What are you thinking, banging on the door so late?"

It's just a few minutes past seven and the little girls down the street are still out on the sidewalk playing hopscotch. I present a small plate of cookies covered in Saran Wrap. "Teddy and I made gingersnaps."

Her eyes go wide. "I'll put on coffee."

She grabs my wrist and pulls me into a darkened living room, and I blink my eyes to adjust to the gloom. The house is dirty. The air has a musty, skunky smell that's part cannabis and part high school locker room. The sofa and armchairs are shrouded in clear plastic slipcovers, but I can see a layer of grime on the surfaces, as if they haven't been wiped down in months.

Mitzi leads me into the kitchen and I find the back of her house a little more pleasant. Her shades are open and the windows overlook the forest. Spider plants hang from the ceiling in baskets with long leafy tendrils spilling over the sides. The cabinets and appliances are straight out of the 1980s and everything feels familiar, cozy, like my neighbors' kitchens in South Philly. Spread across the Formica kitchen table are sheets of newspaper and several oiled pieces of black metal, including a spring and a barrel and a trigger. I realize that if a person assembled these pieces in the right order, the result would be a handgun.

"You caught me cleaning it," Mitzi explains, and with a sweep of her arm she pushes everything to one side of the table, jumbling all the parts. "Now how do you take your coffee?"

"Do you have decaf?"

"Yuck, no, never. That's just chemicals in a cup. Tonight we're drinking good old-fashioned Folgers."

I don't want to tell her I'm in recovery so I just say I'm very sensitive to caffeine. Mitzi promises one little cup won't hurt me and I figure she's probably right.

"I'll take some milk, if you have it."

"We'll use half-and-half. It has a fuller flavor."

An old Kit-Cat Klock hangs on the wall, grinning mischievously, its tail swishing back and forth. Mitzi plugs an ancient Mr. Coffee machine into the wall and fills its reservoir with water. "How's everything next door? You like the job?"

"It's good."

"Those parents must drive you crazy."

"They're fine."

"I don't know why that woman works, if we're being honest. I'm sure the husband makes plenty. And you know the VA hospital doesn't pay squat. So why not stay home? Who is she trying to impress?"

"Maybe—"

"Some women don't want to be mothers, in my opinion. They want children, they want cute pictures to put on Facebook. But do they want the actual *experience* of mothering?"

"Well—"

"I'll tell you one thing: The boy is adorable. I could gobble him up. I would babysit him for nothing, if they'd asked me nicely, if they just showed me a little common courtesy. But that's the problem with Millenniums! They don't have any values!"

She keeps talking while we wait for the coffee, sharing her frustrations about Whole Foods Market (overpriced), #metoo victims (whiny and entitled), and daylight saving time (never mentioned anywhere in the Constitution). I start to wonder if coming here was a mistake. I need to talk to someone, and I'm not sure if Mitzi is much of a listener. I'm developing a theory about Teddy's drawings but I don't want to worry Russell and I definitely can't tell the Maxwells; they're such devout atheists, I know they'll never consider my ideas. Mitzi is my last best hope.

"Can you tell me more about Annie Barrett?"

This stops her short.

"Why are you asking?"

"I'm just curious."

"No, Princess, that's a very specific question. And forgive me for saying this but you don't look so hot."

I make Mitzi promise not to say anything—especially to the Maxwells—then I place Teddy's latest artwork on the table.

"Teddy's drawing some unusual pictures. He says he's getting these ideas from his imaginary friend. Her name is Anya, and she visits him in his bedroom, when no one else is around."

Mitzi examines the drawings and a shadow falls over her face. "So why are you asking about Annie Barrett?"

"Well, it's just that the names are so similar. Anya and Annie. I know it's normal for children to have imaginary friends. Lots of kids do. But Teddy says Anya told him to draw these pictures. A man dragging a woman through a forest. A man burying a woman's body. And then Anya told Teddy to give these pictures to me."

A silence settles over the kitchen—the longest silence I've yet experienced in Mitzi's presence. All I can hear is Mr. Coffee gurgling and the steady *swish-swish-swish* of the Kit-Cat's tail. Mitzi studies the illustrations carefully—almost like she's trying to see *through* the illustrations, past the pencil marks and into the fibers of the paper. I'm not sure she fully understands what I'm driving at, so I spell it out for her:

"I know this sounds crazy, but I guess I'm wondering if Anya's spirit is somehow bound to the property. If she's trying to communicate using Teddy."

Mitzi stands up, goes over to the coffeepot, and fills two mugs. With trembling hands, she carries the mugs back to the table. I pour in some cream and take a sip and it is the strongest, most bitter coffee I've ever tasted. But I drink it, anyway. I don't want to insult her. I'm desperate for someone to listen to my theory and tell me I'm not crazy.

"I've done some reading about this," Mitzi finally says. "Historically, children have always been more receptive to the spirit community. A child's mind doesn't have all the barriers we adults put up."

"So—it's possible?"

"Depends. Have you mentioned anything to his parents?"

"They're atheists. They think—"

"Oh, I know, they think they're smarter than everyone else."

"I want to do more research before I sit down with them. Try to connect the dots. Maybe something in these pictures overlaps with Annie Barrett's story." I lean across the table, talking faster. Already I can feel the caffeine waking up my central nervous system. My thoughts are sharper, my pulse is quickening. I'm no longer bothered by the bitter taste and I take another sip. "According to Teddy, the man in these drawings stole Anya's little girl. Do you know if Annie had any children?"

"That's a really interesting question," Mitzi says. "But the answer will be clearer if I start at the beginning." She settles back in her chair, getting comfortable, and pops a cookie into her mouth. "Just remember, Annie Barrett died before I was born. So these are stories I heard growing up, but I can't guarantee they're actually true."

"That's fine." I take another sip of coffee. "Tell me everything."

"The original owner of your house was a man named George Barrett. He was an engineer for DuPont, the chemical company, up in Gibbstown. He had a wife and three daughters, and his cousin Annie came to live here in 1946, right after World War II. She moved into your guest cottage and she used it as a kind of studio-slash-guesthouse. She was about your age and very pretty, long black hair and just knockout gorgeous. All the GIs are coming home from Europe and they go nuts for her, they forget all about their high school sweethearts. They start coming around George's house day and night, asking if his cousin is free to talk.

"But Annie's shy, she's quiet, she keeps to herself. She doesn't dance or go to the movies, she turns down all their invitations. And she doesn't even go to church, which was a big no-no back then. She just stays in her cottage and paints. Or she walks around Hayden's

Glen, looking for subjects to sketch. And so gradually the whole town kind of turns on her. Word gets around that she's an unwed mother, that she put her child up for adoption and moved to Spring Brook in disgrace. Then the rumors get even worse. People say she's a witch, and she's luring all the husbands into the woods to have sex with them." Mitzi laughs at the absurdity of the idea. "Because that's just how women talk, you know? I'm sure all the moms on this block say the same things about me!"

She takes another sip of coffee and continues: "Anyway, so one day George Barrett walks over to the cottage, knocks on the door, no answer. He goes inside and there's blood everywhere. All over the bed, all over the walls. 'Up to the rafters,' he told my father. But there's no body. No sign of Annie anywhere. George calls the police and the whole town searches the forest, combing all the trails, dragging nets through the creek, search dogs, the whole nine yards. And you know what they found? Nothing. She vanished. End of story."

"Has anyone lived in the cottage since the '40s?"

Mitzi shakes her head no. "My parents said George nearly knocked it down. To erase the memory of the tragedy. Instead he turned it into a toolshed. And like I told you, when I was growing up in the '50s and '60s, we all called it the Devil House. We were all afraid of it. But it was just a tall tale, a local legend in our own backyard. I never saw anything that truly frightened me."

"What about the next owners? After George died?"

"Well, after George passed, his wife sold the house to Butch and Bobbie Hercik. They were my neighbors forty years. They built the pool that you and Teddy go swimming in. We were real close, terrific friends."

"Did they have children?"

"Three girls, two boys, and zero problems. And I was close with Bobbie. If her kids were drawing dead people, she'd have told me." Mitzi takes another sip of her coffee. "Of course they had the good sense to leave the guest cottage alone. Maybe when the Maxwells fixed it up, they disturbed something. Unlocked some kind of hostile energy."

I imagine myself approaching Ted and Caroline and warning that they'd released a malevolent spirit. I'm pretty sure they would start searching Craigslist for a new babysitter. And then what would I do, where would I go? My heartbeat surges, like a revving engine stuck in neutral, and I rest a hand on my chest.

I need to relax.

I need to calm down.

I need to stop drinking coffee.

"Would you mind if I used your bathroom?"

Mitzi points me back toward the living room. "First door on your left. The light's on a string, you'll see it."

The bathroom is small and cramped, with an old-fashioned clawfoot tub that's cocooned in vinyl shower curtains. The instant I turn on the light, a silverfish skitters across the tiled floor and disappears through a crack in the grout. I lean over the sink, turn on the faucet, and splash my face with cold water. My heart palpitations level off and I reach for a guest towel, only to find they're all covered with a fine layer of dust, like they haven't been touched in years. There's a pink terry cloth robe hanging on the back of the door and I use its sleeve to blot my face dry.

Then I open Mitzi's medicine cabinet and take a quick look around. Back in high school I used to snoop in bathrooms all the time, because you'd be amazed at the prescription pharmaceuticals that people left unsupervised; I could skim pills and sometimes entire bottles without anyone getting suspicious. And I guess with my heart racing and my legs shaking I feel like I'm back in high school again. Mitzi's medicine chest is stocked like a freaking Walgreens, four crowded shelves of Q-tips and cotton balls, medicated pads and petroleum jelly, tweezers, antacids, and half-flattened tubes of Monistat and hydrocortisone. Plus a dozen orange prescription bottles, everything from Lipitor and Synthroid to amoxicillin and erythromycin. And way, way, way in the back, hidden behind all the others, is my old friend oxycodone. I had a hunch I'd find some. These days, almost everyone has Oxy in their house, a half-finished bottle of pills left over from a minor surgical procedure. And few people ever notice when these pills go missing. . . .

I twist off the cap and peer inside the bottle: empty. Then Mitzi taps on the door and I nearly drop everything in the sink. "Make sure you hold the handle when you flush, okay? I've got a problem with my flapper."

"Sure," I tell her. "No problem."

And suddenly I'm furious with myself for snooping, for backsliding. I feel like Mitzi's caught me red-handed. I blame the coffee—I never should have had the coffee. I put back the bottle and turn on the tap and take long slurps of cold water, hoping to dilute the toxins in my system. I'm ashamed of myself, nineteen months sober and snooping around an old lady's medicine cabinet. What the hell is happening to me? I flush the toilet and hold the lever until all the water goes down.

When I return to the kitchen, Mitzi is waiting at the table with a wooden board that's covered with letters and numbers. I realize it's some kind of Ouija board—but it's nothing like the flimsy cardboard sets I remember from childhood sleepovers. This one is a thick slab of maple engraved with arcane symbols. It looks less like a toy and more like a butcher's block.

"Here's what I'm thinking," Mitzi says. "If this spirit wants to tell you something, let's cut out the middleman. Bypass Teddy and contact her directly."

"Like a séance?"

"I prefer the term 'gathering.' But not here. We'll get better results in your cottage. How about tomorrow?"

"I have to watch Teddy."

"Right, I know, we need Teddy involved. This spirit has attached herself to him. We have a much better chance of communicating if he joins us."

"No way, Mitzi. I can't."

"Why not?"

"His parents would kill me."

"I'll talk to them."

"No, no, no," I tell her, and panic creeps into my voice. "You promised you wouldn't say anything to them. Please, Mitzi, I cannot lose this job."

"Why are you so worried?"

I tell her about the House Rules from my job interview—how I've been hired to teach science, not religion or superstition. "I can't bring Teddy to a séance. If he sneezes, I can't even say 'God Bless You.'"

Mitzi taps the drawings with her finger. "These pictures aren't normal, sweetie. Something weird is happening in that house."

I take back the drawings, stuff them into my bag, and thank her for the coffee. My pulse is revving again—more heart palpitations. I thank Mitzi for the advice and open the back door to leave. "Just don't say anything to them, okay? I'm trusting you to keep this secret."

She covers her wooden board with a sheath made of black velvet. "My offer stands if you change your mind. And I pretty much guarantee you will."

I'm back at my cottage by eight o'clock and still awake at four in the morning. Sleeping is impossible. The coffee was a huge mistake. I try all the usual tricks—deep breaths, a glass of warm milk, a long hot shower—but nothing helps. The mosquitoes are relentless, and the only way to quiet them is to pull the sheets up over my head, exposing my bare feet. I'm just so disappointed in myself. I can't believe I opened her goddamn medicine cabinet. I toss and turn and obsess over my two minutes in Mitzi's bathroom, trying to pinpoint the exact moment my brain switched to autopilot. I thought I could manage my addiction, but apparently I'm still Anything-for-a-Bump Mallory, still raiding medicine cabinets for ways to get high.

I wake to my alarm at seven o'clock, feeling groggy and ashamed of myself—and determined not to backslide again.

No more coffee, ever.

No more obsessing over pictures.

And no more talk of Annie Barrett.

Thankfully, when I get to the big house, there's a brand-new crisis to distract me. Teddy's favorite charcoal pencils have gone missing and he can't find them anywhere. We walk to the art store to buy a new pack and as soon as we're home, he hurries upstairs for Quiet Time. I'm still exhausted from my sleepless night so I move into the den and collapse on the sofa. I only mean to close my eyes for a few minutes, but once again Teddy has to shake me awake.

"You're napping again!"

I leap to my feet. "Sorry, Teddy Bear."

"Are we going swimming?"

"Definitely. Put your suit on."

I feel a million times better. The nap was just enough sleep to recharge my batteries, to bring me back to baseline normal. Teddy runs to get his swimsuit and I see he's left a new drawing facedown on the coffee table. And I know I ought to leave it there. Let his mother or father deal with it. But I can't help myself. Curiosity gets the better of me. I turn the paper over, and this is pretty much the last straw.

Look, I know there are many different kinds of parents—liberal parents and conservative parents, atheist parents and religious parents, helicopter parents and workaholic parents and totally toxic parents. And I know all these different parents have wildly different ideas about the best way to raise children. But when I study this picture and see Anya with her eyes squeezed shut and two hands wrapped tight around her neck—well, I think all parents would agree this is pretty fucked-up?

9

Caroline is home from work at five thirty and I resist the temptation to ambush her as soon as she walks through the door. She's busy, she's distracted, she needs to greet her son and start making dinner. So when she asks about our day, I just smile and tell her everything is fine.

I go out for a run but I'm still tired from the night before and after thirty minutes I give up. I walk past the Flower Castle, but there's no sign of Adrian or his family. I go home and shower; I microwave a frozen burrito and try to lose myself in a Hallmark movie. But I'm too distracted to concentrate. My mind keeps going back to the last drawing, to the picture of the hands squeezed tight around Anya's throat.

I wait until nine o'clock, until I'm certain Teddy will be asleep in his bedroom. Then I gather the three most recent drawings and step outside. I hear voices whispering in the wind and I recognize two figures sitting out by the pool. Ted and Caroline are dressed in white robes and sharing a bottle of wine. They look like the happy couples you see in advertisements for cruise ships—like they've just embarked on a seven-day excursion with Royal Caribbean. Caroline is lying back in Ted's lap and he is gently massaging her shoulders.

"Just a quick dip," he's saying. "To relax you."

"I'm already relaxed."

"Then should we go upstairs?"

"What about Teddy?"

"What *about* Teddy? He's asleep."

I step lightly over the soft springy grass and I'm halfway across the yard when my heel comes down on a sprinkler head. My ankle twists and I fall on my tailbone, slamming my elbow into the ground, and I can't help it: I cry out in pain.

Caroline and Ted come running across the yard. "Mallory? Are you all right?" I've got my hand cupped over my elbow—the pain is so sudden and searing, I'm certain I'm bleeding. But when I lift my fingers to look, I see the skin is bruised but not broken.

"I'm okay. I just tripped."

"Let's get you into the light," Ted says. "Can you stand up?"

"I just need a minute."

Ted doesn't wait. He slides his arm under my knees, then stands and carries me like a child. He walks me back to the pool deck and gently lowers me into a patio chair.

"I'm fine," I tell them. "Really."

Caroline inspects my elbow anyway. "What were you doing in the yard? Did you need something?"

"It can wait."

Through it all, I've managed to keep my grip on the three drawings, and Caroline sees them. "Did Teddy do these?"

At this point I decide I have nothing left to lose. "He asked me not to show you. But I think you ought to look at them."

Caroline studies the pictures and her face falls. Then she shoves the papers into her husband's hands.

"This is *your* fault," she says.

Ted sees the first picture and laughs. "Oh, dear. Is this person being strangled?"

"Yes, Ted, she's being murdered and her body is being dragged through a forest and I wonder where our sweet gentle little boy got all these terrible ideas?"

Ted raises both hands in a show of surrender. "Brothers Grimm," he explains. "I read him a different story every night."

"These aren't the Disney versions," Caroline tells me. "The original stories are much more violent. You know that scene in Cinderella, where the wicked stepsister tries on the glass slipper? In the original, she slices off her toes to make it fit. The slipper fills with blood. It's horrifying!"

"He's a boy, Caroline. Boys love this stuff!"

"I don't care. It's not healthy. Tomorrow I'm going to the library and getting some Disney storybooks. No strangling, no murders, just good clean G-rated fun."

Ted tips the bottle of wine into his glass and gives himself an extra-large pour. "Now that's *my* idea of horror," he says. "But what do I know? I'm just the boy's father."

"And I'm the licensed psychiatrist."

They look at me like they're waiting for me to choose a side, to declare which parent is right.

"I don't think this is a fairy tale," I tell them. "Teddy says he's getting these ideas from Anya. He says Anya is telling him what to draw."

"Of course he does," Caroline says. "Teddy knows we won't approve of these pictures. He knows it's wrong to draw women being strangled and killed and buried. But if Anya says it's okay, then he's allowed to proceed. He can achieve a kind of cognitive dissonance."

Ted's nodding along with his wife, like this all makes perfect sense, but I have no idea what she's talking about. Cognitive dissonance?

"Teddy says he's drawing Anya's story. He says the man in the pictures stole Anya's little girl."

"That's classic Brothers Grimm," Ted explains. "Half their stories have children gone missing. Hansel and Gretel, the Pied Piper, Godfather Death—"

"Godfather Death?" Caroline shakes her head. "Please, Ted. These stories. They're too much. You need to stop."

Ted takes another look at the drawings and at last he surrenders. "All right, fine. From now on, I'll stick with Dr. Seuss. Or Richard Scarry. But I will not read those awful Berenstain Bears, that's where I draw the line." He puts an arm around Caroline and squeezes her shoulder. "You win, hon, okay?"

And he's acting like the matter is resolved, like now we should all go inside and call it a night. But I worry that if I don't ask my question now, I might never have another opportunity. "I just thought of one other possibility," I tell them. "What if Anya is Annie Barrett?"

Caroline is confused. "Who?"

"The woman murdered in my cottage. In the 1940s. What if Teddy goes into his bedroom for Quiet Time and communicates with her spirit?"

Ted laughs like I've made a joke—and Caroline shoots another angry look in his direction. "What, seriously? You mean like a ghost?"

There's no turning back now. I need to outline my case: "The names are so similar. Annie and Anya. Plus, you said that Teddy never liked to draw in Barcelona. But as soon as you moved back to the United States—as soon as you moved onto *this property*—where Annie Barrett disappeared—he started drawing like crazy. Those were your exact words: 'like crazy.'"

"I just meant he has an active imagination."

"But he's talking to someone. In his bedroom. I stand at his door listening, and he's having long conversations."

Caroline narrows her eyes. "Do you hear the ghost, too? Do you hear the sad baleful voice of Annie Barrett giving art direction to my son?" I admit that I don't, and Caroline reacts like this proves something. "Because he's talking to himself, Mallory. It's a sign of intelligence. Gifted children do it all the time."

"But what about his other problems?"

"Problems? Teddy has problems?"

"He wets his bed. He wears the same striped shirt every day. He refuses to play with other children. And now he's drawing pictures of a woman getting murdered. You add all that up, Caroline, I don't know. I'm worried. I think he should see a doctor."

"I *am* a doctor," Caroline says, and all-too-late I realize I've struck a nerve.

Ted reaches for her wineglass and fills it.

"Honey, here."

She waves it off. "I am fully capable of assessing my child's mental health."

"I know—"

"Really? You don't sound like you do."

"I'm just worried. Teddy is such a sweet, gentle, innocent boy. But these drawings feel like they're coming from a different place. They feel dirty to me. Impure. Mitzi thinks—"

"Mitzi? You showed these pictures to Mitzi?"

"She thinks maybe you disturbed something. When you renovated the guest cottage."

"You talked to *Mitzi* before you came to us?"

"Because I knew you would react this way!"

"If you mean rationally, then yes, you're right, I don't believe a word that woman says. Neither should you. She's a burnout, Mallory. She's a drugged-up, fucked-up mess!"

And the words just hang between us. I've never heard Caroline swear before. I've never heard her use this kind of language to describe an addict.

"Look," Ted says. "We appreciate your concern, Mallory." He rests a hand on his wife's knee. "Don't we, hon? We're big believers in honest communication."

"But we will *not* blame Teddy's bedwetting on ghosts," Caroline says. "You understand that, right? The state would take away my license. Bedwetting is normal. Being shy is normal. Having a pretend playmate is normal. And these pictures—"

"Mommy?"

We all turn and there's Teddy—standing on the far side of the pool fence, dressed in his fire truck pajamas and holding his Godzilla doll. I have no idea how long he's been waiting or how much he's heard.

"I can't fall asleep."

"Go back to your room and try again," Caroline says.

"It's late, big guy," Ted says.

Their son looks down at his bare feet. The light from the swimming pool casts his body in a murky blue glow. He looks anxious, like maybe he doesn't want to go back alone.

"Go on," Caroline tells him. "I'll check on you in twenty minutes. But you need to try on your own."

"Oh, and buddy?" Ted calls. "No more pictures of Anya, okay? You're scaring Mallory."

Teddy turns to me—wounded, eyes wide with betrayal.

"No, no, no," I tell him. "It's fine—"

Ted holds up the three drawings. "No one wants to see these, buddy. They're too scary. From now on, draw nice things, okay? Horses, sunflowers."

Teddy turns and runs across the lawn.

Caroline scowls at her husband. "That was *not* the right thing to say."

Ted shrugs and takes another sip of wine. "The kid needs to hear it sooner or later. He starts school in two months. You think his teachers won't have the same concerns?"

She stands up. "I'm going inside."

I stand up, too. "Caroline, I'm sorry. I didn't mean to offend you. I was just worried."

She doesn't stop or turn around, just marches across the lawn toward the house. "It's fine, Mallory. Good night."

But it's obviously not fine. This is even worse than the last time she yelled at me. She's so angry, she won't even look at me. And I feel silly for crying but I can't help myself.

Why did I have to mention Mitzi?

Why couldn't I keep my mouth shut?

Ted pulls me close and lets me rest my head on his chest. "Listen, it's okay, you were just being honest. But when it comes to raising children, the mother is always right. Even when she's wrong. Do you know what I mean?"

"I'm just worried—"

"Leave the worrying to Caroline. She'll worry enough for the both of you. She's very protective of Teddy, haven't you noticed? We struggled a long time to have him. It was a lot of work. And the ordeal—I guess it left her feeling insecure. Now, on top of all that, she's gone back to work—a whole new reason to feel guilty! So anytime something goes wrong, my wife takes it very personally."

I hadn't considered this before, but everything Ted is saying rings true. In the mornings, when Caroline is running out the door for work, she always seems guilty about leaving the house. Maybe even jealous that I'm the person who gets to stay home and bake cupcakes with Teddy. I've been so busy admiring Caroline, I've never stopped to think that she might be envious of me.

I've managed to catch my breath and stop crying. Ted seems anxious to get back to his house, to check on his wife, and I have one more request before he goes. I hand him the three drawings, absolving myself of all responsibility. "Would you mind taking these? So I don't have to look at them anymore?"

"Of course." Ted folds the pages in half and then rips them into pieces. "You'll never have to see these pictures again."

10

I sleep poorly and wake up feeling awful. Caroline Maxwell has treated me better than I deserve—she's welcomed me into her home, she's trusted me with her child, she's given me everything I need to start a new life—and I can't stand knowing she's angry with me. I lie in bed imagining a hundred different ways to say I'm sorry. And eventually I can't put it off any longer, I have to get out of bed and face her.

When I arrive at the main house, Teddy's down under the kitchen table, dressed in his pajamas, playing with his Lincoln Logs. Caroline's at the kitchen sink, washing the breakfast dishes, and I offer to take over. "Also, I wanted to say I'm sorry."

Caroline turns off the water. "No, Mallory, *I'm* sorry. I had too much wine, and I was wrong to blow up at you. It's been bothering me all morning."

She opens her arms and we hug and we both apologize again, at the same time. And then we're laughing together and I know everything is going to be fine.

"You're still welcome here in the main house," she reminds me. "You could take the bedroom next to Teddy's. I'd only need a day to get it ready."

But I don't want to cause her any more inconvenience. "The cottage is perfect," I tell her. "I love it out there."

"Okay, but if you change your mind—"

I take the dish towel from her hand and nod at the clock on the microwave oven. It's 7:27 and I know Caroline likes to be on the road by 7:35, before the traffic turns horrendous. "Let me finish," I tell her. "Go have a great day."

So Caroline leaves for work and I get down to business. There isn't really much to clean—just a few cups and cereal bowls, and the wineglasses from the night before. After I load everything into the dishwasher, I get down on my hands and knees and crawl under the kitchen table. Teddy has built a two-story farmhouse out of Lincoln Logs, and now he's surrounding it with tiny plastic animals.

"What are we playing?"

"They're a family. They live together."

"Can I be the pig?"

He shrugs. "If you want."

I push the pig around the other animals and make it *beep-beep-beep* like a car. Normally Teddy loves this joke. He loves it when I make the animals honk like a truck or choo-choo like a train. But this morning he just turns his back to me. And, of course, I know what's wrong.

"Teddy, listen. I want to talk about last night. I think your daddy misunderstood me. Because I love *all* your drawings. Even the ones with Anya. I always look forward to seeing your pictures."

Teddy pushes a plastic cat up a table leg, like it's climbing a tree. I try to move in front of him, try to force eye contact, but he swivels away. "I want you to keep sharing your drawings, okay?"

"Mommy says no."

"But I'm saying you can. It's fine."

"She says you're not well, and scary pictures could make you sick again."

I sit up so fast I bang my head on the bottom of the table. The pain is white hot and for the next few moments I can't move. I just squeeze my eyes shut and hold my hand to my scalp.

"Mallory?"

I open my eyes and I realize I finally have his attention. He looks frightened. "I'm fine," I tell him. "And I need you to listen very carefully. There's nothing you can do that would make me sick. You don't have to worry. I am one hundred percent fine."

Teddy gallops a horse up my leg and parks it on my knee. "Is your head okay?"

"My head is fine," I tell him, even though it's throbbing like crazy and I can feel a bump swelling on my scalp. "I just need to put something on it."

I spend the next few minutes sitting at the kitchen table, pressing a sandwich bag of ice to the top of my skull. Down at my feet, Teddy is pretend-playing with all his different farm animals. Each creature has its own distinct voice and personality. There's stubborn Mr. Goat and bossy Mama Hen, a brave black stallion and a silly baby duckling, more than a dozen characters in all.

"I don't want to do my chores," the horse says.

"But rules are rules," Mama Hen tells him. "We all have to follow the rules!"

"It's not fair," Mr. Goat complains.

On and on it goes—the conversation pivots from chores to lunch to a secret treasure buried in the forest behind the barn. I'm impressed by Teddy's ability to remember all the different characters and their voices. But, of course, this is what Ted and Caroline have been saying all along: Their son has an extremely active imagination. End of story.

Later that afternoon, when Teddy goes to his bedroom for Quiet Time, I wait a few minutes then follow him upstairs. By the time I press my

ear to the door of his bedroom, he's already in the middle of a conversation.

". . . or we could build a fort."

". . . . ."

"Or play tag."

". . . . ."

"No, I can't. I'm not allowed."

". . . . ."

"They said I can't."

". . . . ."

"I'm sorry but—"

". . . . ."

"I don't understand."

". . . . ."

Then he laughs, like she's proposed something ridiculous. "I guess
we could try?"

". . . . ."

"How do we—okay. Right."

". . . . ."

"Oh, it's cold!"

There's no more speaking after that—but as I strain to hear what's happening, I detect a kind of whisper—the sound of a pencil scratching on paper.

Drawing?

Is he drawing again?

I go downstairs, sit at the kitchen table, and wait.

Normally Quiet Time isn't much more than an hour, but Teddy stays in his room twice as long. And when he finally comes down to the kitchen, he's empty-handed.

I smile at him. "There he is!"

He climbs up onto a kitchen chair. "Hello."

"No drawing today?"

"Can I have cheese and crackers?"

"Sure."

I go over to the refrigerator and fix him a plate. "So what were you doing upstairs?"

"Can I have some milk?"

I pour him a small cup of milk, then carry everything over to the kitchen table. As he reaches for a cracker, I notice his palms and fingers are covered with black smudges. "Maybe you should wash your hands," I suggest. "It looks like you've got pencil on them."

He hurries over to the sink and washes his hands without comment. Then he returns to the table and starts eating the crackers. "Do you want to play LEGOs?"

And for the next few days, things are pretty normal. Teddy and I fill the hours with LEGOs and puppet shows, Play-Doh and Shrinky Dinks, coloring books and Tinkertoys and endless trips to the grocery store. He is a brave, adventurous eater and he loves to sample strange and exotic foods. Some days we'll walk to Wegmans and buy jicama or a kumquat, just to see what they taste like.

He's one of the most curious children I've ever met, and he loves to challenge me with imponderable questions: Why are there clouds? Who invented clothes? How do snails work? I am constantly reaching for my phone and checking Wikipedia. One afternoon in the swimming pool, Teddy points at my chest and asks why I have bumps poking through my swimsuit. I don't make a big deal out of it. I just say they're part of my body and the cold water makes them hard.

"You have them, too," I tell him.

He laughs. "No, I don't!"

"Sure you do! Everybody does."

Later, when I'm rinsing off in the outdoor shower stall, I hear him knocking on the wooden door.

"Hey, Mallory?"

"Yeah?"

"Can you *see* your girl parts?"

"How do you mean?"

"If you look down? Can you see them?"

"It's hard to explain, Teddy. Not really?"

There's a long pause.

"Then how do you know they're there?"

And I'm glad there's a door between us, so he can't see me laughing. "I just know, Teddy. They're definitely there."

That night I mention the incident to Caroline and instead of laughing she seems alarmed. The next day she comes home with a giant stack of picture books with titles like *It's Perfectly Normal!* and *Where Did I Come From?* They're way more explicit than the books I had growing up. There are detailed definitions of anal sex, cunnilingus, and genderqueer expression. With full-color drawings and everything. I mention that it all seems a bit much for a five-year-old, but Caroline disagrees. She says it's essential human biology and she wants Teddy to learn the facts at an early age so he won't get misinformation from his friends.

"I understand, but cunnilingus? He's five."

Caroline glances at the cross hanging from my neck, like somehow *that's* the problem. "Next time he has questions, just send him to me. I want to answer them."

I try to assure her that I am totally capable of answering Teddy's questions but she makes it clear the conversation is over. She's already opening kitchen cabinets and noisily gathering pots and pans to make dinner. It's the first night in a while she doesn't invite me to stay and eat with them.

Two-hour Quiet Times are getting more and more common, and I don't know how Teddy passes the time. Sometimes I'll lurk outside his door and I'll hear him speaking to himself, weird nonsensical fragments of conversation. Or I'll hear him sharpening pencils or ripping pages from his spiralbound sketch pad. Clearly, he's still drawing—and somehow hiding his work from me and his parents.

So Friday afternoon I decide to do a little snooping. I wait until Teddy goes to make number two, because I know I'll have a good ten or fifteen minutes (he sits on the toilet for a long time, flipping through a stack of picture books). As soon as I hear him lock the door, I hurry upstairs to the second floor.

Teddy has a bright sunny bedroom that always smells a little bit like urine. There are two big windows overlooking the backyard, and Caroline has instructed me to leave them open all day long, even if the central air is running, because I think this helps to diminish the smell. The walls are painted a cheerful sky-blue and adorned with posters of dinosaurs, sharks, and *The LEGO Movie* characters. Teddy's furniture consists of a bed, a short bookshelf, and a dresser, so you might think a search wouldn't take very long. But I know a thing or two about hiding stuff. During my first year on OxyContin I was still living at home and I had little stashes of pills and paraphernalia all over my bedroom, crammed into places my mother would never think to look.

I roll back his rug, I pull down all his picture books, I remove the dresser drawers and peer inside the empty cavities. I shake the curtains and stand on his bed to carefully inspect the valances. I sift through a mountain of stuffed animals piled high in a corner of his bedroom—a pink dolphin, a tattered gray donkey, a dozen Ty Beanie Babies. I tug the sheets off his mattress and reach beneath the mattress pad and finally I lift the entire mattress off the frame, turning it onto its side, so I have a clear view of the floor.

"Mallory?" Teddy is shouting through the door of the first-floor powder room. "Can you bring me toilet paper?"

"Just a second!"

I'm not finished yet. I still have to go through the closet. I sift through all the adorable outfits that we can never convince Teddy to wear—beautiful collared shirts, miniature khakis and designer blue jeans, tiny leather belts for his twenty-two-inch waist. I spy three board games on the top shelf of the closet—Clue, Mousetrap, and Sorry!—and I'm certain I've found my treasure trove. But then I open the boxes and shake out the boards and all I find are game pieces and playing cards. No drawings.

"Mallory? Did you hear me?"

I put the games back in the closet, close the door, and make sure the room is more or less as I found it.

Then I grab a roll of toilet paper from the laundry room and hurry downstairs to the first-floor bathroom. "Here you go," I tell him. He opens the door a crack, just wide enough for me to pass the paper.

"Where were you?" he asks.

"Just tidying up."

"All right."

He pushes the door closed and I hear the button lock click.

I spend the weekend convinced I'm being paranoid. I have no proof that Teddy is still drawing pictures. The scratching sounds from his bedroom could be anything. The black grit on his fingers could be dirt from our gardening projects, or the normal grimy smudges of a five-year-old boy. Everything else seems to be going fine, so what am I worried about?

Monday morning, I awaken to the sound of sanitation trucks making their slow rumbling crawl down Edgewood Street. They come twice a week—on Mondays for recycling, and again on Thursdays for regular trash. And in an instant I remember the one spot I didn't think to check: the wastebasket in Ted's second-floor office. Teddy has to walk right past it to get downstairs. It would be an easy place for him to discard his drawings, on his way out of his bedroom.

I spring out of bed, grateful that I sleep in running shorts and a T-shirt, and I sprint out my door and across the lawn. The grass is still wet with morning dew and I nearly wipe out rounding the side of the house. The truck is three doors away so I only have a minute to spare. I run to the end of the driveway, where Ted drags the blue containers every Sunday night—one for metals and glass, the other for papers and cardboard. I plunge my hands deep inside, past shreds of junk mail and utility bills, take-out menus and credit card statements and a heaping stack of mail order catalogs: Title Nine, Lands End, L.L.Bean, Vermont Country Store, they arrive every day by the dozen.

The recycling truck pulls alongside me, and a skinny guy wearing work gloves smiles at me. There's a tattoo of a dragon coiled around his bicep.

"Lose something?"

"No, no," I tell him. "You can take it."

But then he reaches for the bin and all its contents shift, revealing a giant ball of crumped paper, with the same confetti edges familiar to Teddy's drawings.

"Wait!"

He holds out the bin, allowing me to grab the ball, and I carry it back up the driveway to my cottage.

Once inside, I boil some water, make myself a mug of tea, and then sit down to study the papers. It's a bit like peeling an onion. There are nine pages total and I use my palm to smooth out all the wrinkles. The first few drawings don't look like anything. They're just scribbles. But as I turn the pages there's more control and more detail. The composition improves. There's light and shadow. It's like a sketchbook for some strange work in progress; some of the pages are cluttered with drawings, many of them half-finished.

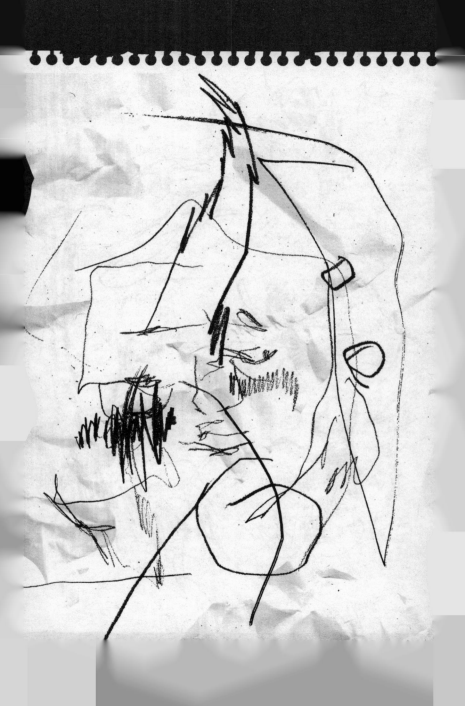

11

And I'm sorry but there's no way Teddy drew these pictures. Most adults can't draw this well—let alone a five-year-old boy who sleeps with stuffed animals and can't count past twenty-nine.

But how else did they end up in the recycling bin?

Did Ted draw them? Caroline?

Are the Maxwells studying illustration in their free time?

All my questions lead to more questions, and pretty soon I'm wishing I never got out of bed. I wish I'd just let the sanitation trucks carry away the clues, so I wouldn't have to wonder what they meant.

Monday passes in a daze—LEGOs, mac and cheese, Quiet Time, swimming pool—but by nightfall I'm ready to do some serious research. I take a shower and wash my hair and put on one of Caroline's nicest outfits, a breezy blue midi dress with pretty white flowers. Then I walk a mile into town to The Raconteur, Spring Brook's local independent bookstore.

I'm surprised to find it crowded on a Monday night—a neighborhood author has just finished a reading and the mood is festive, like a party. People are drinking wine in plastic cups and eating sheet cake off tiny paper plates. I have to push through the crowd to reach the parenting section, but I'm grateful for all the distractions; I don't want any store clerks offering to help me find something. If they heard what I was researching, they'd think I was crazy.

I gather some books and head out the back door to a large brick patio—a crowded café that's ringed with twinkling Christmas lights. There's a small bar selling snacks and drinks, and a very earnest teenage girl sitting on a barstool with an acoustic guitar, dressed in overalls and singing "Tears in Heaven." I can't hear this song without thinking about my sister's memorial service; it was part of a playlist that looped over and over. The song is constantly sneaking up on me in supermarkets and restaurants, and even after a thousand times it still has the power to make me cry. But this girl's version is brighter than the Eric Clapton original. There's something about her young age that makes the song seem almost hopeful.

I walk over to the coffee bar and order a mug of tea and a pastry, only to find that I don't have enough hands to carry everything. Plus, all the tables are full and no one seems anxious to leave, so I can't believe my good luck when I see Adrian sitting alone at a table for two, reading a Star Wars novel.

"Can I join you?"

And it's funny—this time, *he* doesn't recognize *me*, not right away, not in Caroline's gorgeous $500 dress. "Yes! Definitely! Mallory! How are you?"

"I didn't realize it would be so crowded."

"It's always busy here," Adrian says. "This is the third-hottest spot in Spring Brook."

"What are the other two?"

"Number one is Cheesecake Factory, obviously. Number two is the Wegmans hot food buffet." He shrugs. "We don't have much of a night life."

The girl with the guitar finishes "Tears in Heaven" to tepid applause but Adrian claps long and loud, and she shoots an annoyed look in our direction. "My cousin Gabriella," he says. "She's only fifteen, can you believe it? She marched in here with a guitar and they gave her a job."

Gabriella leans closer to the microphone and says she's going to switch to the Beatles, and then she starts singing a sweet cover of "Blackbird." I look at the book Adrian is reading. The cover shows Chewbacca firing lasers at an army of robots, and the title is printed in giant silver-foil letters: *Wookiee Vengeance*.

"Is that any good?"

Adrian shrugs. "It's not canon? So they take a lot of liberties. But if you liked *Ewok Vengeance*, you'll love this one."

And I can't help myself—I start laughing. "You're really something. You look like a landscaper. You've got a Florida tan and dirt under your fingernails. But it turns out you're actually a country club kid *and* a Star Wars nerd."

"I spend my whole summer pulling weeds. I need some escapist entertainment."

"I understand. I watch Hallmark Channel for the same reason."

"Seriously?"

"No joke. I've seen all five *Murder, She Baked* mysteries. And I don't share this information with a lot of people so I'm trusting you to keep it secret."

Adrian crosses an X over his heart. "Your secret's safe with me," he says. "What books are *you* reading?" And I don't have to answer the question because my books are already on the table and Adrian can read the spines: *Abnormal Child Psychology* and *The Encyclopedia of Supernatural Phenomena*. "This is how you unwind after a long day of babysitting?"

"If I told you why I'm reading these books, there's a good chance you'll think I'm crazy."

Adrian closes *Wookiee Vengeance* and sets it aside, giving me his full and undivided attention. "All my favorite stories come with that kind of warning," he says. "Tell me everything."

"It's a really long story."

"I have nowhere to be."

"I'm warning you. The bookstore might close before I can finish."

"Start from the beginning and don't leave out any details," he tells me. "You never know what's going to be important."

So I tell him about my job interview with the Maxwells, about the guest cottage, about my daily routine with Teddy. I describe the evolution of Teddy's drawings and the strange conversations happening inside Teddy's bedroom. I tell him about my discussions with Mitzi and the Maxwells. I ask him if he knows the story of Annie Barrett, and he assures me that every kid in Spring Brook knows the story of Annie Barrett. Apparently she's the local boogeyman, always ready to prey on children who stray into the forest after dark.

And after nearly an hour of talking (and after his cousin packs up her guitar and heads home, after all the surrounding tables have emptied out and it's just me and Adrian and the café staff wiping down tables) I reach into my bag and produce my latest discovery—the drawings from the recycling bin.

Adrian flips through the pictures in astonishment. "You're saying Teddy drew these? Five-year-old Teddy?"

"That paper comes from Teddy's sketch pad. And I can hear him drawing in the bedroom. He comes out with pencil all over his fingers. The only thing I can think of is—" I tap the *Encyclopedia of Supernatural Phenomena*. "Maybe he's channeling someone. Maybe it's the spirit of Annie Barrett."

"You think Teddy is possessed?"

"No. This isn't *The Exorcist*. Annie isn't trying to destroy Teddy's soul or take over his body. She just wants to borrow his hand. She uses it during Quiet Time, when he's alone in his bedroom. And for the rest of the day, she leaves him alone."

I pause so Adrian can laugh or make fun of me, but he doesn't say anything, so I outline the rest of my theory: "Annie Barrett is a good artist. She already knows how to draw. But this is her first time drawing with *someone else's arm*. So her first few efforts are terrible. They're just scribbles. But after a couple pages she gets better. She gains control and there's more detail. Texture, light, and shadow. She's mastering her new tool—Teddy's hand."

"So how did these pages end up in the trash?"

"Maybe Anya put them there. Or maybe Teddy did, I'm not sure. He's become very private about his drawings."

Adrian cycles through the pictures again, this time studying them more closely. He turns some of the drawings upside down, searching the scribbles for a deeper meaning. "You know what they remind me of? Those picture-puzzles in *Highlights* magazine. Where the artist hides stuff in the background. Like, the roof of the house is actually a boot, or a pizza, or a hockey stick, you remember those?"

I know the puzzles he's describing—my sister and I used to love them—but I think these pictures are more straightforward. I point to the drawing of the woman crying out in anguish. "I think this is a self-portrait. I think Annie's drawing the story of her murder."

"Well, there's one easy way to find out. Let's get a photo of the real Annie Barrett. Compare her to the woman in this picture. See if they match."

"I already looked. There's nothing online."

"Well, lucky for you, my mother works summers at the Spring Brook public library. They have a massive archive of town history. A whole basement full of materials. If anyone's going to have a picture of Annie Barrett, it's them."

"Could you ask her? Would she mind?"

"Are you kidding? She lives for this stuff. She's a teacher and a part-time librarian. If I tell her you're researching local history, she'll be your new best friend."

He promises to ask her first thing in the morning, and I feel so much better, now that I've shared my problems. "Thank you, Adrian. I'm glad you don't think I'm crazy."

He shrugs. "I think we have to consider every possibility. 'When you eliminate the impossible, all that remains, however improbable, must be the truth.' That's Spock in *Star Trek VI*, but he's paraphrasing Sherlock Holmes."

"My God," I tell him. "You really are a nerd."

We walk home in the dark and we have the sidewalks to ourselves. The neighborhood feels safe, quiet, peaceful. Adrian plays tour guide, pointing out the houses of his most notorious high school classmates, like The Dude Who Rolled His Parents' SUV and The Girl Who Had to Change Schools After a Scandalous TikTok Video. I get the sense he knows everyone in Spring Brook, that his high school years were like a glossy Netflix teen drama, one of those silly soap operas where everyone is beautiful and the outcome of a varsity football game has life-altering consequences.

Then he points to a house on the corner and tells me it's where Tracy Bantam grew up.

"Should I know who that is?"

"The point guard for the Lady Lions. Penn State's women's basketball team. I figured you knew each other."

"Penn State is enormous," I tell him. "There are fifty thousand students."

"I know, I just figured all the jocks went to the same parties."

I don't answer Adrian right away. He's giving me the perfect opportunity to come clean. I should tell him it was a stupid joke, a game I play with strangers. Clear up the truth before our relationship goes any further. I think it's possible he'll understand.

Except I can't tell Adrian part of the truth without telling him the whole truth. If I tell him that I never actually went to college, I'll have to explain how I've spent the last few years—and there's no way I'm ready to get into all that, not right now, not when we're having such a nice conversation. So I just change the subject.

We arrive at the Flower Castle but Adrian says he'll walk me home and I don't object. He asks where I'm from and he's surprised to learn that I grew up in South Philly, that I could see Citizens Bank Park from my bedroom window. "You don't sound like you're from the city."

I give him my best Rocky Balboa: "Yo, Adrian! You tink we all tawk like dis?"

"It's not your voice. It's the way you present yourself. You're so positive. You're not jaded like everyone else."

Oh, Adrian, I think to myself. You really have no idea.

He asks, "Are your parents still in South Philly?"

"Just my mom. They split up when I was young, and my dad moved to Houston. I hardly know him."

This is all true, so I think my answer sounds fairly convincing, but then Adrian asks if I have any siblings.

"Just one sister. Beth."

"Older or younger?"

"Younger. She's thirteen."

"Does she go to your meets?"

"All the time. It's three hours in the car, one way, but if it's a home race my mother and sister always come." And my voice catches—I don't know why I'm saying all this stuff. I want to be honest with him, to have a real relationship, and instead I'm just piling on more lies.

But as I walk these moonlit sidewalks with this very sweet and handsome lawn boy, it's so easy to surrender to fantasy. My real past feels a million miles away.

When we finally reach the Maxwells' house, it's dark. It's after ten thirty and everyone must be in bed. We follow the tiny flagstone path around the side of the house and it's even darker out back, with just the shimmering blue light of the pool to guide the way.

Adrian squints across the yard, scanning the trees for the outline of my cottage. "Where's your house?"

I can't see it, either. "Somewhere back in those trees. I left the porch light on, but I guess the bulb burned out."

"Hmmph. That's weird."

"Is it?"

"After all the stories you just told me? I don't know."

We walk across the lawn to the cottage, and Adrian waits on the grass while I climb the steps to my porch. I try the door and it's still locked, so I reach for my keys. Suddenly I'm grateful to Caroline for insisting I put the Viper on my key chain. "Maybe I'll just look inside for a minute. Would you mind waiting?"

"No problem."

I unlock the door, reach inside, and toggle the switch for the porch light—definitely dead. But the interior light works fine, and the cottage looks just as I left it. Nothing in my kitchen, nothing in the bathroom. I even get down on my knees and take a quick peek under the bed.

"Everything okay?" Adrian calls.

I walk back outside. "It's fine. I just need a new bulb."

Adrian promises to call when he has more information about Annie Barrett. I watch and wait as he crosses the yard and rounds the side of the house, disappearing from view.

And as I turn to enter the cottage, my foot brushes an ugly gray rock about the size of a tennis ball. I look down and realize I'm standing on paper, three sheets of paper with ragged edges, and the rock is holding them in place. Keeping my back to the door of the cottage, I reach down and pick them up.

Then I go inside, lock the door, and sit at the edge of my bed, turning the pages one at a time. They're like the three drawings that Ted Maxwell ripped into pieces—the three drawings he swore I'd never see again. Only they've been drawn by a different hand. These drawings are darker and more detailed. They use so much pencil and charcoal, the paper has warped and buckled. A man is digging a grave. A woman is being dragged through a forest. And someone is looking up from the bottom of a very deep hole.

12

The next morning I walk over to the main house and Teddy is waiting for me at the sliding glass patio doors, holding a small notepad and pencil. "Good morning and welcome to my restaurant," he says. "How many are in your party?"

"Just one, Monsieur."

"Right this way."

All his stuffed animals are seated in chairs around the kitchen table. Teddy leads me to an empty seat between Godzilla and Blue Elephant. He pulls out a chair and hands me a paper napkin. I can hear Caroline upstairs, frantically crisscrossing her bedroom. It sounds like she'll be late leaving the house again.

Teddy stands patiently at my side, pencil and notepad in hand, ready to take my order. "We don't really have a menu," he says. "We can make anything you want."

"In that case I'll have scrambled eggs. With bacon and pancakes and spaghetti and ice cream." This makes him laugh, so I milk the joke for all it's worth. "And carrots, hamburgers, tacos, and watermelon."

He doubles over with giggles. The kid has a way of making me feel like Kate McKinnon on *SNL*, like everything I do is comedy gold. "If you say so!" he says, and then he wobbles over to his play chest to fill my plate with plastic food.

The landline starts ringing and Caroline calls downstairs to me. "Let that go to voice mail, please, I don't have time!"

After three rings, the machine picks up, and I can hear the message being recorded: "Good morning! This is Diana Farrell at Spring Brook Elementary . . ."

It's their third message in a week and Caroline swoops into the kitchen, hurrying to catch the caller before she hangs up. "Hello, this is Caroline." She shoots me an exasperated look—*can you believe this freaking school system??*—and carries the phone into the den. Meanwhile Teddy brings me a plate that's piled high with play toys: plastic eggs and plastic spaghetti and several scoops of plastic ice cream. I shake my head and pretend to be outraged. "I'm pretty sure I ordered bacon!"

Teddy laughs, runs across the room to his toy chest, and returns with a strip of plastic bacon. I'm trying to eavesdrop on Caroline's call but she's not saying very much. It's like the conversations happening at Quiet Time in Teddy's bedroom, where the other person is doing most of the talking. She's just saying "Right, right" and "of course" and "no, thank *you*."

I pretend to stuff myself with plastic food like a fat hog at a trough. I make a lot of snuffing and snorting noises, and Teddy roars with laughter. Caroline enters the kitchen with the cordless phone and puts it back in the cradle.

"That was your new school principal," she tells Teddy. "She cannot wait to meet you!"

Then she gives him a big hug and kiss and hurries out the door, because it's already 7:38 and she's crazy-late.

After I've finished "eating" my breakfast, I pay my pretend bill with pretend money and ask Teddy what he feels like doing. And I guess he's really in the mood to pretend because he wants to play Enchanted Forest again.

We follow Yellow Brick Road and Dragon Pass down to the Royal River, and then we climb the branches of the Giant Beanstalk until we're ten feet above the ground. There's a small hollow in one of the limbs, and Teddy dutifully fills it with small rocks and sharp sticks—an arsenal of weapons, in case we're ever attacked by goblins.

"Goblins can't climb trees because their arms are too short," Teddy explains. "So we can hide in these branches and throw stones at them."

We spend the morning immersed in a game of endless invention and improvisation. In the Enchanted Forest, everything is possible, nothing is off-limits. Teddy stops on the banks of the Royal River and tells me I should drink the water. He says the river has magical properties that will keep us from getting captured.

"I already have a gallon back at my cottage," I tell him. "I'll share it with you when we get home."

"Perfect!" he exclaims.

And then he skips off down the path, leading the way to the next discovery.

"By the way," I call after him. "I found the pictures you left for me."

Teddy looks back and smiles, waiting for me to elaborate.

"The pictures you left on my porch."

"Of the goblins?"

"No, Teddy, the pictures of Anya being buried. They're really well done. Did someone help you?"

Now he looks confused—like I've abruptly changed the rules of the game without telling him.

"I don't draw Anya anymore."

"It's okay. I'm not upset."

"But I didn't do it."

"You left them on my porch. Under a rock."

He throws up his hands in exasperation. "Can we just play regular Enchanted Forest? Please? I don't like this other way."

"Sure."

I realize that maybe I've introduced the subject at the wrong time. But after we head back to the house for lunch, I don't want to bring it up anymore. I make us some chicken nuggets and Teddy goes upstairs for Quiet Time. I wait a little while, and then I follow him upstairs and put my ear to his bedroom door. And I can hear the whisper of his pencil moving across the page, *scritch scritch scritch*.

Later that afternoon Russell calls and invites me to dinner. I'm still tired from the night before so I suggest pushing it off, but Russell says he's leaving for a two-week vacation—it has to be tonight. "I found a restaurant near your house. A Cheesecake Factory."

I almost laugh because Russell is such a stickler for healthful eating. His diet is almost entirely plants and proteins—no added sugars or carbs, just occasional spoonfuls of carob chips and organic honey.

"Cheesecake? You're serious?"

"I already booked a table. Seven thirty."

So after Caroline goes home, I shower and put on a dress and on my way out of the cottage I reach for the pile of Teddy's latest drawings. And then I stop in the doorway, hesitating. After sharing the whole story with Adrian at the bookstore, I know I'd need an hour to get through everything. And so I decide to leave the drawings at home. I want Russell to feel proud of me. I want to project the image of a strong, capable woman thriving in recovery. I don't want to burden him with all my worries. So I stash the drawings in my nightstand.

The restaurant is big, crowded, thrumming with energy—a typical Cheesecake Factory. The hostess leads me to a table where Russell is waiting. He's dressed in a navy-blue tracksuit and his favorite HOKA sneakers, the ones he wore in the New York City Marathon. "There she is!" He gives me a hug, then looks me up and down. "What happened, Quinn? You look wiped out."

"Thanks, Coach. You look good, too."

We settle down in our seats, and I order a seltzer.

"I'm serious," he says. "Are you sleeping okay?"

"I'm fine. The cottage is a little noisy at night. But I'm managing."

"Have you told the Maxwells? Maybe they can do something."

"They offered me a room in the main house. But I told you, I'm fine."

"You can't train if you're not resting."

"It was just one bad night. I swear."

I try changing the subject to the menu, which has calorie counts and nutritional information under every entrée. "Did you see the Pasta Napolitano? It's twenty-five hundred calories."

Russell orders a tossed green salad with grilled chicken and vinaigrette dressing on the side. I get the Glamburger with a side of sweet potato fries. We talk a bit about his upcoming vacation—two weeks in Las Vegas with his lady friend, Doreen, a personal trainer at his YMCA. But I can tell he's still troubled. After we've finished eating, he steers the conversation back to me.

"So how's Spring Brook? How are the NA meetings?"

"It's an older crowd, Russell. No offense."

"Are you going once a week?"

"Don't need to. I'm steady."

I can tell he doesn't like this answer, but he doesn't give me any flak.

"How about friends? Are you meeting people?"

"I went out with a friend last night."

"Where'd you meet her?"

"*He* is a student at Rutgers, and he's home for the summer."

My sponsor narrows his eyes, concerned. "It's a little early for dating, Quinn. You're only eighteen months sober."

"We're just friends."

"So he *knows* you're sober?"

"Yes, Russell, that was our very first topic of conversation. I told him how I nearly overdosed in the back of an Uber. Then we talked about the nights I slept at the train station."

He shrugs, like these would be perfectly sensible things to discuss. "I've sponsored a lot of college kids, Mallory. These campuses—the fraternities, the binge drinking—they're breeding grounds for addicts."

"We had a very quiet evening in a bookstore. We drank seltzer water and listened to music. Then he walked me back to the Maxwells' house. It was nice."

"The next time you see him, you should tell him the truth. This is part of your identity, Mallory, you need to embrace it. The longer you wait, the harder it gets."

"Is this why you invited me here? To lecture me?"

"No, I invited you here because Caroline called me. She's worried about you."

I'm blindsided. "Seriously?"

"She said you started off great. She called you a dynamo, Quinn. She was really happy with your performance. But the last few days, she said she's noticed a change. And anytime I hear those words—"

"I'm not using, Russell."

"Good, okay, that's good."

"Did she *say* I was using?"

"She said you were acting strangely. She saw you outside at seven in the morning, digging through her trash cans. What the heck was that all about?"

I realize Caroline must have spotted me through her bedroom window. "It was nothing. I threw something away by mistake. I had to get it back. Big deal."

"She says you're talking about ghosts. You think maybe her son is possessed?"

"No, I never said that. She misunderstood me."

"She says you're getting chummy with a user who lives next door."

"You mean Mitzi? I've talked to Mitzi two times. In four weeks. Does that make us BFFs?"

Russell gestures for me to keep my voice down. Even in the crowded noisy dining room, some of our neighbors are turning to stare. "I'm here to help you, okay? Is there anything you want to talk about?"

Can I really tell him? Can I really outline all my concerns about Annie Barrett? No, I cannot. Because I know all my worries sound ridiculous. And I just want my sponsor to be proud of me.

"Let's talk about dessert. I'm thinking Chocolate Hazelnut Cheese-cake."

I offer him a laminated menu, but he won't accept it. "Don't change the subject. You need this job. If you get fired, there's no going back to Safe Harbor. They've got a wait list longer than your arm."

"I'm not going back to Safe Harbor. I'm going to do an amazing job, and Caroline is going to rave about me to all her neighbors, and when the summer's over I bet she keeps me on. Or I'll go work for another family in Spring Brook. That's the plan."

"What about the father? How's Ted?"

"What about him?"

"Is he nice?"

"Yes."

"Is he *too* nice? Maybe a little handsy?"

"Did you really just use the word *handsy*?"

"You know what I'm talking about. Sometimes these guys lose sight of boundaries. Or they see the boundary and they don't care."

I think back to my swimming lesson from two weeks ago, the night Ted complimented me on my tattoo. I guess he'd put a hand on my shoulder, but it's not like he grabbed my ass. "He's not handsy,

Russell. He's fine. I'm fine. We're all fine. Now can we please order dessert?"

This time, he grudgingly accepts a menu. "Which one are we looking at?"

"Chocolate Hazelnut."

He flips to the back of the menu, to the index listing all the nutritional information. "Fourteen hundred calories? Are you shitting me?"

"And ninety-two grams of sugar."

"Good lord, Quinn. People must die in this restaurant every week. They must have heart attacks walking out to their cars. There should be medics in the parking lot, waiting to revive them."

Our waitress sees Russell browsing the desserts. She's a teenager, smiling and cheerful. "Looks like someone's thinking cheesecake!"

"Not a chance," he says. "But my friend's going to have some. She's healthy and strong and she has her whole life ahead of her."

After dessert Russell insists on driving me back to the Maxwells', so I won't have to cross the highway after dark. It's almost nine thirty when we pull up to the house.

"Thank you for the cheesecake," I tell him. "I hope you have a great vacation."

I open the door to the car and Russell stops me. "Listen, are you sure you're okay?"

"How many times are you going to ask me?"

"Just tell me why you're shaking."

Why am I shaking? Because I'm nervous. I'm afraid I'm going to walk up to the cottage and find more drawings on the porch—that's why I'm shaking. But I'm not about to explain any of this to Russell.

"I just ate fifty grams of saturated fat. My body's going into shock."

He looks skeptical. This is the classic sponsor's dilemma: You need to trust your sponsee, you need to show you believe in them and have absolute faith in their recovery. But when they start acting weird—when they start shivering in cars on hot summer nights—you need to be the bad guy. You need to ask the tough questions.

I open his glove box and it's still full of dip cards. "You want to test me?"

"No, Mallory. Of course not."

"You're obviously worried."

"I am, but I trust you. Those cards are not for you."

"Let me do it anyway. Let me prove I'm fine."

He's got a sleeve of paper cups rattling around the floor of the back seat so I reach down and grab one. Russell takes a dip card from the glove box and we both get out of the car. More than anything, I just want company walking back to my cottage. I'm afraid to go home by myself.

Once again, the backyard is dark. I still haven't replaced the dead bulb that's over my porch. "Where are we going?" Russell asks. "Where's your house?"

I point toward the trees. "Back here. You'll see."

We step closer and I begin to discern its shape. I already have my keys in hand, so I test-fire the Viper and it makes a loud crackling noise, illuminating the backyard like a flash of lightning.

"Jesus," Russell says. "What the hell is that?"

"Caroline gave me a stun gun."

"There's no crime in Spring Brook. What do you need a stun gun for?"

"She's a mom, Russell. She worries about stuff. I promised her I would keep it on my key chain."

The Viper has a tiny LED flashlight and I use it to scan the cottage porch: no new rocks and no new pictures. I unlock the door and turn on the lights and lead Russell into the cottage. His eyes wander the room—ostensibly he's admiring what I've done with the place, but Russell is a veteran sponsor and I know he's also scanning the room for signs of trouble. "This is really nice, Quinn. Did you do all this work yourself?"

"No, the Maxwells decorated before I moved in." I take the plastic cup from his hand. "Give me a minute. Make yourself at home."

You might think it's gross, coming home from a nice dinner and peeing into a paper cup and then sharing that cup with a close friend so he can analyze its contents. But if you spend any time in rehab you get used to it pretty fast. I go into the bathroom and do what needs to happen. Then I wash my hands and return with the sample.

Russell is waiting anxiously. Since my living room is also my bed-room, I think he's feeling a little awkward, like he's breached some kind of sponsor-sponsee protocol. "I'm only doing this because you volunteered," he reminds me. "I'm not really worried."

"I know."

He dips the card in the cup, holding it in place until the strips are saturated, and then he lays it across the top of the cup while we await the results. He talks a little more about his vacation, about his hopes of hiking down to the bottom of the Grand Canyon if his knees coop-erate. But we don't have to wait very long. The test panels show single lines for negatives and double lines for positives—and negative results always appear quickly.

"Squeaky clean, just like you said."

He takes the cup, walks it back to my bathroom, and flushes the urine down the toilet. Then he crumples it up and pushes it deep down into my wastebasket, along with the test card. Finally he washes his hands, patiently and methodically, under warm water. "I'm proud of you, Quinn. I'll call you when I'm back. Two weeks, okay?"

After he leaves, I lock the door and change into my pajamas, full of delicious cheesecake and feeling rather proud of myself. I've left my tablet computer charging in the kitchen, and since it's still early I think I might watch a movie. But as I walk around the kitchen counter to retrieve the tablet, I see the drawings I've been dreading—not pinned by a rock to my porch, but pinned by magnets to my refrigerator.

I yank the drawings off the refrigerator and the magnets clatter to the floor. The pages are limp with moisture and a little warm, like they've just come from an oven. I put them facedown on the counter so I won't have to look at them.

Then I hurry around my cottage and lock both my windows. The night ahead will be warm and stuffy and possibly sleepless but after my discovery I'm not taking any chances. I roll back the rug and check the hatch in the floor—it's still securely nailed shut. Then I drag my bed across the cottage and use it to barricade the door. If anyone tries to open it, the door will bang into the footboard and jolt me awake.

As I see it, there are three possible ways these drawings ended up on my refrigerator.

#1: The Maxwells. I know they have a key to my cottage. I suppose it's possible that Ted or Caroline drew these pictures and then—while I was out having dinner with Russell—one of them entered my cottage and left the drawings on my refrigerator. But why? I can't think of a single plausible reason for either one of them to do this. I'm responsible for the safety and welfare of their child. Why would they want to gaslight me, to make me feel like I'm going crazy?

#2: Teddy. Perhaps this sweet five-year-old child swiped a spare key from his parents, then sneaked out of his bedroom, crept across the backyard, and carried the drawings inside my cottage. But to believe this theory, you also have to believe that Teddy is some kind of magical artistic savant—that he's gone from drawing stick figures to fully realistic three-dimensional illustrations with convincing light and shadow—all in a matter of days.

#3. Anya. I have no idea what happens in Teddy's bedroom during Quiet Time—but what if Anya really is controlling him? Taking possession of his body and using his hand to draw these pictures? And then somehow "carrying" these finished drawings into my cottage?

I know, I know: It sounds crazy.

But when I look at all three theories? When I compare them to each other? The most impossible explanation seems like the most likely explanation.

And that night—while I'm tossing and turning in bed, struggling to fall asleep—I figure out a way to prove I'm right.

13

The next day at lunch, I head downstairs to the Maxwells' basement and start opening boxes. The basement is filled with shipping cartons they've yet to unpack and I only have to open three before I find what I'm looking for. I knew the Maxwells would have a baby monitor, and to my delight it looks pretty state-of-the-art. The transmitter is an HD camera with infrared night vision and regular/wide-angle lenses. The receiver is a large screen about the size of a paperback book. I stash everything in a small shoebox and carry it upstairs. When I return to the kitchen, Teddy is waiting.

"What were you doing in the basement?"

"Just poking around," I tell him. "Let's get you some ravioli."

I wait until he's busy eating his lunch, and then I sneak upstairs to his bedroom and look for a place to hide the camera. I've realized that if I want to know where the pictures are coming from, I need to *see* where they're coming from—I need to see inside his bedroom during Quiet Time.

But hiding the camera isn't easy. It's big, clunky, and difficult to conceal. Even worse, it has to be plugged into a power outlet. But I find a solution in Teddy's mountain of stuffed animals—I bury the camera ever so carefully, so the lens peeks out between Snoopy and Winnie-the-Pooh. I make sure it's plugged in and set to transmit, and then I kiss the cross that hangs from my neck, hoping to God Teddy won't notice anything unusual.

I return to the kitchen and sit with Teddy while he finishes his lunch. He's chatty this morning. He's complaining about going to the barbershop—Teddy hates going to the barbershop, he says he wants to grow his hair long, like the Cowardly Lion—but I barely listen. I'm too nervous. I'm about to get answers to many of my questions, but I'm not sure I'm ready for them.

After what feels like hours, Teddy finishes his food and I send him upstairs for Quiet Time. Then I hurry into the den and plug in the receiver. Teddy's bedroom is directly above me, so the audio and video are crystal clear. The camera is pointed toward his bed and I can see most of the floor—the two places where he's most likely to sit and draw.

I hear the door to his bedroom open and close. Teddy enters the frame from the right, crosses over to his desk, and then grabs his sketchbook and pencil case. Then he leaps on top of his bed. I hear the soft *thump* of his mattress through the receiver *and* through the ceiling above my head, like it's being broadcast in stereo.

Teddy sits with his back against the headboard, legs bent, using his knees to support the sketchbook. He arranges a row of pencils on the nightstand beside his bed. Then he removes a miniature pencil sharpener—the kind that collects the shavings in a clear plastic dome. He twists a pencil inside—*skritch*, *skritch*, *skritch*—then takes it out, examines the point, and decides it's not sharp enough. He puts it back in—*skritch*, *skritch*—and then decides it's ready.

I look away for an instant—just long enough to take a sip of water—and when I look back, the video is sputtering, freezing and skipping frames, like it can't keep up with the audio. I can still hear the sharpening sounds but the video is frozen on an image of Teddy reaching for a pencil.

And then a single word, spoken softly, not much louder than a whisper: "Hello."

It's followed by a quick hiss of static. The video skips forward, then freezes again. The image has turned blurry, lo-res. Teddy is looking up from his sketch pad, directing his attention toward the door of his bedroom, to someone or something just outside the frame.

"Getting the pencils ready," he says, and then laughs. "The pencils? For drawing."

There's a longer hiss of static, and the noise rises and falls with a rhythm that reminds me of breathing. Something in the microphone crackles and pops and again the picture skips forward—now Teddy is looking right at the camera, and his head has doubled in size. It's like a reflection in a fun house mirror; his features are stretched to impossible proportions, his arms are short little flippers but his face is enormous.

"Careful," he whispers. "Gently."

The static gets louder. I try turning down the volume but the knob doesn't do anything; the sound gets louder and louder until I hear it all around me, like it's escaped the speaker and filled the room. The video skips ahead and there's Teddy sprawled out on his mattress, arms extended, his body convulsing, and I can hear his bed *thump-thump-thumping* on the ceiling.

I run out of the den, through the foyer, and up the stairs to the second floor. I reach for Teddy's doorknob but it won't turn, it's stuck, it's locked.

Or something is holding it closed.

"Teddy!"

I bang my fists on the door. Then I step back and kick it, like I've seen people do in movies, but all this does is hurt my foot. I try smashing my shoulder into the door and this hurts so much I sink to the floor, clutching my side. And then I realize I can see into Teddy's room. There's a tiny half-inch gap beneath his door. I lie on my side, rest my head on the floor, close one eye, and peer into the gap, and the smell hits me hard—a toxic punch of concentrated ammonia, venting from the room like warm exhaust. It fills my mouth and I roll away, coughing and gagging and clutching at my throat like I've been pepper-sprayed. Tears stream down my face. My heart is going a mile a minute.

And as I'm lying in the hallway wiping the snot from my nose and trying to recover, trying to muster the energy to simply sit up, I hear the tiny mechanism in the doorknob click.

I scramble to my feet and open the door. Again I'm hit by the stench—it's the smell of urine, extremely concentrated, suspended in the air like steam from a shower. I pull my shirt up and over my mouth. Teddy seems unaffected by the odor; he's oblivious to all my shouting. He's sitting on his bed with a sketch pad in his lap and a pencil in his right hand. He's working quickly, slashing thick black lines across the page.

"Teddy!"

He doesn't look up. Doesn't seem like he's heard me. His hand keeps moving—shading the page with darkness, filling in the black night sky.

"Teddy, listen, are you all right?"

Still he ignores me. I step closer to his bed and my foot comes down on one of his stuffed animals, a plush horse that emits a noisy high-pitched whinny.

"Teddy, look at me." I place my hand on his shoulder and finally he looks up and I see that his eyes are completely white. His pupils have rolled back into his head. But still his hand keeps moving, drawing without seeing. I grab his wrist and I'm shocked by the heat of his skin, by the strength that's coiled in his arm. Normally his body is loose and floppy like a rag doll's. I often joke that he has hollow bones, because he's light enough to lift off the ground and spin in a circle. But now there's a strange energy thrumming beneath the skin; he feels like all his muscles are clenched, like a small pit bull terrier poised to attack.

Then his eyes snap back into place.

He blinks at me. "Mallory?"

"What are you doing?"

He realizes he's holding a pencil and he instantly drops it. "I don't know."

"You were drawing, Teddy. I was watching. Your whole body was shaking. Like you were having a seizure."

"I'm sorry–"

"Don't apologize. I'm not angry."

His lower lip is quivering. "I said I was sorry!"

"Just tell me what happened!"

And I know I'm yelling but I can't help myself. I'm too freaked out by everything I'm seeing. There are two pictures on the floor and a third in process on the sketch pad.

"Teddy, listen to me. Who is this girl?"

"I don't know."

"Is she Anya's daughter?"

"I don't know!"

"Why are you drawing these things?"

"I didn't, Mallory, I swear!"

"Then why are they in your room?"

He takes a deep breath. "I know Anya isn't real. I know she's not really here. Sometimes I *dream* we're drawing together, but when I wake up there are never any pictures." He flings the sketch pad across the room, like he's trying to deny its existence. "There shouldn't be any pictures! We just *dream* them!"

And I realize what's happening: Anya must be taking the pictures out of the bedroom, before Teddy wakes up, so he won't have to look at them. And I've come along and interrupted their usual process.

It's all too much for Teddy because he explodes into tears and I pull him into my arms and his body is soft and loose again; he feels like a regular boy again. I realize I'm asking him to explain something he doesn't understand. I'm asking him to explain the impossible.

He places his right hand in mine, and I see his tiny fingers are smudged with dirty pencil marks. I hold him tight and calm him down and assure him that everything is going to be okay.

But really, I'm not so sure.

Because I know for a fact this kid is a lefty.

14

That night, Adrian comes over and together we review all the illustrations. There are nine drawings in total—the three pictures left on my porch, the three pictures pinned to my refrigerator, and the three pictures I collected today from Teddy's bedroom. Adrian keeps re-shuffling the pages, like he's trying to put them in a proper order, as if there's some kind of magical sequence that might reveal a story. But I've been thinking about them all afternoon and I still can't make sense of them.

It's dusk and the sun is almost down. The air in the backyard is hazy and gray. The forest is full of fireflies blinking on and off. Across the way at the big house, through the windows of the kitchen, I can see Caroline loading the dishwasher; she's cleaning up dinner while Ted is upstairs putting their son to bed.

Adrian and I sit side by side on the steps of the cottage, scrunched so close our knees are nearly touching. I tell him about my experiment with the baby cam, how I watched Teddy draw without the use of his eyes, without the use of his dominant hand. And by all rights Adrian should tell me I'm crazy—I know my story *sounds* crazy—so I'm relieved when he takes me seriously. He holds the drawings close to his face and coughs. "God, these really stink."

"That's the smell of Teddy's bedroom. Not all the time but some of the time. Caroline says he wets the bed."

"I don't think this is pee. Last summer, we had a job in Burlington County? Near the Pine Barrens? Some guy hired us to clear his vacant lot. It was a half acre of land gone wild, weeds taller than your head, we were literally hacking with machetes. And trash like you wouldn't believe—old clothes, beer bottles, bowling pins, just the weirdest junk you can imagine. But the worst thing we found was a dead deer. In the middle of July. And we're hired to clear the lot, so we need to bag it and get it out of there. I won't go into details, Mallory, but it was awful. And the thing I will never forget—and you hear this in movies all the time, but it's true—the smell was horrible. It smelled like these pictures."

"What should I do?"

"I don't know." He takes the stack of drawings and puts them at a distance, like maybe it's not safe to be sitting so close to them. "Do you think Teddy's okay?"

"I have no idea. It was really weird. His skin was broiling. And when I touched him, he didn't feel like Teddy anymore. He felt like . . . something else."

"Have you told his parents?"

"Tell them what? 'I think your son is possessed by the ghost of Annie Barrett?' I already tried. They freaked out."

"But it's different now. You have proof. All these new pictures. It's like you said: Teddy couldn't have drawn these without help."

"But I can't prove Anya helped him. I can't prove she's sneaking into my cottage and leaving them on my refrigerator. It sounds crazy."

"That doesn't mean it's not true."

"You don't know his parents like I do. They won't believe me. I need to keep digging, I need real proof."

We're drinking seltzers and sharing a large bowl of microwave popcorn—the best refreshments I could provide on short notice. I feel inadequate about my hosting skills, but Adrian doesn't seem to mind.

He updates me on the situation with the Spring Brook Public Library. His mother has started combing through the archives, but she hasn't found anything yet. "She says the files are a mess. Land deeds, old newspapers, nothing's organized. She thinks she'll need another week."

"I can't wait another week, Adrian. This thing—this spirit or ghost, whatever it is—she's getting inside my cottage. Some nights I feel her watching me."

"How do you mean?"

I've never really found the words to describe the sensation—the strange fluttery feeling on the periphery of my senses, sometimes accompanied by a high-pitched whining noise. I'm tempted to mention the research experiment at the University of Pennsylvania, to ask Adrian if he's ever heard of terms like "gaze detection." But I don't want to say anything that might steer the conversation toward my past. I've already told him too many lies; I'm still wrestling with the best way to come clean.

"I have an idea," he says. "My parents have a small apartment over their garage. No one's using it right now. Maybe you could stay with us for a few days. Work here, but sleep someplace safe until we figure out what's going on."

I try to imagine myself explaining the situation to the Maxwells—telling five-year-old Teddy that I'm moving out, because I'm too scared to live in his backyard.

"I'm not leaving. I was hired to look after Teddy, and I'm going to stay here and look after Teddy."

"Then let me stay over."

"You're joking."

"I'll crash on your floor. No funny business, just a measure of added security." I look at him and it's nearly dark but I'm pretty sure he's blushing. "If the ghost of Annie Barrett sneaks into your cottage, she'll trip over me and wake me up and we'll talk to her together."

"Are you making fun of me?"

"No, Mallory, I'm trying to help."

"I'm not allowed to have sleepovers. It's one of the House Rules."

Adrian drops his voice to a whisper: "I'm up at five-thirty every morning. I can sneak out before sunrise. Before the Maxwells wake up. They'd have no idea."

And I want to say yes. I would love to keep talking with Adrian until late in the night. I really don't want him to go home.

But the one thing stopping me is the truth. Adrian still thinks he's helping Mallory Quinn, cross-country scholarship athlete and college student.

He doesn't realize I'm Mallory Quinn, ex-junkie and total screwup. He doesn't know that my sister is dead and my mother won't speak to me, that I've lost the two people in the world who meant the most to me. And there's no way I can tell him. I can barely admit these things to myself.

"Come on, Mallory. Say yes. I'm worried about you."

"You don't know anything about me."

"Then talk to me. Tell me. What should I know?"

But I can't tell him now, not when I need his help more than ever. I need to keep my history under wraps for a few days longer. And then I swear I'll tell him everything.

He gently rests his hand on my knee.

"I like you, Mallory. Let me help you."

I realize he's working up the courage to make a move. It's been a long time since anyone has tried to kiss me. And I *want* him to kiss me, but at the same time I don't, so I just sit there, frozen, as he slowly pivots toward me.

And then across the yard, at the big house, the sliding glass doors open and Caroline Maxwell steps outside, carrying a book and a wine bottle and a long-stemmed glass.

Adrian pulls back and clears his throat.

"Well, it's late."

I stand up. "Yeah."

We walk across the yard and around the side of the big house, following the flagstone path to the Maxwells' two-car driveway. "My offer stands if you change your mind," Adrian says. "Although I don't think you need to worry."

"Why not?"

"Well, this thing—this spirit or ghost, whatever she is—have you ever seen her?"

"No."

"And do you ever hear her? Weird groans or noises? Whispers in the middle of the night?"

"Never."

"And does she mess with your stuff? Knocking pictures off the wall, slamming doors, turning on your lights?"

"No, nothing like that."

"Exactly. She's had plenty of chances to scare you. And either she can't or she won't. I think she's trying to communicate. I think there are more drawings coming, and once we have them all, we're going to understand what she's trying to say."

Is he right? I have no idea. But I appreciate the calm and confidence in his voice. He makes all my problems seem completely manageable.

"Thank you, Adrian. Thank you for believing me."

As I'm heading back to my cottage, Caroline calls out to me from the patio. "I see you made a new friend. I hope I didn't scare him away."

I cross the yard so I won't have to yell. "He's one of your landscapers. He works for Lawn King."

"Oh, I know, I met Adrian a few weeks ago. Right before you moved in. Teddy was really impressed with his tractor." She takes a sip of her wine. "He's cute, Mallory. Those eyes!"

"We're just friends."

She shrugs. "It's none of my business. But from here, it seemed like you were sitting pretty close."

I feel myself blushing. "Maybe a *little* close?"

She shuts her book and sets it aside, encouraging me to sit down. "What else do we know about him?"

I explain that he lives three blocks away, that he works for his father's business, that he's studying engineering at Rutgers University in New Brunswick. "He likes to read. I ran into him at a bookstore. And he seems to know everybody in Spring Brook."

"What about warning signs? What are his flaws?"

"I'm not sure I've found any yet. He's kind of a *Star Wars* geek? I mean, it wouldn't surprise me if he dressed up and went to these conventions."

Caroline laughs. "If that's his worst flaw, I'd put on a Princess Leia costume and jump all over him. When are you going to see him again?"

"I'm not sure."

"Maybe you make the next move. Invite him to the house. You're welcome to use the pool, have a picnic lunch together. I'm sure Teddy would love to go swimming with him."

"Thank you," I tell her. "Maybe I will."

We sit in a comfortable silence for a few moments, enjoying the still of the night, and then Caroline reaches for her book—an old paperback that's dog-eared and filled with annotations. The cover shows a naked Eve standing in the Garden of Eden, reaching for the apple while the serpent lurks nearby.

"Is that the Bible?"

"No, it's poetry. *Paradise Lost.* I used to love it back in college but now I can't get through a single page. I don't have the patience anymore. It's like motherhood ruined my attention span."

"I have the first Harry Potter in my cottage. I got it out of the library, to read it to Teddy, but you can borrow it if you want."

Caroline smiles like I've said something amusing. "I think I'll just turn in. It's getting late. Good night, Mallory."

She goes inside the house and I make the long walk across the yard to my cottage. Once again I can hear footsteps padding around in Hayden's Glen—more deer or drunk teenagers or dead people, who knows—but the sound doesn't frighten me anymore.

Because I've decided Adrian is right.

I don't have to be afraid of Anya.

She's not trying to hurt me.

She's not trying to scare me.

She's trying to tell me something.

And I think it's time to bypass the middleman.

15

The next morning, I tell Teddy that Adrian is coming to the house for a lunchtime pool party, and we get to work preparing a mighty picnic feast: grilled chicken sandwiches, pasta salad, fruit salad, and fresh-squeezed lemonade. Teddy proudly carries everything out to the pool deck and I open the patio umbrellas so we can dine in the shade.

I've already briefed Adrian on the plan, and he's agreed to babysit Teddy while Mitzi and I attempt to use the spirit board. He arrives promptly at noon, dressed in a swimsuit and a red Scarlet Knights T-shirt, and Teddy runs across the pool deck to welcome him. Even though Teddy is less than four feet tall, he's somehow figured out a way to open the child-proof gate. Then he puts on his maître d' act, welcoming Adrian to our "restaurant" and escorting him to our table.

Adrian marvels at all the food on display. "I wish I could stay here and eat all day! But El Jefe only gives me an hour. After that he'll come looking for me, and that won't be good for any of us."

"We'll eat fast so we can swim," Teddy tells him. "Then we can play Marco Polo!"

I give Adrian a ton of instructions. I repeatedly remind him that Teddy must wear his floaties, that the water's too deep for him, even in the shallow end. I'm too nervous to eat anything. I keep glancing over at the cottage, where Mitzi has been working for the last hour or so, preparing for "the gathering." She's not positive the plan is going to work. Under ideal circumstances, she says, Teddy would sit beside us at the spirit board. But she agrees that having Teddy some twenty yards away might be close enough, and that's the only shot I'm willing to take.

Teddy is anxious to swim, so he eats only half a sandwich and says he's not hungry anymore. And Adrian knows I'm ready to get started, so he eats quickly, then uses a single arm to scoop Teddy off the ground.

"Are you ready, Mr. T?"

Teddy shrieks and screams with delight.

Now for the tricky part:

"Teddy, would you mind if Adrian watched you for a little while? I need to do something in my cottage."

As I expected, Teddy goes totally bananas. He runs to the far end of the pool deck, waving his arms like a maniac, absolutely thrilled that Adrian—Adrian!!—is going to babysit.

"Please watch him carefully. You can't let him out of your sight. Not for a second. If anything happens to him—"

"We'll be fine," Adrian promises. "It's you that I'm worried about. Is this your first time using a Ouija board?"

"First time since middle school."

"Be careful, okay? Yell if you need anything."

I shake my head. "Don't come anywhere near the cottage. Even if you hear us screaming. I don't want Teddy to know what we're doing. If he tells his parents, they'll flip out."

"But what if there's a problem?"

"Mitzi says she's done a hundred of these things. She says they're totally safe."

"What if Mitzi's wrong?"

I assure him everything's going to be okay but I'm not sure I sound very confident. Mitzi has already called my cell phone six times today, alerting me to important precautions and restrictions. She's forbidden me from wearing any jewelry or perfume. No makeup, no hats or scarves, no open-toed shoes. She's sounded more and more manic with every conversation. She explained that she uses THC to "unblock" her neural pathways, and I worry all the cannabis has made her paranoid.

Teddy comes running back in our direction and slams into Adrian's knees, nearly knocking him into the pool. "Are you ready yet? Can we swim now?"

"You guys have fun," I tell them. "I'll be back in a little bit."

By the time I reach the cottage, Mitzi has finished her preparations. There's a stack of reference books on my kitchen counter and she's hung heavy black fabric over the windows to blot out all the sunlight. When I open the front door, blinking my eyes to adjust to the gloom, I catch her peeking outside and watching Adrian pull off his T-shirt. "Oh my my my. Where did you find this handsome Scarlet Knight?"

She doesn't seem to recognize Adrian without his landscaping gear, doesn't realize he's the same man she profiled as a rapist just a few weeks earlier.

"He lives down the street."

"And you trust him to watch the child? We won't be disturbed?"

"We'll be fine."

I close the door, and it's like sealing myself inside a tomb. The air is thick with the woodsy smell of burning sage; Mitzi explains this will reduce interference from unfriendly spirits. She's placed a half dozen votive candles around the room, giving us just enough light to work by. There's a black cloth draped over my kitchen table and the wooden spirit board sits in the middle, surrounded by a ring of tiny granular crystals. "Sea salt," Mitzi explains. "Kind of an excess precaution, but since it's your first time I'm not taking any chances."

Before we start, Mitzi asks if she can review all the drawings I've received. At this point I've amassed quite a collection; earlier that morning, I'd awakened to find three new ones on the floor of my cottage, as if they'd been slipped under the front door.

Mitzi seems particularly troubled by the last drawing, by the profile of the woman's face. She points to the silhouette on the horizon. "Who's this person walking toward her?"

"I think she's walking away from her."

Mitzi shudders, struck by a chill, then shakes it off. "I guess we'll just have to ask. Are you ready?"

"I don't know."

"Do you have to go to the bathroom?"

"No."

"Is your cell phone turned off?"

"Yes."

"Then you're ready."

We take seats on opposite ends of the table. There's a third chair between us—left empty for Anya. In the darkness of the cottage, it feels like I've left Spring Brook behind. Or rather, it feels like I'm in and out of Spring Brook at the same time. The air is different; it's thicker, harder to breathe. I can still hear Teddy laughing and Adrian shouting "Cannonball!" and water splashing in the swimming pool but all these sounds are slightly distorted, like I'm hearing them over a bad phone connection.

Mitzi places a small heart-shaped planchette in the center of the board and invites me to rest my fingers on one side. The bottom of the planchette is equipped with three small wheels on tiny brass casters; the slightest touch makes it roll away from me. "Steady now, you don't want to push it," Mitzi says. "Let the tool do all the work."

I flex my fingers, trying to relax them. "Sorry."

Mitzi rests her fingers on the opposite side of the planchette. Then she closes her eyes.

"Okay, Mallory, I'm going to start the conversation. I'll make contact. But once we have a good rapport, I'll let you ask your questions. For now, just close your eyes and relax."

I'm nervous and a little self-conscious, but Mitzi's voice is re-assuring. I find myself mirroring her, matching her posture and breathing. The incense relaxes my muscles and quiets my thoughts. All my everyday worries and concerns—Teddy, the Maxwells, running, sobriety—everything starts falling away.

"Welcome, spirits," Mitzi says, and I jolt back in my seat, startled by the volume of her voice. "This is a safe space. We welcome your presence. We invite you to join us in conversation."

Outside the cottage, I can still hear the sounds of the swimming pool—the sounds of frenzied kicking and splashing. But then I con-centrate harder and manage to block them out. I relax my fingertips, keeping contact with the planchette without applying any pressure.

"Annie Barrett, we wish to speak with Annie Barrett," Mitzi says. "Are you there, Annie? Can you hear us?"

The longer I sit in the hard wood-backed chair, the more I'm aware of all the points where it contacts my body—the seat beneath my bot-tom, the crossrail pressing on my shoulder blades. I study the plan-chette, waiting for the slightest signs of movement. The burning sage crackles and pops.

"How about Anya? Is there an Anya present? Can you hear us, Anya?"

My eyelids feel heavy and I allow myself to close them. I feel like I'm being hypnotized, or like I've reached those final moments at the end of the day, when I'm lying in a warm bed under a comfortable blanket, ready to drift off to sleep.

"Are you there, Anya? Will you speak with us?"

No answer.

I don't hear the noises in the backyard anymore. All I hear is Mit-zi's labored breathing.

"Let us help you, Anya. Please. We're listening."

And then something brushes the back of my neck. As if a person has passed behind my chair. I turn and no one's there—but when I look

back at the Ouija board, I feel someone behind me, leaning over me.
Soft long hair falls past my cheek, grazing my shoulder. And then an
invisible weight pushes down on my hand—a gentle, prodding pressure, nudging the planchette forward. One of its wheels makes a tiny
squeak, like the soft cry of a mouse.

"Welcome, spirit!" Mitzi smiles at me, and I realize she has no idea
what's happening; she clearly doesn't see or sense whatever's behind
me. "Thank you for answering our call!"

Warm breath tickles the back of my neck and goose bumps spread
across my skin. There's more pressure on my hand and wrist, guiding
the planchette across the board in slow sweeping circles.

"Is this Anya?" Mitzi asks. "Are we speaking with Anya?"

The board is illustrated with a standard alphabet and the numbers
zero to nine, and the top corners have the words YES and NO. I watch
passively, spectating, as the planchette stops briefly at the letter *I*, then
moves back to *G* and then *E*. Mitzi keeps four fingers on the planchette,
but she's holding a pencil in her free hand to transcribe the results on
a notepad: *I-G-E*? Sweat beads across her forehead. She glances at me
and shakes her head, undaunted.

"Speak slowly, spirit," she says. "We have plenty of time. We wish
to understand you. Is this Anya?"

The planchette moves to *N* and then *X* and then *O*.

"You're leaning," Mitzi whispers, irritated, and I realize she's
talking to me.

"What?"

"On the table. You're pushing, Mallory."

"It's not *me*."

"Sit back in your chair. Sit up straight."

I'm too scared to argue with her, to tell her the truth. I don't want
to interrupt whatever's happening.

"Spirit, we welcome your message! We welcome any information
you'd like to share."

There's more pressure on my hand and the planchette moves faster, veering across the board, stopping at one random letter after another, a string of spiritual static: *L-V-A-J-X-S*. Mitzi is still record- ing everything but she seems more and more annoyed. The results look like alphabet soup.

The wood planchette is thrumming with energy, like the racing heartbeat of a small frightened animal. It's flying all over the board and Mitzi can barely keep up with her one-handed annotations. The air is so thick it's suffocating; my eyes are watering and I don't know why my smoke detector isn't going off. Then Mitzi lifts her fingers and the planchette keeps moving. My hand pushes it across the board and it flies off the edge of the table, clattering to the floor. Mitzi stands up, furious. "I knew it! You were pushing! This whole time, you were pushing!"

All the weight leaves my hand and suddenly I'm out of the trance. The room snaps back into focus. It's twelve forty-five Wednesday afternoon and I can hear Adrian out in the backyard counting "Six Mississippi, Seven Mississippi . . ." and Mitzi is glaring at me.

"Anya did that. Not me."

"I watched you, Mallory. I saw you!"

"Eight Mississippi!"

"Anya moved my hand. She was guiding me."

"This isn't a slumber party. It's not a game. This is my livelihood, I take it very seriously!"

"Nine Mississippi!"

"You've wasted my time. You've wasted the whole day!"

And suddenly I'm blinking into the daylight. The door to my cot- tage has swung open and little Teddy is standing on the porch, peering into the darkness. He raises a finger to his lips, gesturing for us to be quiet. Out in the backyard, Adrian calls out, "Ten Mississippi! Ready or not, here I come!"

Teddy ducks inside and quietly closes the door. Then he looks around the cottage, marveling at the votive candles and the blacked-out windows and my kitchen table with its ring of sea salt. "What are you playing?"

"Honey, this is called a spirit board," Mitzi says, inviting him to take a closer look. "In the right hands, it's a tool for communication. To speak with the dead."

Teddy looks to me for confirmation, like he can't believe Mitzi is telling the truth. "Really?"

"No, no, no." I'm already out of my chair and guiding him back to the door. "It's just a toy. Just a game." The last thing I need is Teddy telling his parents about a séance. "We were just pretending. It's not real."

"It's very real," Mitzi says. "If you respect its powers. If you take it seriously."

I open the door and see Adrian across the yard, searching for Teddy in the trees along Hayden's Glen. "Over here," I call out.

He comes jogging over and Teddy darts past my legs, sprinting across the grass, still caught up in their game of hide-and-seek.

"Sorry about that," Adrian says. "I told him to stay on the pool deck. I hope he didn't ruin anything."

"It was already ruined," Mitzi says. She's gathering her things, snuffing out candles and collecting trays of incense. "There are no spirits in this cottage. There never were. This is just a story she's made up to get attention."

"Mitzi, that is not true!"

"I've used this board a hundred times. It's never acted this way."

"I swear to you—"

"Swear to your Scarlet Knight here, okay? Cry on his shoulder and maybe he'll feel sorry for you. But don't ask me to waste any more time."

She shoves her books into her bag and then storms past me, nearly tripping as she descends the stairs of my cottage.

"What just happened?" Adrian asks.

"Anya was here, Adrian. She was inside the cottage. I swear to you, I could feel her standing over me. Moving my arm. But the letters were gibberish. We couldn't spell anything. And then right in the middle Mitzi lost her shit. She started screaming at me."

We watch from the porch as Mitzi wobbles across the lawn, veering left and then overcompensating to the right, unable to maintain a straight line.

"Is she all right?" Adrian asks.

"Well, she's pretty high, but supposedly that's part of her process."

A dejected Teddy comes walking across the yard. He seems to understand that something bad has happened, that the grown-ups are upset. In a hopeful voice, he asks, "Does anyone want to chase me?"

Adrian apologizes for leaving but says he has to go. "I need to get back or El Jefe will flip."

"I can chase you," I tell Teddy. "Just give us a minute."

Clearly this isn't the answer Teddy wants. He trudges across the yard to the pool patio, unhappy with both of us.

"Are you going to be all right?" Adrian asks.

"I'm fine. I just hope Teddy doesn't say anything to his parents."

But I'm pretty sure he will.

16

After the pool party, Teddy goes up to his bedroom for Quiet Time and I stay downstairs in the den. Maybe I don't want to know what he's doing up there. Maybe things will be better for me if I stop asking so many questions.

In the afternoon we take a long walk in the Enchanted Forest. We follow Yellow Brick Road to Dragon Pass and down to Royal River, and I try to spin a new story about Princess Mallory and Prince Teddy. But all Prince Teddy wants to discuss are spirit boards: Do they need batteries? How do they find the dead person? Can they find *any* dead person? Can they find Abraham Lincoln? I keep saying "I don't know" and hope that he'll lose interest. Instead he asks how much it costs to buy a spirit board, if it's possible to make one.

Caroline gets home from work at her usual time and I hurry out for a long run, eager to get away and burn off stress. It's nearly seven o'clock when I get home, and Ted and Caroline are waiting on my front porch. And as soon as I see their faces, I know that they know.

"Good workout?" Ted asks.

His tone is light, like he's determined to keep things pleasant.

"Pretty good. Almost nine miles."

"Nine miles, really? That's remarkable."

But Caroline has no interest in making small talk. "Do you have anything you want to tell us?"

I feel like I've been dragged into the principal's office and forced to empty my pockets. All I can think to do is play dumb: "What's wrong?"

She pushes a sheet of paper into my hands. "I found this drawing before dinner. Teddy didn't want to show me. He tried to hide it. But I insisted. Now you look at this picture and tell me why we shouldn't fire you on the spot."

Ted rests a hand on her arm. "Let's not overreact."

"Don't patronize me, Ted. We're paying Mallory to watch our child. And she left him with the gardener. So she could play Ouija board. With the pothead who lives next door. How am I overreacting?"

The drawing looks nothing like the dark sinister pictures that were left on my porch and refrigerator. It's just a bunch of Teddy's stick figure characters—me and an angry woman who's obviously Mitzi, gathered around a rectangle covered in letters and numbers.

"I *knew* it!"

Caroline narrows her eyes. "Knew what?"

"Anya was here! At the séance! Mitzi accused me of pushing the pointer thing, but it was Anya! She *was* moving it. Teddy saw her. The picture proves it!"

Caroline is bewildered. She turns to Ted and he raises his hands, pleading with us to settle down. "Let's all take a deep breath, okay? Let's unpack what we're hearing."

But of course they're confused. They haven't seen everything I've seen. They'll never believe me without seeing the pictures. I open the door to my cottage and urge them to follow me inside. I get out the stack of drawings and I arrange them on my bed in a grid. "Look at these. You recognize the paper, right? From Teddy's sketch pads? Last Monday I found the first three drawings on my porch. I asked Teddy and he said he had nothing to do with them. The next night, I went out to dinner with Russell. The door to my cottage was locked. But when I came home, there were three more drawings on my refrigerator. So I hid a camera in Teddy's bedroom—"

"You did *what*?" Caroline asks.

"A baby monitor. From your basement. I put the camera in his room during Quiet Time and I watched him draw." I point to the next three pictures. "I watched him make these. He was using his right hand."

Caroline shakes her head. "I'm sorry, Mallory, but we are talking about a five-year-old boy. We all agree that Teddy's gifted but there's no way he's capable—"

"You're not understanding me. Teddy didn't draw these pictures. Anya did. The spirit of Annie Barrett. She's visiting Teddy in his bedroom. She's using him like a puppet. Somehow she's controlling his body and she draws these pictures and she brings them to my cottage. Because she's telling me something."

"Mallory, slow down," Ted says.

"We tried the séance so Anya would leave Teddy alone. I wanted to communicate with her. Directly. Keep Teddy out of it. But something went wrong. It didn't work."

I stop to pour myself a glass of water and gulp it down. "I know it sounds crazy. But all the proof you need is right here. Look at these pictures. They're coming together, they're telling a story. Help me make sense of it, please."

Caroline sinks into a chair and buries her face in her hands. Ted manages to stay composed, like he's determined to resolve the conversation. "We are committed to helping you, Mallory. I'm glad you're being open and honest with us. But before we make sense of these pictures, we need to agree on a couple of facts, okay? And the biggest one is that ghosts don't exist."

"You can't prove they don't."

"Because you can't prove a negative! Look at the flip side, Mallory—you have no proof that the ghost of Annie Barrett is real."

"These pictures are my proof! They're on Teddy's sketch pad paper. If he didn't draw them—if Annie didn't magically deliver them to my cottage—how did they get here?"

I see that Caroline's attention has drifted to the small end table beside my bed, where I keep my phone, my tablet computer, my Bible—and the blank sketch pad that Teddy gave me a month ago, when I first started working for the Maxwells.

"Oh come on," I tell her. "You think *I'm* drawing them?"

"I never said that," Caroline says. But I can see her mind working, I can see she's probing the theory.

After all: Wasn't I prone to memory lapses?

Didn't a box of Teddy's pencils go missing last week?

"Let's ask your son," I tell them. "He won't lie."

It only takes a minute to cross the yard and get upstairs to Teddy's bedroom. He's already brushed his teeth and changed into his fire truck pajamas. He's down on the floor next to his bed, building a

Lincoln Log house and filling its bedrooms with plastic farm animals. We've never confronted him like this—all three of us entering his bedroom, amped up and stressed out. Immediately, he knows something is wrong.

Ted walks over to the bed and tousles his hair. "Hey, big guy."

"We need to ask you something important," Caroline says. "And we need you to answer with the truth." She takes the pictures and fans them out on the floor. "Did you draw these?"

He shakes his head. "No."

"He doesn't *remember* drawing them," I tell her. "Because he goes into a kind of trance. Like a twilight sleep."

Caroline kneels beside her son and starts playing with a plastic goat, trying to keep the tone light. "Did Anya help you make these drawings? Did she tell you what to do?"

I'm staring at Teddy, trying to get him to make eye contact, but the kid won't look at me. "I know Anya isn't real," he tells his parents. "Anya is just a make-believe friend. Anya could never draw real pictures."

"Of course she couldn't," Caroline says. She puts her arm around his shoulder and squeezes him. "You are absolutely right, sweetie."

And I start to feel like I'm going crazy. It's like we're all willfully ignoring the obvious, like we've all suddenly decided to agree that 2+2=5.

"But you all smell something in this bedroom, right? Look around you. The windows are open, the central air is running, his bedsheets are clean, I washed them today, I wash them every day, but there's always a bad smell in here. Like sulphur, like ammonia." Caroline shoots me a warning with her eyes but she's missing the point. "It's not Teddy's fault! It's Anya! It's her scent! It's the smell of rot, it's—"

"Stop," Ted tells me. "Just stop talking, okay? We understand you're upset. We hear you, all right? But if we're going to fix this problem, we need to deal with facts. Absolute truths. And I'm being honest with you, Mallory: I do not smell an odor in this room. I think Teddy's bedroom smells perfectly fine."

"Me, too," Caroline says. "There's nothing wrong with the way his bedroom smells."

And now I'm certain I'm going crazy.

I feel like Teddy is my only hope but I still can't get him to look at me. "Come on, Teddy, we talked about this. You know the smell, you told me it was Anya."

He just shakes his head and bites his lower lip and suddenly he explodes into tears. "I know she's not real," he tells his mother. "I know she's make-believe. I know she's just pretend."

Caroline puts her arm around him. "Of course you do," she says, trying to comfort him, and then she turns to me. "I think you should go now."

"Wait—"

"No. We've talked enough. Teddy needs to go to bed, and you need to go back to your cottage."

And with all of Teddy's tears, I realize she's probably right, there's nothing else I can do for him. I gather up the pictures and leave the bedroom and Ted follows me downstairs to the first floor.

"He's lying to you," I tell Ted. "He's saying what you want to hear, so he doesn't get into trouble. But he doesn't believe it. He refused to look at me."

"Maybe he was afraid to look at you," Ted says. "Maybe he was afraid you'd get angry if he told the truth."

"So what happens now? Are you and Caroline going to fire me?"

"No, Mallory, of course not. I think we just take the night to cool off. Try to clear our heads. Does that sound good?"

Does it? I don't know. I don't think I want to clear my head. I'm still convinced that I'm right and they're wrong, that I've collected most of the puzzle pieces and now I just need to assemble them in the correct order.

Ted puts his arms around me.

"Listen, Mallory: You're safe here. You're not in any danger. I will never let anything bad happen to you."

And I'm still sweaty from my run—I'm sure I smell terrible—but Ted pulls me closer and smooths the back of my hair with his hand. And in just a few moments it goes from comforting to weird; I can feel his warm breath tickling my neck, I can feel every inch of him pressing against me and I'm not sure how to break free of his grip.

But then Caroline comes stomping down the hallway. Ted springs away and I move in the opposite direction, slipping out the back door so I won't have to see his wife again.

I don't know what just happened but I think Ted is right.

Someone definitely needs a night to cool off.

17

When I return to my cottage, there's a two-word text on my phone from Adrian: **good news**. I call him back and he answers on the first ring.

"The library found something."

"Something like a photo of Annie Barrett?"

"Better. A book of her paintings." I can hear other voices in the background, men and women laughing, like I've reached Adrian in a bar.

"Do you want to meet up?"

"Yes, but I need you to come here. My parents' house. They're hosting a dinner and I promised to eat with their friends. But if you come over, I'll be off the hook."

I'm still in my running clothes, I haven't done any of my stretches, and after 8.78 miles I am insanely thirsty and hungry—but I say I'll be there in thirty minutes. One day without stretching won't kill me.

I chug another glass of water, fix a quick sandwich, and hop in the shower. Three minutes later, I'm stepping into one of Caroline's prettiest outfits—a mint-green minidress with a white baby's breath floral print. Then I hurry over to the Flower Castle.

Adrian answers the door instead of his parents, and I'm relieved.

His clothes are country club casual—a pink polo shirt tucked into belted khaki pants.

"Perfect timing," he says. "We just put out dessert." Then he leans closer and whispers: "By the way, my parents want to know why we're so interested in Annie Barrett. So I said you found some sketches in your cottage, hidden under the floorboards. I said you're trying to figure out if Annie drew them. A little white lie seemed easier than telling the truth."

"I understand," I tell him, and I really do, more than he knows.

The Flower Castle is much bigger than the Maxwells' house but inside it feels smaller and warmer and more intimate. All the rooms are decorated with mission-style furniture; the walls are adorned with family portraits and maps of Central and South America, and it feels like his family has lived here for years. We pass an upright piano and a curio cabinet full of pottery, and there are leafy green houseplants growing in every window. I want to stop and linger over everything but Adrian marches into a noisy dining room with a dozen middle-aged people. They're gathered around a table that's covered in wineglasses and dessert plates. There are five different conversations happening at once, and no one notices that we've arrived until Adrian waves his hands and calls for their attention.

"Everybody, this is Mallory," he says. "She's working as a nanny this summer, for a family on Edgewood Street."

At the head of the table, Ignacio raises his glass in a toast, sloshing red wine on his hand and wrist. "And she's a Big Ten athlete! She's a distance runner for Penn State!"

These people react like I'm Serena Williams fresh off my latest victory at Wimbledon. Adrian's mother, Sofia, is circling the table with a bottle of Malbec, topping off glasses, and she rests a sympathetic hand on my shoulder. "Pardon my husband," she says. "He's a little *achispado*."

"She means tipsy," Adrian translates, and then he points around the dining room, introducing me to everyone. There are too many names for me to remember—the chief of the Spring Brook Fire Department is there, along with a lesbian couple who run the bakery in town, and a couple of neighbors from down the block.

"I understand you're here for a library book," Sofia says.

"Yes, but I don't want to interrupt—"

"Please, I've known these people thirty years. We have nothing left to say to each other!" Her friends laugh, and Sofia grabs a file folder off the counter. "Let's go talk in the yard."

She opens a sliding glass door and I follow her outside to the most extravagant backyard garden I've ever seen. It's the middle of July and everything's blooming: blue hydrangea, bright red zinnia, yellow daylilies, and a host of exotic flowers I've never seen before. There are benches and stepping-stones and archways draped with purple morning glories; there are birdbaths and brick paths and rows of sunflowers taller than my head. In the center of everything is a cedar gazebo with a table and chairs, overlooking a koi pond with a softly splashing waterfall. I wish I had more time to admire everything—I feel like I'm walking through Disneyland—but I can tell that for Adrian and Sofia, it's just their backyard, it's no big deal.

We move into the gazebo and Adrian uses an app on his phone to brighten the party lights strung across the ceiling. Then we all take seats and Sofia gets down to business.

"This is a difficult project to research. The first challenge is that the story's very old, so nothing's on the internet. The second challenge is that Annie Barrett died right after World War II, so all the newspapers were still obsessed with Europe."

"How about local news?" I ask. "Did Spring Brook have some kind of daily paper?"

"The *Herald*," she says, nodding. "They published from 1910 to 1991 but we lost their microfilm in a warehouse fire. Everything went up in smoke." She gestures *poof!* and I glimpse a tiny tattoo on her left forearm: a slender long-stemmed rose, tasteful and elegant, but I'm still surprised. "I checked the library for physical copies but no luck. Nothing before 1963. So I figured I'd reached a dead end, but one of my coworkers pointed me to the local authors shelf. Anytime someone in town publishes a book, we usually order a copy. Just to be nice. Mostly it's mysteries and memoirs, but sometimes it's local history. And that's where I found this."

She reaches inside the folder for a very slender volume—it's more of a pamphlet, really, thirty-some pages with a cardstock cover and bound with thick, rusted industrial staples. The title page looks like it was produced on an old-fashioned manual typewriter:

THE COLLECTED WORKS OF
ANNE C. BARRETT
(1927–1948)

"It wasn't in our computer system," Sofia continues. "I don't think this book has circulated in fifty years."

I hold the book close to my face. It has a musty, pungent odor—like its pages are rotting. "Why is it so small?"

"Her cousin self-published it. Just a small run for friends and family, and I guess someone donated a copy to the library. There's a note from George Barrett on the first page."

The cover feels old and brittle, like a dried husk, ready to crack between my fingers. I open it carefully and begin to read:

In March of 1946, my cousin Anne Catherine Barrett left Europe to begin a new life here in the United States. As a gesture of Christian kindness, my wife Jean and I invited "Annie" to live with our family. Jean and I do not have any siblings, and we looked forward to having another adult relative in our household—someone to help raise our three young daughters.

Annie was just nineteen years old when she arrived in the United States. She was very beautiful but like many young women also very foolish. Jean and I made countless efforts to introduce Annie into Spring Brook society. I'm an alderman for the town council and I also serve on the vestry of St. Mark's Church. My wife Jean is very active in the local Woman's Club. Our closest friends welcomed my cousin into the community with many kind and thoughtful invitations, but Annie turned them all down.

She was silly and solitary and described herself as an artist. She spent her free time painting in her cottage, or walking barefoot in the forest behind our house. Sometimes I would spot her down on her hands and knees, like an animal, studying caterpillars or sniffing at flowers.

Jean compiled a short list of daily chores for Annie to complete, in return for her room and board. Most days, these chores went unfinished. Annie showed no interest in being part of our family, part of our community, or even part of the great American experiment.

I had many disagreements with Annie about her choices. Many times, I warned Annie that she was behaving irresponsibly or even immorally, that all of her bad decisions would catch up with her. I take no satisfaction in knowing that circumstances have proven me correct.

On December 9, 1948, my cousin was attacked and abducted from the small guest cottage at the back of our property. As I write these words nearly a full year later, Annie is presumed dead by the local police, and I fear her body is buried somewhere in the three hundred acres behind my home.

In the aftermath of this tragedy, many of my Spring Brook neighbors have reached out to offer their prayers and fellowship. I have compiled this book as a token of appreciation for their support. Despite my differences with my cousin, I always believed she had a creative spark, and this volume is a memorial to her slight achievements. Collected

*here are all the finished paintings left by Anne Catherine Barrett at
the time of her demise. When possible, I have included titles and dates
of composition. May these paintings stand as a tribute to a sad and
tragic life cut short.*

> *George Barrett*
> *November 1949*
> *Spring Brook, New Jersey*

I start turning the pages. The book is filled with blurry black-and-
white photographs of Annie's canvases. Paintings called *Daffodils* and
Tulips have wiggly rectangles that don't look anything like flowers.
And a painting called *Fox* features diagonal lines slashed across the
canvas. There's nothing remotely realistic in the book—just abstract
shapes and splatters and blobs of paint, like something off the spin-
art machines at a church carnival.

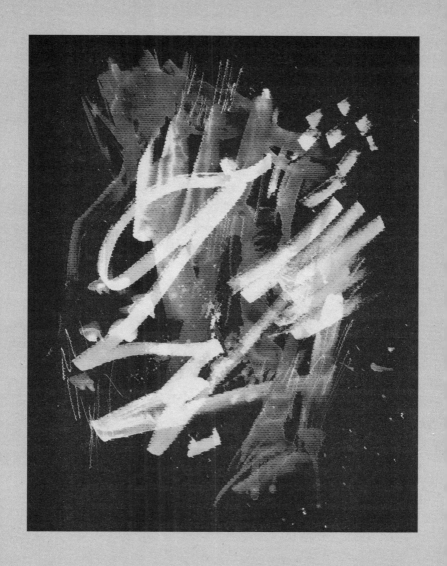

It's a massive disappointment. "These look nothing like the drawings in my cottage."

"But painting is one thing and drawing is another," Sofia says. "Some artists use different styles for different mediums. Or they just like to mix it up. One of my favorites, Gerhard Richter, he spent his whole career moving between very abstract and very realistic paintings. Maybe Annie liked both."

"But if that's true, the book doesn't answer anything."

"Ah, but wait," Sofia says. "There's still one more thing I need to show you. Yesterday I called over to the courthouse, because that's where they keep the old wills. They're a matter of public record, anyone can view them. And you'd be amazed by the things people are willing to share after they're dead." She opens the folder and removes a pair of blurry photocopies. "I didn't expect Annie Barrett to have a will—she died much too young—but I did find the last will and testament of George Barrett. He passed in 1974 and left everything to his wife, Jean. And here's where things get really interesting. Jean retired to Florida and lived until 1991. And when she passed, she left most of her estate to her daughters. But she also left fifty thousand dollars to a niece, Dolores Jean Campbell of Akron, Ohio. Now, do you know why I find that surprising?"

And at once I understand why the book is such a revelation. "Because Jean and George didn't have siblings. George said so in his introduction."

"Exactly! So who is this mystery niece and where did she come from? I wondered to myself: What if Jean *thinks* of this girl as a niece, but she's really the child of a cousin? What if she's a consequence of Annie's 'irresponsible' and 'immoral' behavior? I started wondering: Maybe there's more to the story than George is letting on. Maybe Jean felt some obligation to look after the girl."

I do the arithmetic in my head. "If Dolores was born in 1948, she wouldn't be that old. She could still be alive."

"She could indeed." Sofia pushes a small square of paper across the table. It has the name "Dolores Jean Campbell" and a ten-digit phone number. "That's the area code for Akron, Ohio. She's living in a retirement community called Rest Haven."

"You talked to her?"

"And deny you the thrill of calling this number? Not a chance, Mallory. But I'm very curious to know who answers the phone. I'd love to hear what you find out."

"Thank you. This is incredible."

From inside the house, there's a sound of breaking glass, followed by uproarious laughter. Sofia glances at her son. "I think your father's telling dirty jokes again. I should get inside before he embarrasses me." She stands up. "But tell me again why you're interested in all of this?"

"Mallory found some pictures in her cottage," Adrian says. "Stashed under her floor. We already went over this."

Sofia laughs. "*Mijo*, you were a horrible liar at age four and you're even worse now. This morning you said Mallory found the pictures in a closet."

"Under the floor of a closet," Adrian insists.

Sofia gives me a look that says: *Do you believe this kid?* "If you guys don't want to tell me, that's fine. But I'm going to suggest you both be careful. If you start poking your noses into family secrets, someone may bite them off."

I'm tempted to call Dolores immediately, but it's late, nearly ten o'clock, and Adrian suggests I'll get better results in the morning. "She's probably asleep."

I know he's right, I'm just impatient. I need information and I need it quickly. I tell him about my latest confrontation with the Max-wells. "I showed them Anya's drawings. I explained how the pictures keep turning up in my cottage. But they don't believe me, Adrian. And I mean of course they don't believe me! It sounds crazy. I know it sounds crazy. Caroline acted like maybe *I'm* drawing the pictures, like I'm making up the whole story to get attention."

"We're going to prove you're telling the truth," Adrian says. "But first we should go to the house and get some churros."

"Why?"

"Because they're awesome, and they will make you forget about all your problems. Trust me."

We return to the house and find the dinner party has kicked into a higher gear. There's Top 40 on the stereo, everyone has moved into the living room, and Ignacio seems more *achispado* than ever. He's demonstrating the paso doble, a dance he claims to have mastered in his youth, and Sofia is his surprisingly game partner, shaking her skirts and following his lead. Their guests are clapping and cheering and Adrian just shakes his head, embarrassed and exasperated. "This happens every time they have people over," he says. "My dad's such a ham."

We grab two cans of seltzer from the refrigerator. Then Adrian fills a plate with churros, drizzles them with chocolate sauce, and brings me outside for a walking tour of the garden. He says his father's been working on it for thirty years, that it's his own personal Versailles.

"What's a Versailles?"

"Like the palace? In France?"

He seems surprised that I've never heard of it, but what can I tell you? People in South Philly don't spend a lot of time talking about French royalty. Still, I don't want to look like an idiot, so I shovel on more lies.

"Oh, *Versailles*," I say, laughing. "I misheard you."

We wander the trails and Adrian introduces me to all the garden's secrets: the family of cardinals nesting in the sour cherry tree. A small alcove for private prayer with a shrine to the Virgin Mary. And a wooden bench on the banks of the koi pond, next to the waterfall. We stop and share our churros with some of the fish. There must be seven or eight of them, bobbing openmouthed on the surface of the water.

"This is a really special place."

Adrian shrugs. "I'd be happier with a swimming pool. Like the Maxwells have."

"No, this is better. You're lucky."

I feel his hand on my waist, and when I turn to look he kisses me. His lips taste sweet, like cinnamon and chocolate, and I want to pull him closer, I want to kiss him again.

But first I need to tell him the truth.

I put my hand on his chest.

"Wait."

He stops.

He looks into my eyes, waiting.

And I'm sorry but I don't know how to tell him. The whole scene is just too perfect: All the soft little lights are twinkling, the waterfall sounds like music, and the smell of the flowers is intoxicating—and it's another perfect moment I can't bring myself to ruin.

Because clearly I am past the point of no return. Lying to Adrian was bad enough. But now I've lied to his parents and even his parents' friends. Once these people learn the truth, there's no way they'll ever accept me. My relationship with Adrian doesn't stand a chance. We're like one of Teddy's playtime soap bubbles—magical, buoyant, lighter than air—and doomed to explode.

He realizes something's wrong and pulls back.

"Sorry about that. I think I misread the moment. But if I talk long enough and fast enough we can just act like it didn't happen, right?" He stands up, looking sheepish. "We've got Ping-Pong in the garage. Do you feel like playing?"

I take his hand and pull him back toward the bench. This time, I kiss him. I put my hand on his heart and lean into his body so there's no mistaking how I feel.

"No," I tell him. "I don't want to leave here."

But I do leave, eventually.

The dinner party breaks up around ten thirty. From our bench in the shadows of the garden, we can hear car doors slamming and engines starting and guests pulling out of the grand circular driveway.

Adrian and I stay in the garden past midnight. Eventually all the lights inside the house blink off and it seems his parents have gone to bed and I decide I should probably get going.

Adrian offers to walk me home. I tell him it's not necessary, that it's just a few blocks, but he insists.

"This isn't South Philly, Mallory. The streets of Spring Brook get pretty rough after dark."

"I have a stun gun on my key chain."

"That's no match for a drunk mom behind the wheel of a minivan. I'd feel much better if I walked you home."

The neighborhood is silent. The streets are empty, the houses are dark. And as soon as we leave the garden, I feel like a spell has been broken. As the Maxwells' house comes into view, I'm reminded of all my old problems, I'm reminded of the person I really am. And once again I feel compelled to be honest. Maybe I can't muster the courage to tell him everything—not tonight, not yet. But I want to say at least one thing that's true.

"I haven't had a boyfriend in a while."

He shrugs. "I've *never* had a boyfriend."

"I'm just saying, we shouldn't rush into anything. Until we get to know each other better. Let's take things slowly."

"What are you doing tomorrow night?"

"I'm serious, Adrian. You might learn some things about me that you don't like."

He takes my hand and squeezes it. "I want to learn everything about you. I want to change my major to Mallory Quinn and learn as much as I can."

Oh you have no idea, I think to myself. You really have no idea.

He asks if I've ever eaten at Bridget Foy's, his favorite restaurant in all of Philadelphia. I say I haven't been to Philly in six weeks and I'm in no hurry to get back. "Then how about Princeton? The town, not the university. They have a really good tapas place. Do you like tapas? Should I get a table?"

By this point we've crossed the Maxwells' yard and we're standing outside my cottage and of course I say yes, I tell him I can be ready by five thirty.

And then we're kissing again and if I close my eyes it's easy to pretend we're back in the castle gardens, that I'm Mallory Quinn Cross-Country Superstar with a promising future and no worries in the world. I'm leaning against the side of my cottage. Adrian has one hand in my hair and another hand moving up my leg, sliding under my dress, and I don't know how I'm going to tell him the truth, I really don't.

"This is not taking things slow," I tell him. "You need to go home now."

He lifts his hands from my body, steps backward, and takes a deep breath. "I'll be back tomorrow."

"Five thirty," I tell him.

"See you then. Good night, Mallory."

I stand on the porch and watch him walk across the yard, vanishing into the blackness of the night, and I know I must tell him the truth. I decide I will tell him everything over dinner tomorrow in Princeton. So even if he's upset, he won't be able to leave me, he'll be forced to drive me home. And in that time, maybe I can convince him to give me a second chance.

Then I unlock the door to my cottage, turn on the light, and discover Ted Maxwell lying in my bed.

18

He sits up, shielding his eyes from the light. "Jesus, Caroline, can you turn it down?" His voice is an octave lower than normal, thick with sleep.

I don't move from the doorway.

"It's Mallory."

He peeks out between his fingers and seems surprised to find himself in my cottage, in my bed, under my blankets. "Oh, Jesus. Oh, fuck. I'm sorry." He swings his legs out of bed and stands up and immediately loses his balance. He grabs the wall to steady himself and waits for the room to stop spinning. Ted is so drunk he doesn't seem to notice that he's not wearing pants, that he's huddled against the wall in a polo shirt and black boxer-brief underwear. There are gray chinos splayed across the foot of the bed, like he peeled them off just before tucking himself in.

He says, "This isn't what it looks like."

It looks like Ted is being frisked by the police. He's got both legs spread apart and both hands pressed against the wall.

"Maybe I should get Caroline?"

"No! God, no." He turns to look at me. "I just need you to—oh Jesus, oh no." He looks back at the wall and steadies himself. "Can you bring me some water?"

I walk over to the sink and fill one of the small plastic tumblers that I serve to Teddy. It's illustrated with polar bears and penguins. I carry it over to Ted and I can smell the booze on him; he reeks of scotch and sour sweat. He drinks from the cup, sloshing most of it across his neck and chest. So I fill it again and this time he manages to get most of the water into his mouth. But his body is still anchored to the wall, like he's not quite ready to take on gravity.

"Ted, why don't you stay here? I'll go to the big house. I can sleep on the sofa."

"No, no, no, I need to get back."

"I really think I should get Caroline."

"I'm better now. The water helps. Watch."

He stands up straight and takes a wobbly step toward me. Then he reaches out, flailing, desperate for help. I take his hand and guide him to the foot of the bed. He sinks onto the mattress, not releasing my hand until I'm seated beside him.

"Five minutes," he promises. "It's getting better."

"Do you want more water?"

"No, I don't want to throw up."

"How about a Tylenol?"

I want an excuse to stand and move away from him, so I go into my bathroom and come back with three chewable baby aspirin. I put them in Ted's sweaty palm and he dutifully grinds them between his teeth.

"Caroline and I had a fight. I just needed some space, a little room to clear my head. I saw your light was off. I figured you were out for the night. I didn't mean to fall asleep."

"I understand," I tell him, even though I really don't; I have no idea why he climbed into my bed.

"Of course you understand. You're a very empathetic person. That's why you're such a great mother."

"I'm not a mother yet."

"You'd *make* a great mother. You're kind, you're caring, and you'd put the child first. It's not rocket science. Are you wearing Caroline's dress?"

His eyes are roaming all over my body and I move behind the kitchen counter, grateful to have a barrier between us. "She gave me some clothes last month."

"Castoffs. Hand-me-downs. You deserve better, Mallory." He mumbles some things I can't make out except the very end: "You're stuck in this shithole and there's a whole big world out there."

"I like it here. I like Spring Brook."

"Because you haven't been anywhere else. If you'd traveled, if you'd been to Whidbey Island, you'd understand."

"Where's that?"

He explains that it's part of a chain of islands in the Pacific Northwest. "I spent a summer there in college. Best summer of my life. I worked on a ranch, I spent all day in the sun and at night we sat on the beach drinking wine. No TVs, no screens. Just good people and nature and the most gorgeous views you've ever seen."

Then he notices the chinos on top of the bedspread. He seems to understand that they belong to him, that they ought to be on his legs. He shakes out the pants and lowers them to his feet and promptly drops them on the floor. I realize I will need to help. I kneel in front of him, holding open the pants so he can pull them on—first one leg, then the other. He raises them just past his hips, then stares into my eyes. "I swear to you, Mallory, if you saw Puget Sound, you'd forget Spring Brook in five minutes. You'd realize Spring Brook is a shithole, it's a trap."

I'm not really listening to anything he's saying. When you grow up in South Philly, you have lots of encounters with lots of drunks, and you learn that most of their comments are nonsense. None of this means anything.

"Spring Brook is beautiful. And you have a wonderful life here. A beautiful family, a beautiful wife."

"She sleeps in the guest room. She won't touch me."

Ted is mumbling and looking down at his pants, so it's easy for me to pretend I didn't hear that.

"You have a beautiful house," I continue.

"She bought it. Not me. This is the last place on Earth I'd choose to live."

"What do you mean?"

"Caroline's father was very wealthy. We could afford to live anywhere. Manhattan, San Francisco, you name it. But she wanted Spring Brook, so here we are in Spring Brook." He speaks as if events have spiraled beyond his control. "Don't get me wrong, Mallory. She's a good person. She has a big heart. And she would do anything for Teddy's well-being. But this is not the life I wanted. I never signed on for any of this."

"Can I get you some more water?"

He shakes his head, like I'm failing to grasp some essential point. "I'm not asking you to take care of me. I'm saying *I* would take care of *you*."

"I understand. And I'll think about it. But right now we should get you home. Caroline is probably worried."

Ted is increasingly incoherent—he says something about Seneca Lake and wine country and running away from everything. He manages to stand without my help, then lifts his chinos and buttons them. "We should burn these."

"Tomorrow," I tell him. "Let's burn them tomorrow."

"But not in the cottage." He points to the smoke detector on the wall. "All your wiring is knob and tube so it's very delicate. Very fragile. Don't fix it yourself. Ask me for help."

I open the door to the cottage and Ted stumbles outside onto the porch. Somehow he manages to descend the three steps to the lawn without tripping, and then he veers off into the dark, heading toward the big house.

"Good night," I call after him.

"We'll see," he calls back.

I close the door to my cottage and lock it. I spy a crumpled wad of Kleenex on the nightstand beside my bed. I pick it up with a paper towel and shove it deep down to the bottom of my wastebasket. Then I pull off my blankets and strip off my sheets and discover three of my bras mixed up in everything. I don't know how they ended up in my bed and I don't want to know. Tomorrow I will put everything in the laundry and I will try to forget this happened.

Since I don't have any other sheets, I have to spread my bath towels over the mattress and lie down on them. It's not as uncomfortable as it sounds. All I have to do is close my eyes and I'm transported back to the beautiful castle garden with its gentle waterfalls and sweet-smelling floral archways. Nothing can spoil this night for me—not my argument about the séance with Caroline, and certainly not discovering Ted in my cottage. And before I fall asleep I ask God to forgive me for lying to Adrian. I pray that He'll help me find the right words to tell him the truth. I pray that Adrian will see past all the horrible things I've done—that he'll see me as the person I am now, not the disaster I used to be.

19

The next morning I get to the big house and find Caroline and Ted dressed for work and sitting in the breakfast nook. Caroline is drinking tea and Ted is sipping black coffee and they're staring at each other in stony silence. I realize they're waiting for me.

"Can you join us?" Caroline asks. "Ted has something he'd like to say."

Ted looks like hell. He's clearly hungover. The man belongs upstairs in bed. Or down on his knees in the bathroom, hunched over a toilet. "I want to apologize for my behavior last night. It was completely unacceptable and—"

"Ted, it's fine. I've already forgotten about it."

Caroline shakes her head. "No, Mallory, we're not going to pretend this didn't happen. We need to fully acknowledge everything that occurred last night."

Ted nods and dutifully continues, like he's reciting some kind of memorized public statement. "My actions were arrogant and disrespectful. I'm ashamed of my behavior, and I'm looking inward to understand why I chose to abuse my privilege."

"Apology accepted," I tell them. "You don't need to say anything else. I'd feel better if we just moved on, okay?"

Ted looks to Caroline, and she shrugs. Fine.

"Thank you for understanding, Mallory. I promise it won't happen again."

He stands up and grabs his briefcase and then walks unsteadily toward the foyer. Moments later, I can hear the front door slam, and the sound of his car starting in the driveway.

"He's afraid you're going to sue us," Caroline explains. "Can you please tell me what happened? In your own words?"

"Caroline, I promise you, it was nothing. Last night, I went to Adrian's house. His parents were having a party. I got home after midnight and Ted was in my cottage. He was drunk. He said you guys had a fight, and that he needed a quiet place to cool off."

"I thought he was downstairs. Sleeping on the sofa."

"As soon as I came home, he said he was sorry and he left. That was it."

"Did he tell you about our fight?"

"No, he just said you were a good person. With a good heart. He said you would do anything for your family."

"And?"

"And that was it. He wasn't making a lot of sense. He talked about some island? Where he spent a summer in college?"

"'Working in the sun and sleeping under the stars,'" Caroline says, and I realize that she's parodying her husband, gently mocking him. "Whenever he gets drunk, he talks about Whidbey Island."

"I didn't mind. I gave him some water and some baby aspirin and I opened the door and he left. End of story."

She studies my face like she's searching for clues. "I'm embarrassed to ask this next question, but since technically you're my employee, I feel like I have to. Did he try anything?"

"No. Not at all."

I mean, I guess I could mention that he took off his pants, and raided my underwear drawer, and did God-knows-what in my bed before I arrived. But what would be the point? Poor Caroline already looks miserable, and Ted has apologized. I don't see the point in dragging this out. I'm certainly not going to quit over what happened.

"Caroline, I swear to you, he didn't put a hand on me. Not even close."

She releases a deep long sigh. "Ted turned fifty-three this summer. I'm sure you've heard about men and their midlife crises. They start questioning all the choices they've made. And on top of that, his business is struggling. It's taking a toll on his ego. He was hoping to hire some new people this fall, but it's looking doubtful."

"How big is the company?"

She gives me a funny look. "He'd like a staff of forty but right now it's just Ted. It's a one-man operation."

Just Ted? My sense was that he worked in a big Center City skyscraper full of secretaries and fancy computers and big glass windows overlooking Rittenhouse Square. "He told me he works with Cracker Barrel. And Yankee Candle. Big companies."

"He's taken meetings with them," Caroline explains. "He goes around to different companies and offers to run their websites. Direct their e-commerce businesses. But it's hard to land these big clients when you're just one person."

"He's mentioned coworkers. Guys named Mike and Ed. He says they all eat lunch together."

"Right, they're all in the same WeWork. One of those office-shares where people rent desks by the month. Because Ted needs to have a mailing address in the city. A big part of his business is making a good impression. Trying to appear more important than you really are. He's been under a lot of stress this summer—and last night, I think you saw the first cracks in the facade."

Her voice breaks and I realize she's worried not just for Ted but also for their marriage, for their entire family. And I truly have no idea what to say to her. I'm relieved to hear Teddy's footsteps coming down the stairs. Caroline sits up straight and dabs her eyes with a napkin.

Teddy enters the kitchen carrying an iPad. He's swiping his finger across the surface and the screen responds with loud, cacophonous explosions.

"Hey there, Teddy Bear! Whatcha got?"

He doesn't look up from the screen. "Mommy gave it to me last night. It used to be Daddy's but now it's mine." He grabs a plastic tumbler and fills it with water from the sink. Without another word of explanation, he carries the cup and iPad into the den.

"Teddy's taking a break from drawing," Caroline explains. "In light of all the confusion, we think he needs some new interests. And the App Store has a ton of educational resources. Math games, phonics, even foreign languages." She walks across the kitchen and opens a cabinet above the refrigerator, way beyond Teddy's reach. "I gathered all his crayons and markers and put them up here. Teddy's so excited about the iPad, I don't think he's even noticed."

I know the first rule of babysitting is never second-guessing the mother, but I can't help feeling like this is a mistake. Teddy took a real joy in drawing and I think it's wrong to deprive him of the privilege. Worse, I feel like it's happening because of me, because I wouldn't keep my mouth shut about Annie Barrett.

Caroline registers my disappointment. "It's an experiment. Just for a couple days. Maybe it can help us understand what's happening." She closes the door to the cabinet, as if the matter is settled. "But now tell me about this party at Adrian's house. Did you have a nice time?"

"Really nice." And I guess I'm happy to change the subject, because I've been thinking about our dinner date since I got out of bed. "We're going out tonight. He wants to drive to Princeton. Some kind of tapas restaurant."

"Oooh, those places are so romantic."

"He's picking me up at five thirty."

"Then I'll try to get home early. Give you some extra time to get ready." Then she checks the time. "Shoot, I better go. I'm so excited for you, Mallory! You're going to have so much fun tonight!"

After Caroline leaves, I find Teddy sitting in the den, mesmerized by a game of Angry Birds. He's using his finger to stretch and release a giant slingshot; he's launching colorful birds at a series of wood and steel structures occupied by pigs. With each new attack, there's a cacophony of screeches, explosions, bangs, blasts, and slide whistles. I sit across from Teddy and clap my hands together. "So, what are we doing this morning? A little stroll in the Enchanted Forest? Or how about a Bake-Off?"

He shrugs, swiping furiously. "I don't care."

One of the birds misses its target and Teddy furrows his brow, frustrated by the results. He hunches closer to the screen, almost like he's trying to disappear inside it.

"Come on, Teddy. Put the game away."

"I'm not done."

"Mommy says it's for Quiet Time. She doesn't want you using it all morning."

He turns away from me, shielding the tablet with his body. "Just one more level."

"How long is a level?"

It turns out that one more level takes a good half hour. After he's finished, Teddy pleads with me to charge the iPad, so he'll have enough batteries for later.

We spend the morning trampling around the Enchanted Forest. I try to make up a new adventure story for Prince Teddy and Princess Mallory, but all Teddy wants to discuss is Angry Birds strategy. Yellow birds are best for attacking wood structures. Black birds can destroy concrete walls. White birds accelerate after dropping their egg bombs. It's not really a conversation; he's just reciting a string of facts and data, like he's trying to organize the rules in his mind.

I spy a glint of silver in a bed of leaves and I kneel down to investigate. It's the bottom half of an arrow; the top part with the feathers is missing and all that remains is the aluminum shaft and a pyramid-shaped tip.

"This is a magic missile," I tell Teddy. "It's used for slaying goblins."

"That's cool," Teddy says. "Also, the green bird is a boomerang bird. He gets double-damage when he attacks. So I like to play him first."

I suggest that we hike to the Giant Beanstalk and add the arrow to our arsenal of weapons. Teddy agrees, but his participation feels half-hearted. It's like he's just biding his time, running down the clock until morning is over and we can go back to the house.

I offer to make Teddy anything he wants for lunch but he says he doesn't care so I just make grilled cheese. As he wolfs down the sandwich, I remind him that he doesn't have to use the iPad during Quiet Time. I suggest it might be fun to play LEGOs or Lincoln Logs or farm animals. And he glances at me like I'm trying to swindle him, like I'm trying to cheat him out of a privilege he has rightfully earned.

"Thanks, but I'll do my game," he says.

He carries the tablet up to his bedroom and after a few minutes I climb the stairs to the second floor and press my ear to his bedroom door. There are no whispered words, no half-conversations. Just occasional laughter from Teddy, and the sounds of stretching slingshots, squawking birds, and imploding buildings. He sounds giddy with delight, but something in his happiness makes me sad. Overnight, like flipping a switch, I feel as if something magical has been lost.

I go downstairs, take out my phone, and call the number of the Rest Haven Retirement Community. I tell the receptionist that I'm looking to speak with one of the residents, Dolores Jean Campbell. The phone rings several times before a default voice mail greeting kicks on.

"Um, hi, my name is Mallory Quinn? We don't know each other, but I think maybe you can help me?"

I realize I have no idea how to explain my question, that I should have practiced what to say before the call, but now it's too late and I just need to blunder ahead.

"I wondered if your mother was someone named Annie Barrett. From Spring Brook, New Jersey. Because if she is, I would really love to talk with you. Can you please call me back?"

I leave my number and end the call feeling like I've already hit a dead end. I'm convinced I'll never hear from her.

I clean up the lunch dishes and then go around the kitchen with a soapy sponge, cleaning the counters and trying to make myself useful. More than ever, I'm feeling vulnerable in my job. It's like every day brings some new reason for Caroline to replace me. So I busy myself with tasks outside my job description. I sweep and mop up the floors, and wipe down the inside of the microwave. I open the toaster oven and empty the little tray of crumbs. I reach under the sink and fill the liquid soap dispensers, then stand on a chair and wipe the dust off the ceiling fan.

All these little chores make me feel better, but I'm not sure Caroline will notice. I decide I need a bigger and more ambitious project, something she could never miss. I move into the den and lie down on the sofa and I'm considering all my different options when I'm struck by the perfect idea: I will bring Teddy to the supermarket, we will buy a bunch of food, and we'll prepare a surprise dinner for his parents. I'll have the whole meal warming in the oven so it's ready to eat as soon as they get home. I'll even set the table so they won't have to lift a finger.

They can just enter the house, sit down with some delicious food, and be grateful that I'm part of their family.

But before I can actually act on this idea, before I can sit up and start a shopping list, I fall asleep.

I'm not sure how it happens. I'm not particularly tired. I only meant to rest my eyes for a minute. But the next thing I know, I'm dreaming about a place from my childhood, a tiny family-owned amusement park called Storybook Land. It was built in the 1950s to celebrate all the classic fairy tales and Mother Goose nursery rhymes. Kids could climb a giant beanstalk or visit the three little pigs or wave through a window to the Old Woman Who Lived in a Shoe, a creaky animatronic puppet with a dead-eyed stare.

In my dream, I'm walking Teddy past the carousel and he's incredibly excited and he pleads with me to hold all his pencils and crayons so he can start going on rides. He empties an entire box into my hands, more than I can possibly carry, and the pencils fall all around my feet. I try to stuff them into my pockets because there's no way I can carry all of them. And by the time I've collected everything, Teddy is gone. I've lost him in the crowd. My dream has turned into a nightmare.

I start running through the park, shoving past the other parents, shouting Teddy's name and searching all over. Storybook Land is full of five-year-old children and from the back they all look identical, any one of them could be Teddy, I can't find him anywhere. I pull some parents aside and beg them to help me, please please help me, and they're appalled. "But this is *your* responsibility," they tell me. "Why would we help?"

I have no choice but to call the Maxwells. I don't want to tell them what's happened, but it's an emergency. I take out my cell phone and I'm calling Caroline's number when suddenly I see him! All the way across the park, sitting on the steps of Little Red Riding Hood's cottage. I elbow my way through throngs of people, trying to move as fast as I can. But by the time I reach the cottage it's not Teddy anymore. It's my sister, Beth! She's wearing a yellow T-shirt and faded jeans and checkered black-and-white Vans.

I run over and hug her and lift her off the ground. I can't believe she's here, she's alive! I squeeze her so tight she starts laughing, and sunlight glints off her orthodontic braces. "I thought you were dead! I thought I killed you!"

"Don't be a dork," she says, and my dream is so realistic I can actually smell her. She smells like coconut and pineapple, like the piña colada bath bombs that she and her girlfriends used to buy at Lush, the overpriced soap shop at the King of Prussia Mall.

She explains the accident was just a big misunderstanding and all this time I've been blaming myself for nothing.

"Are you sure you're okay?"

"Yes, Mal, for the one millionth time I am totally okay. Now can we ride the Balloon Bounce?"

"Yes, Beth, yes! Anything! Anything you want!"

But then Teddy is back, he's pulling on my arm, he's gently shaking me awake. I open my eyes and I'm lying on the sofa in the den and Teddy is holding out the iPad.

"It went dead again."

I'm certain he's mistaken. I just charged the iPad over lunch and the battery went to 100 percent. But as I sit up, I realize the light in the den is significantly darker; the sun has stopped streaming through the north-facing windows. The clock over the mantel says it's 5:17 but that can't be right, that's impossible.

I reach for my phone and confirm it's actually 5:23.

I've been asleep four hours.

And the Maxwells will be home any minute.

"Teddy, what happened? Why didn't you wake me up?"

"I got to level thirty," he says proudly. "I unlocked eight new feather cards!"

My hands are filthy. My fingers and palms are smeared with dark black soot, like I've been digging outside in the garden. There's a worn-down nub of pencil in my lap—and more pencils and markers and crayons scattered on the floor, all the art supplies that Caroline stashed away in the kitchen.

Teddy looks around the den in wide-eyed wonder.

"Mommy's going to be so mad."

I look where he's looking and the walls are covered with sketches—many, many sketches, dense and detailed and spanning from floor to ceiling.

"Teddy, why did you do this?"

"Me? *I* didn't do anything!"

And of course he didn't. He couldn't! He's not tall enough! He's not the one with charcoal and graphite smeared all over his hands. I walk across the room to take a closer look. These are Anya's drawings, there's no doubt in my mind. They're all over the walls, drawn in the blank spots between windows and thermostats and light switches.

"Mallory? Are you okay?"

He's tugging on my shirttail, and I am not okay.

I am definitely *not* okay.

"Teddy, listen to me. We need to fix this before Mommy and Daddy get home. Do you have any erasers in your bedroom? Big fat pink rubber erasers?"

He looks at all the pencils and crayons and markers on the floor. "This is everything I have. But I'm not supposed to use these anymore. Not until we get to the bottom of things."

It's too late, anyway. I can hear a car pulling into the driveway. I look outside and see not just Ted and Caroline but Adrian, too. He's parking his landscaping truck in front of the house. Right now I'm supposed to be putting on one of Caroline's summer dresses, getting ready for my big dinner date in Princeton.

"Go upstairs, Teddy."

"Why?"

"Because I don't want you to be here."

"Why?"

"Please just go upstairs? Please?" There's a USB cable on the coffee table and I pass it to him. "Go charge the iPad in your bedroom."

"Okay, cool."

Teddy takes the iPad and the cable and runs out of the den, like he thinks he's getting away with something. I can hear his little feet running upstairs to his room.

And then the sound of the front door opening, the soft swish of the door sweep whisking over the tiled floor. I can hear Caroline talking to Adrian, welcoming him into their home. "Where are you going for dinner?"

"A really good tapas place," he says. "They make a killer patatas bravas."

"Mmmm, what are those?" Ted asks.

"Mr. Maxwell, they're the best French fries you've ever tasted, I guarantee it."

I know I need to intercept them and somehow prepare them for what I've done. I head into the kitchen and Caroline is asking Adrian if he'd like something to drink. The cabinet above the refrigerator is still hanging open, its contents have been looted, but Caroline hasn't noticed yet.

And Adrian is so handsome it's almost heartbreaking. He looks like he's just stepped out of the shower. His hair is a little damp, and he's smartly dressed in dark jeans and a crisp white button-down shirt. No one sees me enter the kitchen until I announce my presence.

"Something happened."

Caroline stares at me. "Mallory?"

"What's on your hands?" Ted asks.

Adrian hurries to my side. "Are you okay?"

And I know he's my only hope.

He's the only one who *might* believe me.

"This is going to sound crazy but I swear I'm telling the truth. After Teddy went upstairs for Quiet Time, I started feeling tired. I lay down on the sofa to rest. I figured I would close my eyes, just for a few minutes. And then somehow—I don't know how—Anya's spirit took possession of my body."

Caroline stares at me. "What?"

"I know. I know it sounds crazy. But while I was sleeping, she made me get out all the pencils and markers and crayons." I point to the empty cabinet above the refrigerator. "And since you took all the paper, she made me draw on your walls. She couldn't get inside Teddy so she put herself in me."

Adrian puts an arm around my waist. "Hey, it's okay. You're safe now. We're going to figure this out."

Caroline shoves past me, storming into the den, and we all follow. She draws in her breath sharply, staring at the walls in disbelief.

"Where's Teddy?"

"In his room. He's fine."

Caroline looks to her husband. He hurries upstairs.

I try to walk Caroline through the afternoon. "He went into his bedroom at one o'clock. For Quiet Time. I let him take the iPad, just like you said. He didn't come downstairs until ten minutes ago. Right when you got home."

"Four hours?" she asks.

I show Adrian my right hand, all covered with graphite and charcoal and blisters. "I'm left-handed, just like Teddy. I couldn't have done this on my own. These are just like the pictures in my cottage."

"Yes, exactly! The style is identical!" He takes out his smartphone and walks around the room, capturing photographs of the various scenes. "The first thing we should do is compare them to the other pictures. See how they fit in the sequence."

"No," Caroline says. "The first thing we're doing is a tox screen. Right now. Or I'm calling the police."

Adrian stares at her. "Tox screen?"

"I can't believe I left you alone with our son. I can't believe I trusted you! What the hell was I thinking?"

"I'm not using," I tell her. I try to speak softly, as if it's somehow possible to have the conversation in a sidebar. As if Adrian wasn't standing right there listening. "I swear to you, Caroline, I'm clean."

"Then you'll have no problem with the test. When you started working here, you agreed to random testing every week. You volunteered. On days of our choosing." She takes my wrist and studies my arm for marks. "I guess we should have started a lot sooner."

Ted returns from the second floor, and with a single look he assures Caroline that Teddy is fine. Meanwhile Adrian is trying to persuade Caroline that she's got the situation all wrong.

"Mrs. Maxwell, I don't know what you're talking about, but Mallory's not on drugs. Do you really think she'd have an athletic scholarship if she was doing heroin? Penn State would kick her off the team in a heartbeat."

An awkward silence settles into the room, and I realize Caroline is giving me a chance to explain myself. I can feel my tears welling up because this isn't how it was supposed to happen. "Okay, wait," I tell him. "Because, the thing is, I haven't been completely honest with you."

Adrian still has his arms around me, but his grip goes loose. "What does that mean?"

"I was going to tell you the truth tonight."

"What are you talking about?"

And I still can't do it.

I still have no idea where to begin.

"Mallory doesn't go to Penn State," Ted explains. "She's spent the last eighteen months in rehab. In a halfway house. She was abusing prescription painkillers and heroin."

"Plus other drugs she doesn't even remember," Caroline adds. "The brain needs time to heal, Mallory."

Now Adrian isn't holding me at all. Now I'm just hanging on to his body like a big sad pathetic monster, like a parasite. He shakes me off so he can see my face.

"Is this for real?" he asks.

"I'm not using," I tell him. "I swear to you, Adrian, I am twenty months sober next Tuesday."

And he takes a step back like I've struck him. Caroline rests a gentle hand on his shoulder. "This must be hard for you to hear. We just assumed Mallory had been honest with you about her history. We thought she told you the truth."

"No, not at all."

"Adrian, I work with a lot of addicts at the VA hospital. They're good people, and our main goal is moving them back into society. But sometimes the timing isn't right. Sometimes, we launch people before they're ready."

I look up at Caroline, furious. "That is NOT what's happening here! I am not on drugs. And I am not a fucking illustrator! I swear to you, Caroline. Something is wrong with this house. The ghost of Annie Barrett is haunting your son, and now she's haunting me, and this is her message." I point all around the room, at all of the walls. "This is her story!"

And I know I must look crazy and sound crazy because Adrian studies me in a kind of bewilderment. He looks like he's seeing me for the first time.

"But is the rest of it true?" he asks. "You lived in a halfway house? You used *heroin*?"

I'm too ashamed to answer, but he can read the truth on my face. Adrian turns and leaves the den and I go to follow him but Caroline blocks my way. "Let him go, Mallory. Don't make this any harder for him."

I turn toward the window and watch Adrian cross the flagstone walkway and his face is all twisted up with hurt. Halfway down the driveway he breaks into a kind of trot, like he can't wait to get the hell away from me. He gets inside a black pickup truck and peels away from the curb.

And when I look back at Caroline, she's holding a plastic cup. "Come on. Let's get this over with."

She walks me to the powder room. I go inside and reach to close the door, but she stops me, shaking her head. As if she's worried I'm going to somehow manipulate my sample, like I carry around vials of clean urine just in case. Caroline does me the courtesy of turning her head while I drop my shorts and squat over the toilet. Having been tested many hundreds of times, I am well practiced in collecting clean samples. I can fill a four-ounce cup without spilling a drop. I set the cup on the edge of the sink, then pull up my shorts and wash my hands. The water runs black, filling the basin with grainy residue. I use a bar of soap to scrape at my fingers and palms, but the graphite clings to my skin like ink, like stains that will never come out.

"I'll wait for you in the den," Caroline says. "We won't start until you get there."

All my handwashing leaves a filthy gray ring on the immaculate white pedestal sink. Yet another thing to feel guilty about. I try to clean it up with some toilet paper, then I dry my hands on my shorts.

When I reach the den, Caroline and Ted are seated on the sofa and they've got my sample on the coffee table, resting atop a paper towel. Caroline shows me a dip card that's still wrapped in cellophane, to prove it hasn't been tampered with. Then she unwraps the card, exposes the five test strips, and lowers them into the cup.

"Look, I understand why you're doing this, but it's not going to come up positive. I swear to you. I've been sober for twenty months."

"And we want to believe you," Caroline says, and then she glances at the drawings all over the walls. "But we need to understand what happened here today."

"I already told you what happened. Anya took possession of my body. She used me like a puppet. I didn't draw any of these pictures! She did!"

"If we're going to talk about this," Caroline says, "we need to stay calm. We can't shout at each other."

I take a breath. "All right. Okay."

"Now before you came to work here, we had a long talk with Russell about your history. He told us about your struggles—the false memories, the lapses—"

"This is different. I don't have those problems anymore."

"You know just a couple days ago, Teddy lost his box of drawing pencils. He came to me crying. He was upset because he couldn't find them anywhere. And soon after that, all these pictures start magically appearing in your cottage. Doesn't that seem like an extraordinary coincidence?"

I look down at the cup. It's only been a minute. It's still way too early for results.

"Caroline, I can barely draw a straight line. I took one art class in high school. I got a C plus. There's no way I drew these pictures, I'm not that good."

"My patients always say the same thing: 'I can't draw to save my life!' But then they try art therapy and the results are extraordinary. They draw the most amazing images to work through their trauma. To process truths they're not ready to face."

"That's not what this is."

"Look at the woman in your pictures. She's young, she's tall. She has an athletic build. She's actually *running*, Mallory. Does she remind you of anyone?"

I see where she's going but she's wrong. "That's not a self-portrait."

"It's a symbolic representation. A visual metaphor. You've lost your younger sister. You're upset, you're panicking, you're desperate to bring her back—but it's too late. She's fallen into a valley of death." She moves around the den, directing my attention from one picture to the next. "And then an angel comes to help her—nothing too subtle about that metaphor, right? The angel is leading Beth toward the light and you can't stop them. Beth has crossed over, she's never coming back. You know this, Mallory. It's all here on the wall. This isn't Anya's story. It's *your* story. It's *Beth's* story."

I shake my head. I don't want to drag Beth into this. I don't even want Caroline saying her name.

"We know what happened," she continues. "Russell told us your story and it's awful, Mallory. I am so sorry it happened. I know you're carrying a lot of guilt, a lot of grief. But if you don't address these feelings—if you just keep tamping them down—" She gestures around the room to my artwork. "They're like steam under pressure, Mallory. They're going to look for cracks and find a way to escape."

"What about all the other pictures? The woman being strangled?"

"An abstract concept made literal," Caroline says. "Maybe grief, or addiction. The stranglehold that drugs put on your body."

"And the woman getting dragged through the forest?"

"Perhaps there's someone who pulled you out of danger? A sponsor or mentor? Like Russell?"

"Then why is he burying me?"

"He's not burying you, Mallory. He's *freeing* you. Excavating you from a mountain of heroin and bringing you back to society. And look at you now!"

Caroline turns the dip card so I can see the results. All five tabs— the indicators for THC, opioids, cocaine, amphetamines, and meth— they've all come up negative.

"Twenty months sober," Ted says. "That's amazing."

"We're really proud of you," Caroline says. "But it's clear you have a lot more work to do, isn't that right?"

And I don't know what to say.

I agree there are some very puzzling parallels between Anya's drawings and my own personal history.

And yes, I have struggled with lapses and false memories and all the other psychological fallout of drug addiction.

But I have twelve more drawings back at my cottage that stink of death and there's only one person responsible.

"Anya drew these. Not me."

"Anya is an imaginary friend. Teddy knows she's made up. He understands she doesn't really exist."

"Teddy is scared and confused and he's repeating everything you're teaching him. I know you guys went to great schools and you think you have the whole world figured out. But you're wrong about these pictures, you're wrong about this house, and you're wrong about Teddy. There is some seriously weird shit happening right under your nose and you're living in denial!"

By this point I'm yelling, I can't help myself, but Ted and Caroline are unshaken. I realize that they've stopped listening to me, that they're ready to move on.

"I think we should just agree to disagree," Caroline tells me. "Maybe she's a ghost or maybe she's just guilt. It doesn't matter, Mallory. The key takeaway is that you left our son unattended for four hours, and I don't trust you to watch him anymore."

Ted agrees that "a change needs to happen" and Caroline says it's good to think of this moment as a crossroads, an opportunity to improve things for everyone.

And they both sound so positive, so supportive and encouraging, it takes me a moment to realize I'm being fired.

20

I'm back in my cottage for ten minutes when my phone rings.

It's Russell. Calling from a tiny motel on Route 66, somewhere in the desert between Las Vegas and the Grand Canyon. It's a bad connection, and the line crackles and pops.

"Quinn! What happened?"

"I think I lost the job."

"No, you *definitely* lost the job! Caroline texted me pictures of your crazy ape-shit art project. What the hell is going on over there?"

"There's something in this house, Russell. Some kind of presence. First she went after Teddy and now she's coming after me."

"Presence?" Most days, Russell is a font of limitless energy and enthusiasm—but suddenly he sounds tired and just a tiny bit disappointed. "You mean like a ghost?"

"I'm not using. Caroline tested me."

"I know."

"This is something else. This is—"

We're interrupted by a hiss of static, and for a moment I'm worried I've lost him. Then his voice comes back.

"You should get to a meeting. What time is it there? Six thirty? Friday night? Try Holy Redeemer. They start at seven, I think."

"I don't need a meeting."

"Are there friends you can call? Someone you can stay with? I don't want you alone tonight." And I guess he can tell from my silence there's no one here to help me. "All right, listen. I'm coming home."

"No!"

"It's fine. I hate it here anyway. The weather's impossible. I have to do all my running indoors, on treadmills, because if you step outside for ten minutes the heat'll stop your heart."

He explains that he'll need two or three days to come get me. He's currently en route to the Grand Canyon, so he'll have to drive back to Las Vegas and book a new flight. "So maybe Sunday but definitely Monday. You just need to make it to Monday, okay? Doreen and I will pick you up. You can stay with me a few weeks, we'll have a doctor look you over. Figure out a Plan B."

"Thank you, Russell."

I let my phone drop to the floor and close my eyes. I know I should get out of bed, I should go to a meeting or at the very least make myself dinner. But outside the cottage, it's started to rain, one of those abrupt summer thunderstorms that come out of nowhere. Wind shakes the roof and water cascades down my windows. I'm trapped inside the cottage and I wish there was someone I could call. I'm dreading the long weekend ahead of me, the long lonely wait until Russell comes to get me. My only other friends are back at Safe Harbor, but I'm too ashamed to tell them what I've done.

Of course, there are also my friends *before* Safe Harbor. I've erased all their names and numbers from my contacts, but it wouldn't be hard to track them down. Philadelphia is a thirty-minute train ride from Spring Brook. If I could just get to Kensington Avenue, I know I'd recognize plenty of faces, old friends happy to see me, ready to welcome me home. I have twelve hundred dollars in my checking account. I can pick up and go, and no one here would ever miss me.

Except Teddy.

Teddy *would* miss me, I know he would.

I can't leave him without saying goodbye.

I need to stick around long enough to explain things, to let him know that none of this was his fault.

And so I stay in my perfect little cottage, the nicest place I've ever lived, a beautifully furnished reminder of everything I've just lost. It rains and rains and the buzzing in my brain is worse than ever—like my head is full of mosquitoes. I smash a pillow into my face and scream but nothing will silence the noise.

That night I sleep for ten, twelve, fourteen hours. Every time I wake up, I remember what happened, and then I burrow under my blankets until I'm asleep again.

At ten o'clock Saturday morning I stand up and drag myself into the shower. It makes me feel better, a little, I guess. Then I step outside and there's a rock holding a sheet of paper on my porch.

Oh sweet Jesus, I think to myself, I'm really going crazy.

But it's just a note from Caroline:

Dear Mallory,

Ted and I are taking Teddy to the shore. We told him you'll be moving away, and of course he's upset. Hopefully a day of beach and boardwalk rides will take his mind off things. We'll be gone until late so you'll have the pool and yard to yourself.

Also: Russell called this morning with an update. He has booked a red-eye ticket for tomorrow night, and he'll be here Monday morning, between 10 and 11 a.m.

We'd like to spend tomorrow afternoon celebrating your time with our family—with swimming, dinner, dessert, etc. Starting around 3:00 if that works for you. Please call if you need anything or just want to talk. I am here to support you during this transition.

Love, Caroline

I walk over to the big house to get some orange juice, but when I try to enter my passcode on the keypad, it doesn't work. Of course it doesn't. Ted and Caroline might trust me with their backyard, but there's no way they'll let me back in their house, not after I drew all over the walls.

I know I should go for a run. I know I'll feel better if I get out and log a few miles. But I'm too embarrassed to leave the backyard, too ashamed to show my face around the neighborhood. I imagine that news of my deception has spread quickly, and now everyone in Spring Brook knows my secret. I walk back to my cottage, pour myself a bowl of Cheerios, and then remember I'm out of milk. I eat them dry, with my fingers. I lie on my bed with my tablet and go to the Hallmark Channel, scanning the selection of movies, but suddenly they all seem fake and horrible and awful—full of false promises and bullshit happy endings.

I'm ten minutes into something called *A Shoe Addict's Christmas* when I hear footsteps on my porch and a soft knock at my door. I figure it's probably Mitzi, coming to apologize for her behavior during the séance. I yell out "I'm busy" and raise the volume on my tablet.

Adrian's face appears in the window.

"We need to talk."

I leap out of bed and open the door. "Yes, we really do, because—"

"Not here," he says. "I've got my truck out front. Let's go for a drive."

He doesn't say where we're going, but as soon as reach the on-ramp for 295 I figure it out. We merge into fast-flowing traffic, connect with 76 West, and cross the Walt Whitman Bridge, soaring high above the shipyards and seaports of the Delaware River. We are going to South Philadelphia. Adrian is bringing me home.

"You don't have to do this. Turn the truck around."

"We're almost there," he says. "Five more minutes."

It's too early for football and the Phils must be out of town because the expressway is clear, no traffic. Adrian takes the exit for Oregon Avenue. He keeps glancing at his GPS, but from this point I could direct him blindfolded. I still know every road and stop sign and traffic light. All the old businesses are still here: the fast-food places and the cheesesteak shops, the Asian supermarkets and the cell phone retailers and the sports bar/strip club that recruited two of my classmates straight from high school. No one was ever going to mistake my old neighborhood for Spring Brook. The roads are full of potholes; the sidewalks are littered with broken glass and chicken bones. But many of the rowhouses have new aluminum siding and look better than I remember, like people have been making an effort to keep everything nice.

Adrian stops at the corner of Eighth and Shunk. I'm guessing he found my address online because we're right in front of the short squat rowhouse I used to call home. The bricks have been repointed, the shutters have a fresh coat of paint, and there's bright green grass where our white gravel "yard" used to be. Next to the front door is a man standing on a ladder; he's wearing work gloves and scooping dead leaves from the rain gutters.

Adrian shifts into park and turns on his flashers. I haven't seen any of my neighbors since high school and I'm afraid of being spotted. The houses are all packed tight together and it's easy to imagine everyone opening their doors and streaming outside to gape at me.

"Please just drive."

"Is this where you grew up?"

"You already know it is."

"Who's the man on the ladder?"

"I don't know. Just drive, all right?"

The man turns to study us. He's middle-aged, balding, not too tall and dressed in an Eagles jersey. "You need something?"

I've never seen him before. Maybe my mother has hired a handy-man. More likely, she's sold the house and moved away and this man is the new owner. I wave an apology and turn to Adrian. "If you don't go right now, I am getting out of this truck and walking back to Spring Brook."

He shifts into drive and we move through the green light. I direct him through traffic to FDR Park, South Philly's go-to spot for pic-nics, birthdays, and wedding party photography. Growing up, we all called it "the Lakes," because it's speckled with ponds and lagoons. The largest one is Meadow Lake and we find a bench with a good view of the water. Off on the horizon, against the gray sky, we can see the elevated roadways of Interstate 95, six lanes of cars hurtling to and from the airport. And for a long time we don't say anything, because neither of us knows where to start.

"I wasn't lying about the scholarship," I tell him. "In my junior year, I ran a 5K in seventeen minutes, fifty-three seconds. I was the sixth-fastest girl in Pennsylvania. You can google it."

"I already googled it, Mallory. The first day we met, I ran home and searched for every Mallory Quinn in Philadelphia. I found all your high school stats. Just enough to make your story feel credible." Then he laughs. "But nothing on Twitter, nothing on social media. I thought it was cool—this aura of mystery. The girls at Rutgers, they're on In-stagram twenty-four/seven, posting glamour shots and fishing for compliments. But you were different. I thought you were confident. I never imagined you were hiding something."

"I was mostly honest."

"*Mostly*? What does that mean?"

"I only lied about my past. Nothing else. Not the pictures from Anya. And definitely not the way I feel about you. I was going to tell you the truth last night, over dinner, I swear."

He doesn't say anything. He just stares out over the lake. Some nearby kids are playing with a drone; it looks like a miniature UFO with eight furiously spinning propellers, and every time it passes by, it sounds like a swarm of bees. I realize Adrian is waiting for me to continue, that he's giving me the chance to come clean. I take a deep breath.

"All right, so—"

21

All my problems started with a simple sacral stress fracture—a tiny break in the triangle-shaped bone at the base of my spine. This was September of my senior year of high school, and the recommended treatment was eight weeks of rest—right at the start of cross-country season. It was bad news but not a complete disaster. The injury was common among young women runners, easily treatable, and wouldn't impact my offer from Penn State. The doctors prescribed OxyContin for the pain—a single forty-milligram tablet twice a day. Everyone said I would be fine for winter track in November.

I still went to all the practices and I lugged around equipment and helped to tally everyone's scores—but it was hard to watch my teammates from the sidelines, knowing I should be running alongside them. Plus, since I had more time on my hands, my mother expected me to do more around the house. More cooking and cleaning and shopping and looking after my sister.

Mom raised us single-handedly. She was short, overweight, and she smoked a pack a day—even though she worked at Mercy Hospital, as a billing administrator, so she knew all the health risks. Beth and I were always after her to quit, always hiding her Newports under the sofa or other places she would never look. She would just go out and buy new ones. She said they were her coping mechanism, that we needed to get off her case. She was always quick to remind us we had no grandparents, no aunts or uncles, and there was definitely no second husband on the horizon—so the three of us had to show up for each other. That was our big refrain growing up: showing up for each other.

Three or four Saturdays a year, the hospital would summon my mother for "Surprise Mandatory Overtime" to plow through all the outstanding billing disputes that nobody could make sense of. One Friday evening Mom got the call and told us she had to go to work the next day. Then she told me I had to drive my sister to Storybook Land.

"Me? Why me?"

"Because I promised I would take her."

"Take her Sunday. You're off Sunday."

"But Beth wants to bring Chenguang, and Chenguang can only go Saturday."

Chenguang was my sister's best friend, a weirdo with pink hair who drew cat whiskers on her cheeks. She and Beth were in some kind of anime club.

"I've got a meet tomorrow! In Valley Forge. I won't be back until three."

"Skip the meet," my mother said. "You're not running. The team doesn't need you."

I tried explaining to my mother that my presence delivered a huge psychological boost to my teammates, but she wasn't buying it. "You're driving Beth and Chenguang."

"They're too big for Storybook Land! It's a kiddie park!"

"They're going ironically." My mother opened the back door, lit a cigarette, and exhaled smoke through the screen. "They *know* they're too big for it, that's why they want to go." She shrugged like this was a perfectly rational thing for people to do.

The next morning—Saturday, October 7—Chenguang arrived at our house wearing a yellow shirt with a glittery white unicorn and faded jeans. She was eating a bag of sour spaghetti gummy candy and she offered me some. I shook my head and said I would rather die. Beth came downstairs and she was wearing the same unicorn T-shirt and the same jeans. Apparently they had planned the matching outfits in advance, and it was all part of our weird freakish adventure.

I insisted on leaving the house at 9:00 A.M. My plan was to be on the highway while my teammates were running, and then call to hear the results as soon as we got to Storybook Land. But Chenguang had a spider bite that wouldn't stop itching, so we had to stop at a Walgreens to get Benadryl. This set us back a half hour and we didn't cross the Walt Whitman Bridge until nine thirty, didn't merge onto the Atlantic City Expressway until nine forty-five. There were three lanes of cars hell-bent for the Jersey shore at eighty miles an hour. I had the windows rolled down and Q102 turned up loud so I wouldn't have to hear Beth and Chenguang giggling in the backseat. They chattered nonstop, they were constantly interrupting and talking over each other. My phone was resting on the console between the front seats. I had it charging in the cigarette lighter adapter. Over the music, I could hear the chirp of an incoming text message—and then another and another. I knew it was likely my friend Lacey, who never sent one text when five would suffice. The lane ahead of me was clear. I looked down at my phone, at the incoming notifications scrolling up my screen:

HOLY SHIT

OMFG

!!!!!!!!

you wont believe who placed 3rd

The clock on the dash read 9:58. I realized that the girls' race must have ended and Lacey was dutifully sending me the results. I checked the road again, then lifted the phone with one hand, entered my password, and carefully typed my reply: **tell me.**

There were three blinking dots on the side of the screen, signaling that Lacey was typing a response. I remember Ed Sheeran on the radio singing about the castle on the hill. And I remember glancing into the rearview mirror. There was an SUV tailgating me, the guy was right up on my bumper, and without really thinking, I accelerated, to put a little distance between us. Through the mirror I saw Beth and Chenguang sharing a single strand of gummi spaghetti. They were eating it from both ends like the dogs in *Lady and the Tramp*. They were giggling like lunatics, and I remember thinking: What the hell is wrong with them? How is this normal teenage behavior? And then the phone pulsed in my palm, signaling that Lacey had replied.

And then it was Wednesday and I woke up in a hospital in Vineland, New Jersey. My left leg was broken, I had three cracked ribs, and my body was tethered to half a dozen monitors and machines. My mother was sitting beside my bed, clutching a spiralbound notebook. I tried to sit up but I couldn't move. I was so confused. She started saying things that didn't make sense. There was a bicycle on the expressway. Some family was hauling beach gear on the back of their SUV, and then a mountain bike came loose, and all the cars swerved to avoid it. I said, "Where's Beth?" and her face just collapsed. And that's when I knew.

The driver in front of me broke his collarbone. Everyone in the SUV behind me had various minor injuries. Chenguang walked away from the accident without a scratch. My sister was the only fatality, but doctors said I was a close runner-up. Everyone was quick to say that I shouldn't blame myself, that I didn't do anything wrong. Everyone blamed the family with the mountain bike. A few police officers came to see me in the hospital, but there was never any real kind of investigation. At some point during the barrel roll my cell phone went out the window. Either it was pulverized by the crash, or it vanished in the tall purple wildflowers growing on the side of the highway. I never found out who placed third.

After two weeks I left the hospital with a new prescription for Oxy-Contin to use "as needed for pain," but I felt pain around the clock, every day, from the moment I woke up until the minute I collapsed into bed. The pills blunted it a little and I'd beg the doctors to refill the prescriptions—just to get me through Halloween, through Thanksgiving, through Christmas—but by February I was walking fine and they cut me off.

The hurting was worse than anything I'd ever experienced. That's what people don't understand about OxyContin—or at least, we didn't really understand it back then. Over several months, the drug had completely rewired my brain, hijacking more and more of my pain receptors, and now I needed OxyContin simply to exist. I couldn't sleep, or eat, or focus in class. And no one warned me this was going to happen. No one told me to expect a struggle.

This is when I started leaning on my classmates—asking them to snoop in their bathrooms, in their parents' bedrooms. You would be shocked by how many people have OxyContin in their homes. And when those sources finally dried up, I had a friend with a boyfriend who knew a guy. Buying Oxy from a dealer is a pretty easy thing to rationalize. These were, after all, the very same pills my doctors had required me to take. I was buying medicine, not drugs. But the markup was outrageous, and within a month I had depleted all my savings. I spent three miserable days suffering from cold sweats and nausea before one of my new pill-seeking friends introduced me to a cheaper and more sensible alternative.

Heroin is such a big scary word but it feels like Oxy at a fraction of the price. You just have to get past any squeamishness regarding needles. Fortunately, there were plenty of YouTube videos to help me along—tutorials (ostensibly for diabetics) showing how to find a vein and how to gently draw back the plunger at just the right moment, to make sure you've made contact with the bloodstream. And once I figured that out, everything turned from bad to shit.

I finished high school, barely, thanks to sympathetic teachers who felt sorry for me. But all the coaches understood what was happening, and somehow Penn State weaseled out of their offer. They blamed the car accident and my injuries; they said no amount of physical therapy would have me ready by fall, and I don't remember being disappointed. I don't even remember getting the news. By the time they reached out to my mother, I was already spending my nights in Northern Liberties, crashing on the sofa of my new friend Isaac, who happened to be thirty-eight years old.

There was a long stretch after high school where I lived primarily to take drugs, and to obtain money to buy more drugs—any kind of drugs. If Oxy and heroin were unavailable, I'd sample anything on the menu. My mother spent a great deal of time and money trying to help me, but I was young and pretty and she was old and broke and fat; she didn't stand a chance. One day she got on the 17 bus and found herself having a heart attack; she almost died before the ambulance got her to the hospital. And I didn't even know until six months later, until I landed in rehab and tried calling my mother to tell her the good news. She just assumed I wanted money and hung up.

I called back a couple more times, but she never answered, so I left these long rambling voice mails, confessing that the accident was all my fault and apologizing for everything. By this point I was living at Safe Harbor and completely sober but of course she didn't believe me. *I* wouldn't have believed me, either. Finally one day this man answered the phone. He said his name was Tony and he was a friend of my mother's, and she didn't want to hear from me anymore. And the next time I called, the number was disconnected.

I haven't spoken to my mother in two years. I'm not really sure what happened to her. Still, I know I have many, many reasons to be thankful. I'm grateful that I never got HIV or hepatitis. I'm grateful I was never raped. I'm grateful to the Uber driver who revived me with Narcan after I passed out in the backseat of her Prius. I'm grateful to the judge who sent me to rehab instead of prison. And I'm grateful I met Russell, that he agreed to sponsor me and motivated me to start running again. I never would have come this far without his help.

Adrian doesn't interrupt my story with questions. He just lets me talk and talk until I can finally get to my main point: "I'm always going to feel guilty about what happened. Everyone blames the driver with the mountain bike. But if I had been paying attention—"

"You don't know that, Mallory. Maybe you could have swerved out of the way, or maybe not."

But I know that I'm right.

I'll always know I'm right.

If I went back in time and did everything over, I would just change lanes or cut the wheel or slam on the brakes and everything would still be okay.

"We used to share a bedroom, did I mention that already? We slept in bunkbeds and we hated it, we complained to our mother all the time. We told her we were the only kids on our block who had to share a room, and it wasn't even true! So anyway, after the accident, the day I left the hospital, my mother drove me home and I went upstairs and—" And I can't even describe the rest. I can't tell him how the room was too quiet without Beth, how I couldn't sleep without the sounds of her breathing and her rustling sheets.

"It must be hard," Adrian says.

"I miss her so much. Every day. Maybe that's why I lied to you, Adrian, I don't know. But I swear I never lied about anything else. I didn't lie about my feelings and I didn't lie about the pictures. I have no memory of drawing them. But I guess I must have. I know it's the only logical explanation. I'm leaving Spring Brook on Monday. I'm going to live with my sponsor for a couple weeks. Try to get my head screwed on right. I'm sorry for being such a psycho."

We've reached the part of the conversation where I hope Adrian will say something—maybe not "I forgive you," I know that's asking for too much, but at least some acknowledgment that I've just bared my soul, that I've shared a story I've never shared to anyone outside of an NA meeting.

Instead, he stands and says, "We should get going."

We walk across the grass toward the parking lot. There are three little boys playing next to Adrian's truck, pointing finger-guns and firing imaginary bullets. As we get closer, they all sprint across the asphalt parking lot, whooping and hollering and waving their arms like maniacs. They remind me of the boys at the Big Playground. They're all around five or six years old and they're nothing like quiet and introspective Teddy, always reaching for his picture books and sketch pads.

Adrian doesn't say anything until we're inside his truck. He starts the engine and turns on the air-conditioning but doesn't shift into drive. "Listen, when I left your house yesterday, I was pretty pissed off. Not because you lied to me—that was bad enough. But you lied to my parents and all their friends. It's really embarrassing, Mallory. I don't know how I can ever tell them."

"I know, Adrian. I'm sorry."

"But here's the thing: After I left your house yesterday, I couldn't go back home. My parents knew all about our date and I didn't want to see them, I didn't want to tell them it was a bust. So instead I went to the movies. This new Marvel thing was playing and it seemed like a good way to kill some time. I actually stayed and watched it twice, so I could get home after midnight. And when I finally went upstairs to my bedroom, this was waiting on my desk."

He reached across the front seat and opened the glove box, revealing a sheet of paper covered in dark pencil.

"Now you want to talk about feeling crazy? I guess it's possible you sneaked into my house and found my bedroom and left this drawing on my desk while my parents were home all night? I guess it's also possible that five-year-old Teddy sneaked into my house? Or his parents? But I don't think so, Mallory." Adrian shakes his head. "I think the most likely explanation is that you've been right all along. Anya *is* drawing these pictures. And she wants *me* to know you're telling the truth."

22

We drive back to Spring Brook and get right down to business. I grab all the drawings that I found in my cottage, plus the three pictures I took from Teddy's bedroom. Adrian has the one drawing left on his desk, plus all his photographs of the Maxwells' den. He's already output the images on an inkjet printer so we can add them to the sequence. There are less than forty-eight hours before Russell comes to pick me up—and before that happens, I'm determined to convince the Maxwells we're telling the truth.

We arrange all the pictures on the pool patio, using stones or pinches of loose gravel to hold them in place. Then we spend half an hour moving them around, trying to arrange them in order, looking for some kind of narrative that makes sense.

After much trial and error, we arrive at this:

"The first picture is the hot-air balloon," I begin. "We're in some kind of park or field. An area with a lot of wide-open space. Big skies."

"So definitely not Spring Brook," Adrian says. "There's too much air traffic out of Philly."

"We see a woman painting a picture of the hot-air balloon. Let's assume for now this is Anya. Judging from her sleeveless dress, I'm guessing it's summer, or maybe we're in a warmer climate."

"There's a girl nearby, playing with toys. Possibly Anya's daughter. Teddy mentioned Anya has a daughter. It doesn't seem like Anya is watching her closely."

"Then along comes a white rabbit."

"The little girl is intrigued. She's playing with a stuffed rabbit, but here comes a real one."

"So she follows the rabbit down into a valley . . ."

". . . but Anya doesn't notice the girl walking away. She's too absorbed in her work. But you can see the little girl off on the horizon. Leaving her toys behind. Does that all make sense so far?"

"I think so," Adrian says.

"Good, because here's where it gets confusing. Something goes wrong. The rabbit is gone, the girl looks lost. She might be hurt. She might even be dead. Because in the next picture . . ."

"She's approached by an angel."

"And the angel leads the little girl toward the light."

"But someone's trying to stop them. Someone's chasing after them."

"It's Anya," Adrian says. "It's the same white dress."

"Exactly. She's running to save her little girl, to stop her from being taken away."

"But Anya's too late. The angel won't give her back."

"Or *can't* give her back," Adrian says.

"Exactly. Now here comes a gap."

"The angel and the child are gone. We don't see them anymore. And now someone is strangling Anya. This is the one piece of the puzzle we're still missing."

"Time passes. It's nighttime. Anya's easel is abandoned."

"A man arrives in the forest, carrying tools. They look like a pick and a shovel."

"The man drags Anya's body through the forest . . ."

"He uses his shovel to dig a hole . . ."

"And then he buries the body."

"So the man strangled Anya," Adrian says.

"Not necessarily."

"He moves her body. He buries her."

"But the story starts in the daytime. The man doesn't show up until later, until dark."

Adrian starts moving the pictures around again—arranging them in a different sequence—but I've tried every possible order, and this is the only one that comes close to making sense.

Except something's still missing. It's like the feeling of working through a jigsaw puzzle, putting the whole scene together, only to discover the box has three or four missing pieces, and they're all right in the middle.

Adrian throws up his hands. "Why doesn't she just spell it out for us? Skip the stupid pictures and use words? 'My name is Rumpelstiltskin. I was murdered by the archduke.' Or whoever. Why is she being so cryptic?"

He's just venting, but I realize I've never stopped to ask myself this question: Why *is* Anya being so cryptic?

Instead of using Teddy to draw pictures, why not use words? Why not write a letter? Unless—

I think back to all the one-sided conversations I overheard in Teddy's bedroom—all the guessing games he would play during Quiet Time. "Teddy says Anya talks funny. He says she's hard to understand. What if she doesn't speak English?"

Adrian seems ready to dismiss the idea, but then he reaches for the library book—*The Collected Works of Anne C. Barrett*. "All right, let's think this through for a minute. We know Annie came from Europe after World War II. Maybe she doesn't speak English. Maybe Barrett isn't even her real name. Maybe it's a westernized version of something like Baryshnikov, one of those long impossible-to-pronounce Eastern European names. And the family changed it, just to blend in."

"Exactly," I tell him, warming to the theory. "George writes like he's been in the United States for a long time. He's already assimilated. He's a deacon at the church, he's an alderman on the town council. But suddenly his Bohemian cousin shows up in Spring Brook.

She's a reminder of where he's from, and he's ashamed of her. His letter in the book is so condescending, all his talk about her slight achievements and her foolishness."

Adrian snaps his fingers. "And this explains the spirit board! You said her answers were gibberish! You called them alphabet soup. But what if she was spelling in a different language?"

I think back to the gathering—to the feeling of being entombed inside the cottage, with the planchette trembling beneath my fingertips.

I *knew* we weren't alone.

I *knew* someone was moving my hand and choosing each letter very deliberately.

"Mitzi wrote everything down," I tell him.

We walk across the backyard to Mitzi's house. I rap my knuckles on the front door but there's no answer. Then we walk around to the back of the house, to the rear entrance used by her clients. The back door is open and we can see through the screen door into the kitchen, to the Formica table where Mitzi served me coffee. I bang on the screen door and the Kit-Cat Klock stares back at me, its tail wagging. I can hear the TV playing inside the house, some infomercial for commemorative gold dollars: "These coins are highly prized by collectors, and guaranteed to hold their value. . . ."

I shout Mitzi's name, but there's no way she'll hear me over the sales pitch.

Adrian tries the handle and the door is unlocked. "What do you think?"

"I think she's paranoid and she owns a gun. If we sneak up on her, there's a good chance she'll blow our heads off."

"There's also a chance she's hurt. Maybe she slipped in the shower. If an old person doesn't come to their door, you're supposed to check on them."

I knock again but still no answer.

"Let's come back later."

But Adrian insists on opening the door and calling to her: "Mitzi, are you okay?"

He steps inside, and what else can I do? It's already past three o'clock and the day is passing too quickly. If Mitzi has information that can help us, we need it as soon as possible. I hold the door open and follow him into the house.

The kitchen stinks. It smells like the trash needs to be taken out, or maybe it's all the dirty dishes piled up in the sink. There's a frying pan on the stovetop filled with congealed bacon grease. There are tiny paw prints scattered across the surface, and I don't want to think about all the vermin that might be living behind the walls.

I follow Adrian into the living room. The TV is tuned to Fox News and the hosts are arguing with a guest about the latest threats to American security. They're shouting at each other—shouting over each other—so I grab the remote and mute the volume.

"Mitzi? It's Mallory. Can you hear me?"

Still no answer.

"Maybe she went out for a bit," Adrian says.

And left the back door open? No way, not Mitzi. I move toward the back of the house and check the bathroom—nothing. At last I come to the door of Mitzi's bedroom. I knock several times, calling her name, and then finally open it.

Inside the bedroom, the shades are drawn, the bed is unmade, and there are clothes all over the floor. The air is sour and stale and I'm afraid to touch anything. The door bangs against a wicker wastebasket, knocking the basin on its side, and crumpled wads of Kleenex tumble out.

"Anything?" Adrian asks.

I get down on my knees and look under the bed just to be sure. There's more dirty laundry but no Mitzi.

"She's not here."

As I stand up, I notice the surface of Mitzi's nightstand. Along with a lamp and a telephone I see a handful of cotton balls, a bottle of rubbing alcohol, and a length of latex tourniquet.

"What is it?" Adrian asks.

"I don't know. Probably nothing. We should go."

We walk back to the living room and Adrian finds the notepad on the sofa, tucked beneath the heavy wooden spirit board.

"That's it," I tell him.

I flip past shopping lists and to-do items before arriving at the last used page—her notes from the séance. I rip the page from the pad, then show it to Adrian.

I took Spanish in high school and I had friends who took French and Mandarin, but these words don't look like any language I've ever seen. "The name Anya sounds Russian," Adrian says. "But I'm pretty sure this isn't Russian."

I take out my phone and google IGENXO just to be certain—and it might be the first time I've googled a phrase that doesn't return a single result.

"If Google doesn't know it, it's definitely not a word."

"Maybe it's some kind of cryptogram," Adrian says. "One of those puzzles where every letter is substituted by a different letter."

"We just decided she can't speak English," I tell him. "Do you really think she's making up brainteasers?"

"They're not complicated if you know all the tricks. Give me a minute." He grabs a pencil and sits down on Mitzi's sofa, determined to crack the code.

I start poking around the living room, trying to imagine why Mitzi left the house with her TV on and her back door open, when something crunches beneath my sneaker. It sounds like I've stepped on a beetle, some small insect with a hard brittle shell. I lift my foot and see that it's actually a thin plastic tube, orange and cylindrical, about three inches long.

I lift it off the floor and Adrian looks up from his work.

"What is that?"

"A cap for a hypodermic needle. I think she's been injecting herself. Hopefully with insulin, but this is Mitzi we're talking about so who knows." As I move around the room, I discover three more needle caps—on a bookshelf, in a wastebasket, on a windowsill. When you factor in the rubber tourniquet, I'm pretty sure we can rule out diabetes.

"Are you finished yet?"

I look down at Adrian's notepad and it doesn't seem like he's made any progress.

"This is a tough one," he admits. "Normally you look for the most frequent letter and you replace it with E. In this case, there are four Xs, but when I change them to Es, it doesn't help any."

I think he's wasting his time. If I'm right about Anya's language barrier—and I'm pretty sure I am—then communicating in English would be enough of a challenge. She wouldn't try writing in code. She'd want to make things easier for us, not harder. She'd try to make her message clearer.

"Give me another minute," he says.

And then there's a knock at the back door.

"Hello? Anybody home?"

It's a man's voice, unfamiliar.

Maybe one of Mitzi's customers, visiting to have his energy read?

Adrian stuffs the sheet of notepaper into his pocket. And when we enter the kitchen, I see the man at the back door is wearing a police uniform.

"I'm gonna need you to step outside."

23

The cop is young—he can't be older than twenty-five—with a buzz cut, dark sunglasses, and enormous arms covered in tattoos. There's not an inch of bare skin anywhere between his wrists and his shirtsleeves—it's all Stars and Stripes, Bald Eagles, and passages from the Constitution.

"We were checking on Mitzi," Adrian explains. "Her door was open but she's not here."

"So you what? You just walked inside? Thought you could take a look around?" He offers this theory like it's preposterous, even though it's exactly what happened. "I want you to open the door and slowly step outside, do you understand?"

I realize there are two more cops at the edge of the yard, stretching long ribbons of yellow tape from tree to tree. Farther out, deeper in the forest, I can see flashes of movement, jackets with reflective surfaces. I can hear men shouting discoveries to each other.

"What's going on?" Adrian asks.

"Hands on the wall," the cop says.

"Are you serious?"

Adrian is shocked—clearly, this is his first experience being frisked.

"Just do it," I tell him.

"This is bullshit, Mallory. You're wearing gym shorts! You're not concealing a weapon."

But just the mention of the word "weapon" seems to escalate the confrontation. Now the two cops with the yellow tape are walking toward us with concerned expressions. I just follow the instructions and do what I'm told. I press my palms against the brick wall; I lower my head and stare down at the grass while the cop pats my waist with his hands.

Adrian grudgingly stands beside me and plants his palms on the wall. "Absolute bullshit."

"Shut up," the cop tells him.

And if I wasn't afraid to speak, I would tell Adrian the cop is actually being nice—I've known cops in Philadelphia who would have you pinned, cuffed, and facedown in gravel in the time it takes to say hello. Adrian seems to think he doesn't have to listen to them, that he's somehow above the law.

Then a man and a woman come walking around the side of the house. The man is tall and white and the woman is short and black and they're both a little pudgy and out of shape. They remind me of my high school guidance counselors. They're dressed in business attire that's straight off the racks at Marshalls or TJMaxx, and they both have detective shields hanging from their necks.

"Aw, Darnowsky, come on," the man calls out. "What are you doin' to that girl?"

"She was in the house! You said the victim lived alone."

"Victim?" Adrian asks. "Is Mitzi okay?"

Instead of answering our questions, they separate us. The male detective leads Adrian across the yard while the woman encourages me to sit down at a rusty wrought-iron patio table. She unzips her fanny pack, removes a tin of Altoids, and pops one into her mouth. Then she offers me the open box, but I decline.

"I'm Detective Briggs and my partner is Detective Kohr. Our young associate with the circus tattoos is Officer Darnowsky. I apologize for his exuberance. This is our first dead body in a while, so everybody's jumpy."

"Mitzi's dead?"

"I'm afraid so. Couple kids found her an hour ago. Lying in the woods." She points to the forest. "You could see her from here, if these trees weren't in the way."

"What happened?"

"Let's start with your name. Who are you, where do you live, and how do you know Mitzi?"

I spell my name and show her my driver's license and then point across the yard to my cottage. I explain that I work for the family next door. "Ted and Caroline Maxwell. I'm their babysitter, and I live in their guest house."

"Were you sleeping in the cottage last night?"

"I sleep there every night."

"Did you hear anything unusual? Any noises?"

"No, but I went to bed early. And it was raining hard, I remember that much. With all the wind and thunder I couldn't hear anything. When do you think Mitzi—" I can't bring myself to say the word "died"; I still can't believe Mitzi is actually dead.

"We're just getting started here," Briggs says. "When was the last time you saw her?"

"Not yesterday but the day before. Thursday morning. She came to my cottage around eleven thirty."

"What for?"

It sounds embarrassing when I say it out loud, but I tell her the truth, anyway. "Mitzi was a psychic. She had a theory my cottage was haunted. So she brought over her spirit board—it's like a Ouija board? And we tried to make contact."

Briggs seems amused. "Did it work?"

"I'm not sure. We got some letters but they don't make a lot of sense."

"Did she charge you?"

"No, she offered to help for free."

"And what time did you finish?"

"One o'clock. I'm sure about that because Adrian was here, too. On his lunch break. He had to leave to get back to work. And that was the last time I saw her."

"Do you remember what she was wearing?"

"Gray pants, purple top. Long sleeves. Everything very loose and flowy. And lots of jewelry—rings, necklaces, bracelets. Mitzi always wears lots of jewelry."

"That's interesting."

"Why?"

Briggs shrugs. "She's not wearing any now. She's not even wearing shoes. Just a nightgown. Was Mitzi the sort of woman who'd go walking outside in her nightgown?"

"No, I'd actually say she's the opposite. She put a lot of effort into her appearance. It was a weird look but it's *her* look, if you know what I mean."

"Could she have had dementia?"

"No. Mitzi worried about a lot of different things, but her mind was sharp."

"So why were you inside her house just now?"

"Well, this will probably sound stupid, but I had a question about the séance. We wondered if maybe the spirit was using a different language, and that's why the letters didn't spell anything. We wanted to ask Mitzi if that was a possibility. The back door was open so I knew she had to be home. Adrian thought she might be hurt, so we went in the house to see if she was okay."

"Did you touch anything? Did you handle any of her possessions?"

"I opened her bedroom door. To see if she was sleeping. And I guess I muted her TV. She had it going so loud, we couldn't hear anything else."

Briggs looks down to my waist, and I realize she's studying my pockets. "Did you take anything from the house?"

"No, of course not."

"Then would you mind turning your pockets inside out? I believe you're telling the truth, but it's better for everyone if I check."

I'm glad that Adrian kept the notes from the séance, so I don't have to lie about them.

"Those are all my questions right now," she says. "Do you have any information that might help me?"

"I wish I did. Do you know what happened?"

She shrugs. "There's no sign of injury. I don't think anyone hurt her. And when you find the body of an old person outdoors? Dressed in their nightclothes? Usually it's some kind of medication error. They mixed up their pills or took a double dose. Did she ever mention any prescriptions?"

"No," I tell her, which is the honest answer. I'm tempted to mention the needle caps and the tourniquet and the pungent odor of burned rope that trailed Mitzi like a cloud. But surely Briggs will discover all these things on her own, after a short tour of the house.

"Well, I appreciate your time. And would you mind sending over the Maxwells? Ted and Caroline? I want to speak to all the neighbors."

I explain that they've gone to the beach for the day, but I pass along their cell phone numbers. "They didn't know Mitzi well, but I'm sure they'll help if they can."

She turns to leave—then thinks better of it and stops. "This last question is a little off-topic but I have to know: Who's the ghost you were trying to reach?"

"Her name was Annie Barrett. Supposedly she lived in my cottage. Back in the 1940s. People say—"

Briggs starts nodding. "Oh, I know all about Annie Barrett. I'm a local girl, I grew up in Corrigan, on the other side of these woods. But my daddy always said that story was a fish tale. That was his way of describing a trumped-up story, like a whopper."

"Annie Barrett was real. I have a book of her paintings. Everyone in Spring Brook knows about her."

Detective Briggs seems inclined to disagree but instead she holds her tongue. "I'm not going to spoil a good story. Especially when there's an even bigger mystery out in those woods right now." She hands me a business card. "If you think of anything else, call me."

Adrian and I spend the next hour or so sitting out by the pool, watching the circus in Mitzi's backyard and waiting for new developments. It's clearly a huge deal for Spring Brook because the backyard is teeming with cops, firefighters, EMTs, and a man whom Adrian identifies as the mayor. No one seems to be doing very much; it's just a lot of people talking and standing around. But eventually four somber-faced EMTs emerge from the forest carrying a zippered polyvinyl bag on a stretcher, and soon after that the crowd starts to thin.

Caroline calls from the shore to see how I'm doing. She says she's already heard from Detective Briggs and she is absolutely "wrecked" by the news. "I mean obviously I didn't like the woman very much. But I wouldn't wish this kind of death on anyone. Have they figured out what happened?"

"They think it might be a medication error."

"Do you want to know the strangest thing? We actually heard Mitzi yelling Thursday night. Ted and I were sitting out by the pool. We were having a bit of an argument, which I guess you already know. Then all of a sudden we heard Mitzi shouting at someone in her house. Telling them to get out, saying the person wasn't welcome. We could hear everything she was saying."

"What did you do?"

"I was all set to call the police. I had actually called 911 and the phone was ringing. But then Mitzi came outside. She was dressed in her nightgown, and her voice had totally changed. She was calling after the person, asking the person to wait for her. 'I want to come with you,' she said. And it seemed like things were fine again, so I hung up the phone and forgot about it."

"Did you see the other person?"

"No, I just assumed it was a customer."

This seems unlikely to me. I don't think Mitzi welcomed customers into her home after dark. The first time I went to see her, it was only seven o'clock at night, and she asked why I was banging on her door so late.

"Look, Mallory, do you want us to come home early? I feel bad that you're alone, that you're dealing with this by yourself."

I decide not to mention that Adrian is seated poolside with me, studying the notes we collected from Mitzi's house, still determined to decode them.

"I'm fine," I tell her.

"Are you sure?"

"Stay as long as you want. Is Teddy having fun?"

"He's sad you're leaving, but the ocean is a nice distraction." I can hear Teddy in the background, very excited, shrieking about something he's captured in his sand pail. "Hang on, sweetie, I'm talking to Mallory—"

I tell her to go have fun and not worry about me and I hang up the phone. Then I relay the whole conversation to Adrian—particularly the part about Mitzi's mysterious late-night visitor.

I can tell from his reaction that we are both circling the same conclusion, and we're too nervous to say it out loud.

"You think it was Anya?" he asks.

"Mitzi would never see a customer in her nightgown. Without her jewelry. She was way too vain about her appearance."

Adrian looks to all the cops and EMTs still milling around the woods. "So what do you think happened?"

"I have no idea. I've been telling myself that Anya is nonviolent, that she's some kind of benevolent spirit, but that's just a guess. All I really know is that she was brutally murdered. Someone dragged her body through a forest and dumped her in a ditch. Maybe she's pissed off and wants revenge against everybody who lives in Spring Brook. And Mitzi's the first person she went after."

"Okay, but why now? Mitzi's lived here seventy years. Why did Anya wait all this time to go on her rampage?"

It's a fair question. I have no idea. Adrian chews on the tip of his pencil and returns his attention to the jumble of letters, like they might have answers to all our questions. At the house next door, the circus is slowly winding down. The fire department is gone and all the neighbors have wandered away. There are just a few cops left, and the last thing they do is seal the back door with two long strips of yellow DO NOT CROSS tape. They intersect in the middle, forming a giant X, a barrier between the house and the outside world.

Then I glance down at Mitzi's notes, and the solution is suddenly obvious.

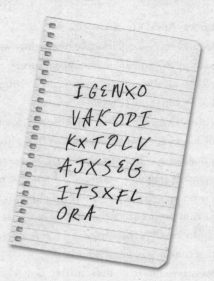

"The Xs," I tell Adrian. "They're not *X*s."

"What are you talking about?"

"Anya knew we didn't speak her language. So she put Xs between the words. Like barriers. They're spaces, not letters."

"Where?"

I take the pencil from him and recopy the letters, placing each word on its own line.

"Now *that* looks like a language," I tell him. "Something Slavic. Russian? Maybe Polish?"

Adrian opens his phone and inputs the first word into Google Translate. The results are instantaneous: *Igen* is the Hungarian word for "yes." From there, it's easy to translate the entire message: YES X BEWARE X THIEF X HELP X FLOWER.

"Help Flower?" Adrian asks. "What does that mean?"

"I don't know." I think back to the drawings that I pulled from the recycling bin—wasn't there a page of flowers in bloom? "But this definitely explains why she's using pictures. Her native language is Hungarian."

Adrian opens his phone and takes a snapshot. "You need to text this to Caroline. It's proof you're not making things up."

I wish I had his confidence. "This doesn't prove anything. It's just a bunch of letters that anyone could have written on paper. She'll accuse me of buying a Hungarian dictionary."

But Adrian is undaunted. He keeps rereading the words, like he's hoping to find some deeper secondary meaning to them. "You need to be careful, you need to beware of the thief. But who's the thief? What did he steal?"

There are so many pieces to the puzzle, my head is starting to hurt. I feel like we're trying to jam a square peg into a round hole—or to force a very easy solution on a very complicated problem. I'm trying so hard to focus and think, I'm annoyed when my cell phone starts to ring, shattering my concentration.

But then I see the name on the caller ID.

The Rest Haven Retirement Community in Akron, Ohio.

24

"Is that Mallory?"

"Yes?"

"Hi, this is Jalissa Bell at Rest Haven Akron. You called here yesterday for Mrs. Campbell?"

"Right, can I speak with her?"

"Well, it's complicated. I could put Mrs. Campbell on the phone, but you wouldn't have much of a conversation. She has late-stage dementia. I've been her caregiver three years and most mornings she won't recognize me. I really doubt she can answer your questions."

"I just need some basic information. Is there a chance you know her mother's name?"

"I'm sorry, hon, I don't. But even if I did, I wouldn't be able to tell you."

"Has she ever mentioned an inheritance? Receiving a large sum of money from an Aunt Jean?"

She laughs. "Now that's something I *definitely* couldn't tell you. There's privacy laws! I'd lose my job."

"Of course. I'm sorry."

I guess she can hear the desperation in my voice, because she offers a compromise: "We have visiting hours tomorrow, noon to four.

If you really want to talk to Mrs. Campbell, you can stop by, and I'll introduce you. Visitors are good for the patients. It keeps their brains active, gets those neurons firing. Just don't come with high expectations, okay?"

I thank her for her time and hang up. Akron is a good six hours away and I only have tonight and tomorrow to convince the Maxwells that I'm telling the truth. I explain everything to Adrian and he agrees that I shouldn't waste any time chasing down long shots.

If there's a solution to my problem, I'm going to have to find it right here in Spring Brook.

At the end of the day, we walk into town to the Bistro, a small sit-down restaurant that serves all the same food that you'd get in a good Jersey diner, but there's soft interior lighting, a full bar, and a jazz trio, so everything costs twice as much as you'd expect. And then after dinner we walk aimlessly around the neighborhood because neither of us is ready to call it a night. Adrian insists he'll come visit me in Norristown, and he says of course I'm welcome to hang out in Spring Brook as much as I want. But I know it's going to feel different without the job—I'll feel like an outsider, like I don't belong here anymore. I just wish there was some way to convince the Maxwells I was telling the truth.

Adrian takes my hand and squeezes it.

"Maybe there will be new pictures when we get back to the cottage," he says. "New clues to help us make sense of everything."

But with Teddy away at the beach all day, I think it's unlikely. "Anya can't draw on her own," I remind him. "She needs hands. She needs to work through a medium."

"Then maybe you should volunteer. Give her a chance to finish the sequence."

"How would that work?"

"We go back to your cottage, you close your eyes, and invite her to take over. It worked yesterday, didn't it?"

Just thinking about the episode in the den makes me shiver. "That's not something I'm anxious to experience again."

"I'll sit nearby and make sure you're safe."

"You want to watch me sleep?"

He laughs. "If you put it like that, it sounds creepy. I'm offering to stay and make sure you're okay."

I don't really love the idea, but it's getting late and I'm running out of options. Adrian seems convinced there's one or more pictures missing from the sequence—and with Teddy away for the whole day, someone needs to volunteer their time and hands, so Anya can finish telling her story.

"What if I fall asleep and nothing happens?"

"I could wait an hour and slip out the door. Or if you prefer I could—" He shrugs. "I could stay until morning."

"I don't want to sleep with you tonight. It's too soon."

"I know, Mallory. I just want to help. I'll crash on your floor."

"Plus I'm not allowed to have overnight guests. It's one of the House Rules."

"But you've already been fired," Adrian reminds me. "I don't think we need to play by their rules anymore."

We stop at Walgreens so Adrian can pick up a toothbrush. The store has a tiny stationery section so we also pick up a sketch pad, a box of pencils, and a thick Sharpie marker. Maybe it's not everything that Anya would prefer, but she'll have to make do.

We arrive at the cottage, and I feel obligated to give Adrian a tour, which takes all of three seconds.

"This is nice," he says.

"I know. I'm going to miss it."

"Don't give up hope yet. I think this plan has a good chance of working."

I put on some music and then we spend a good hour talking, because what we're about to attempt feels so awkward. If I'd brought Adrian home to sleep with him, I'd know exactly what to do. But instead we're getting ready to do something that feels even more intimate and personal.

By midnight I've finally built up the courage to go to bed. I go into the bathroom and change into soft gym shorts and an old Central High T-shirt. I floss and brush my teeth, I wash my face and put on moisturizer. And then I hesitate before opening the door because I feel a little silly, like I'm presenting myself in my underwear. I wish I had nicer pajamas, something prettier than a tattered high school T-shirt with little holes all around the neck.

When I exit the bathroom, I see that Adrian has already turned down the covers for me. All the lights are off except for a small lamp beside the bed. The sketch pad and pencils are on the nightstand—within easy reach if I'm seized by inspiration, or something else.

Adrian is standing in the kitchen with his back to me, reaching into the refrigerator for a can of seltzer. He doesn't notice me until I'm standing right behind him. "I think I'm ready."

He turns around and smiles. "You look ready."

"I hope this isn't too boring for you."

He shows me his phone. "I've got Call of Duty Mobile. I'll be rescuing hostages in Uzbekistan."

I stand on my tiptoes and give him a kiss. "Good night."

"Good luck," he says.

I get into bed and get under the covers, and Adrian settles into a chair at the far end of the cottage. With the ceiling fan spinning and the noisy crickets chirping outside my window, I'm barely aware of Adrian's presence. I turn on my side and face the wall. After two long and exhausting days, I realize I'm not going to have any trouble falling asleep.

As soon as I rest my face on my pillow, I feel all my stress ebbing away; I feel my muscles relaxing, my body letting go. And even with Adrian just a few feet away, it's the first night in a long time when I don't feel like I'm being watched.

I remember only one of my dreams. I'm in the Enchanted Forest, lying on a path of hard-packed earth and looking up at the black night sky. My legs are off the ground. A shadowy figure is pulling me by the ankles, dragging my body through a bed of dry leaves. My arms are raised up and over my head. I can feel my fingers grazing past rocks and roots but I'm unable to grasp them; it's like I'm paralyzed and I'm unable to stop what's happening.

And then I'm looking up from the bottom of a hole; it's like I've fallen to the bottom of a well. My body has been twisted into a pretzel. My left arm is pinned beneath my back and my legs are splayed wide open. I know it ought to hurt more than it does, but somehow I'm in my body and out of my body at the same time. High above me, there's a man looking down into the hole. Something soft and small strikes my chest. It falls away and I see that it's a toy, a child's stuffed bunny rabbit. It's followed by a stuffed bear and a small plastic ball. "I'm sorry," the man says, and his voice sounds hollow, like he's talking underwater. "I am so, so sorry."

Then my face is struck by a clod of dirt. I can hear the soft chop of a shovel spearing into a mound of earth—and then more dirt and rocks fall down upon me. I hear the man grunting; I can feel weight accumulating on my chest, the growing pressure on my body, and then I can't see anymore. It's just blackness.

Then I try to open my eyes, and I'm back in my cottage. The lights are off and the tiny clock on my nightstand says 3:03. I'm lying in bed, clutching a pencil with a broken point. Even in the darkness, I can see that my kitchen chairs are empty; I can only assume that Adrian got tired of waiting for something to happen, and he went home.

I get up to make sure the door is locked. I lift back the sheets and swing my legs out of bed, and only then do I see a bare-chested Adrian sleeping on my floor, lying parallel to my bed, using the crook of his arm and his balled-up shirt as a pillow.

I reach down and gently shake his shoulder. "Hey."

Instantly, he sits up. "What's wrong?"

"Did it work? Did I draw anything?"

"Well, yes and no." He switches on the tiny lamp, then opens the sketch pad to reveal the first page. It's nearly covered in scribbles; the surface of the paper has been obliterated with graphite. There are just two small patches of white—two places where the pencil point gouged through the paper, revealing the blank page underneath.

"It was just past one o'clock," Adrian explains. "You'd been asleep for an hour or so. I was getting ready to give up and go to bed. So I turned off the lights and lay down on the floor. And then I heard you turn over and reach for the pad. You didn't even sit up. You drew this lying down in the dark."

"It's not much of a picture."

"Maybe Anya's telling us she's finished. There are no more pictures. We already have everything we need."

But this can't be right. Something is still missing, I'm sure of it. "I dreamed I was at the bottom of a hole. A man was shoveling dirt on top of me. Maybe this picture is the dirt."

"Maybe, but how would that help us? What do we learn from a picture of dirt?"

I stand up to get the rest of the drawings. I want to spread them out on the floor and see how the all-black scribbles might fit into the sequence. Adrian pleads with me to get some sleep. "You need to rest, Mallory. Tomorrow's our last chance to figure this out. Just go to bed."

He reshapes his T-shirt into the world's saddest pillow and lies back on the hardwood floor. He closes his eyes and I stop thinking about Anya just long enough to register his upper body. He's tan and toned all over, the natural by-product of working outdoors all summer. I could probably bounce a quarter off his stomach. He's been kind and supportive and he might have the best physique I've ever seen on a man, and like a dummy I've made him sleep on the floor.

Adrian opens his eyes and realizes I'm still staring at him. "Can you turn off the light?"

I reach down, skim my fingers across his chest, and take his hand. "Okay," I tell him. "But first I want you to come up here."

2 5

I wake to the smell of butter and cinnamon. Adrian's already dressed and moving around my kitchen. He's found the granny smith apples in my pantry and he's standing over the range with a spatula, flipping some kind of pancake. I glance at the clock and it's just past seven thirty in the morning.

"Why are you awake?"

"I'm driving to Akron. To see Dolores Campbell. If I leave now, Google says I'll be there by two."

"It's a waste of time. You're going to drive four hundred miles to meet a woman who can't even recognize her own nurse."

"It's our last lead. Let me bring the drawings and the library book. I'll show them to her, see if they trigger any kind of reaction."

"They won't."

"You're probably right. I'm going to try, anyway."

He's so determined, I feel obligated to go with him—but I've already committed to spending the afternoon with Teddy. "I need to stay here. They're planning a party for me."

"I'll be fine. I just downloaded a new audiobook, *Heir to the Jedi*. That'll get me all the way to Akron and back." He carries over a mug of tea and a plate of apple-cinnamon pancakes and encourages me to sit up in bed. "Now see what you think of these. It's my father's recipe." I sit up and take a bite and yes, in fact they are remarkable—sweet and tart and buttery and delicious, even better than the churros.

"They're incredible."

He leans over and kisses me. "There's more on the stove. I'll call you from the road and let you know what I find out."

And I'm a little sad that he's leaving. I have a whole day to kill before the pool party starts at three o'clock. But I can sense there's no talking Adrian out of the trip, that he would chase every lead to the end of the earth to keep me from leaving Spring Brook.

I spend the morning packing my things. It doesn't take long. Six weeks ago, I arrived in Spring Brook with a secondhand suitcase and a handful of outfits. Now, thanks to Caroline's generosity, I have a much bigger wardrobe—but nothing to carry all my new clothes. So I fold her five-hundred-dollar dresses very carefully and place them inside a ten-gallon kitchen trash bag—what my friends at Safe Harbor liked to call a sober-living suitcase.

Then I put on my sneakers and go for one last run around the neighborhood. I try not to think about how much I'll miss Spring Brook—all the little shops and restaurants, the ornately detailed houses, the beautiful lawns and gardens. I've been to Russell's condo in Norristown, and his neighborhood isn't nearly as nice. He lives on the tenth floor of a high-rise that's next to an office park and an Amazon fulfillment center. The complex is ringed by highways, many miles of steaming asphalt and concrete. Not a pretty place by any definition, but apparently it's where I'm meant to be.

The pool party is a nice gesture, I guess. Caroline hangs some limp streamers around the back patio, and she and Teddy string up a homemade banner that says *thank you mallory*. Ted and Caroline do a nice job of pretending I haven't been fired. We all act like I'm leaving by choice, which makes the afternoon less awkward. Caroline stays in the kitchen, preparing the food, while I swim in the pool with Ted and Teddy. The three of us compete in a series of silly races that Teddy always manages to win. I wonder aloud if Caroline needs any help—if she'd like some time to swim—and then I realize I've never actually seen her in the pool.

"The water makes her itchy," Teddy explains.

"The chlorine," Ted says. "I've tried adjusting the pH balance but nothing works. Her skin is super-sensitive."

By four o'clock, I've still not heard anything from Adrian. I'm thinking about texting him, but then Caroline calls from the patio that dinner is ready. She's arranged the table with pitchers of ice water and fresh-squeezed lemonade and an abundance of healthful food—there are grilled shrimp skewers and a citrus-seafood salad and bowls of freshly steamed squash and spinach and corn on the cob. She's clearly put a lot of care and effort into everything, and I sense she feels guilty for sending me away. I start to wonder if she's reconsidering my future, if there's still a chance she'll let me stay. Teddy speaks in an animated voice about his day trip to the beach and boardwalk. He tells me all about the fun house and the bumper cars and the crab in the ocean that pinched his tiny toes. His parents chime in with their own stories, and it feels like we're all having a terrific family conversation, like everything has gone back to normal.

For dessert Caroline brings out Chocolate Lava Volcanoes—miniature sponge cakes filled with gooey warm ganache and topped with a scoop of vanilla ice cream. They are baked to perfection and when I take my first bite I literally gasp.

Everybody laughs at my reaction.

"I'm sorry," I tell them. "But this is the best thing I've ever tasted."

"Oh that's wonderful," Caroline says. "I'm glad we can end the summer on a high note."

And that's when I realize nothing has changed.

I offer to help with the dishes but Ted and Caroline insist on tackling the cleanup. They remind me that I'm the guest of honor. They encourage me to go play with Teddy. So he and I return to the pool and cycle through all our favorite games one last time. We play Castaway and Titanic and Wizard of Oz. And then for a long time we lie side by side on the raft and we float.

"How far is Norristown?" Teddy asks.

"Not far. Less than an hour."

"So you can still visit for pool parties?"

"I hope so," I tell him. "I'm not sure."

The truth? I doubt I'll ever see him again. Ted and Caroline will have no trouble finding a new nanny, and of course she will be pretty and smart and charming, and Teddy will have all kinds of fun with her. I'll be remembered as an odd footnote in their family history—the babysitter who only lasted seven weeks.

And here's the part that really stings: I know that many years in the future, when Teddy brings his college girlfriend home for Thanksgiving dinner, my name will be a punchline around the dinner table. I'll be remembered as the crazy babysitter who drew all over the walls, the one who believed Teddy's imaginary friend was real.

He and I lie back on the raft and watch the gorgeous sunset. All the clouds are tinted pink and purple; the sky looks like a painting you'd see in a museum. "We can definitely be pen pals," I promise. "You can send me pictures and I'll write you letters."

"I would like that."

He points up to an airplane soaring across the horizon, trailing long streaks of white vapor. "Do people take airplanes to Norristown?"

"No, buddy, there's no airport."

He's disappointed.

"Someday I'm going to ride on a plane," he says. "My daddy says the big ones go five hundred miles an hour."

I laugh and remind Teddy that he's already been on a plane. "When you came home from Barcelona."

He shakes his head. "We drove from Barcelona."

"No, you drove to the airport. But then you got on an airplane. No one drives from Barcelona to New Jersey."

"We did. It took us all night."

"It's a different continent. There's a giant ocean in the way."

"They built an underwater tunnel," he says. "With super-thick walls to protect you from sea monsters."

"Now you're just being silly."

"Ask my dad, Mallory! It's true!"

And then over on the pool deck, I can hear my telephone ringing. I have the volume turned all the way up, so I won't miss Adrian's call. "Be right back," I tell Teddy. I flip off the raft and swim to the side of the pool, but I'm not fast enough. By the time I reach my phone, the call has already gone to voice mail.

I see that Adrian has texted me a photograph. It's an elderly black woman, wearing a thin red cardigan and sitting in a wheelchair. Her eyes have a vacant stare but her hair is neat and trim. She looks well kept and well cared for.

Then a second photo arrives—the same woman posing next to a black man in his fifties. He has his arm around the woman and he's directing her attention toward the camera, encouraging her to look at the lens.

Adrian calls again.

"Did you get my pictures?"

"Who are these people?"

"That's Dolores Jean Campbell and her son, Curtis. Annie Barrett's daughter and grandson. I just spent two hours with them. Curtis comes every Sunday to visit his mom. And we got everything wrong."

This seems impossible.

"Annie Barrett was black?"

"No, but she's definitely not Hungarian. She was born in England."

"She's British?"

"I've got her grandson standing right next to me. I'm going to put Curtis on the line, let him tell you firsthand, okay?"

Teddy stares at me from the swimming pool, bored, anxious for me to come back and play. I mouth the words "five minutes" and he climbs aboard the raft and starts kicking with his tiny feet, propelling himself around the water.

"Hey, Mallory, it's Curtis. Are you really living in Granny Annie's cottage?"

"I—I think so?"

"Spring Brook, New Jersey. In back of Hayden's Glen, right? Your friend Adrian showed me some pictures. But you don't have to worry, my granny's not haunting you."

I'm so confused. "How do you know?"

"Here's what happened. She moved from England to Spring Brook after World War II, okay? To live with her cousin George. They were on the east side of Hayden's Glen, which back then was very white and well-to-do. Now my Pop-Pop Willie, he lived on the west side of Hayden's Glen. In a neighborhood called Corrigan. The colored section. He pumped gas at a Texaco, and after work he would walk down to the creek to catch his supper. Pop-Pop loved to fish. He ate trout and perch every day if they were biting. One day he sees this pretty white girl walking barefoot. Carrying a sketch pad. She calls out hello and Pop-Pop said he was too afraid to look at her. Because again, this is 1948, remember? If you're a black man and a white woman smiles at you? You look the other way. But Granny Annie comes from Cress-combe, in the UK. A seaside town full of Caribbean migrants. She's not afraid of black people. She says hello to Pop-Pop every afternoon. Over the next year they get friendly, and soon they're more than friendly. Soon Pop-Pop is creeping through the forest in the middle of the night, so he can visit Granny in your cottage. Do you follow what I'm saying?"

"I think so." I glance over to the pool to check on Teddy. He's still drifting in circles on the life raft, and I feel guilty for ignoring him on my last day, but I need to hear the rest. "What happened?"

"Well, so one day Annie goes to cousin George and says she's preg-nant. Only she wouldn't have used that word back then. She probably said she was 'with child.' She tells George that Willie is the father, that she's going to elope with him. They're going to move west to Ohio and live on Willie's family farm, where no one is likely to bother them. And Annie's so stubborn, George knows he can't possibly stop her."

"So what happened?"

"Well, George is furious, obviously. He tells her the child will be an abomination. He says their marriage won't count in the eyes of God. He says Annie will be dead to him, and the family will refuse to ac-knowledge her existence. And she says that's fine, she never really cared for them anyway. Then she packs her things and disappears. Which puts George in a very embarrassing situation. He's a pillar of the community. He's a deacon of the church. He can't tell people that his cousin has run off with a colored man. He'd rather die than have the truth get out. So he makes up a story. He goes to a butcher shop and buys two buckets of pig's blood. There was no forensic science back then, blood was blood. He sloshes it all over the cabin, knocks over the furniture, makes it look like someone ransacked the place. Then he called the police. The town had a manhunt and they dragged nets through the creek but they never found a body because there never was a body. Granny called it the Great Escape. She spent the next sixty years on a farm near Akron. She had my mother, Dolores, in 1949, and my uncle, Tyler, in 1950. By the time she died, she had four grandchildren and three great-grandchildren. She lived to eighty-one."

Curtis tells the story with confidence and conviction, but I still can't believe it. "And no one ever learned the truth? People in Spring Brook still think she was murdered. She's the local boogeyman. Little kids say she's haunting the forest."

"My guess is that Spring Brook hasn't changed much since the 1940s. Back then it was well-to-do, now I bet you just call it 'affluent.' Different words for the same thing. But if you drive over to Corrigan you'll find plenty of people who know the truth."

I'm reminded of my conversation with Detective Briggs. "I think I've already met one. I just didn't believe her."

"Well, I hope this puts your mind at ease," Curtis says. "My wife's waiting for me in the car, so I should put your friend back on."

I thank Curtis for his time and he passes the phone back to Adrian. "Incredible, right?"

"We were wrong about everything?"

"Annie Barrett was never murdered. She's not our ghost, Mallory. All those pictures have to be coming from someone else."

"Teddy?" I look up and see Caroline Maxwell standing at the edge of the pool, calling to her son. "It's getting late, honey. Time to rinse off."

"Five more minutes?" he asks.

I wave to Caroline, signaling that I'll take care of him. "I gotta go," I tell Adrian. "Do you want to come over when you get home? Since it's my last night?"

"If you don't mind staying up late. The GPS says I won't get back until midnight."

"I'll be waiting. Drive safe."

My mind is reeling. I feel like I've run right into a brick wall. I realize I've spent the last few weeks chasing a dead end—and now I need to rethink everything I know about Anya.

But first I need to get Teddy out of the pool.

"Come on, T-Bear. Let's get you rinsed off."

We grab our towels and walk across the yard to the outdoor shower stall. There's a tiny bench outside the stall, and Caroline has set out Teddy's fire truck pajamas and clean underwear. I reach inside the door to turn on the water, adjusting the faucets until the temperature is warm. Then Teddy goes inside and latches the door and I stand outside holding his towel. His swim trunks hit the concrete floor with a splat, and then his tiny feet kick them out to me. I twist the polyester fabric in my hands, wringing out all of the water. Then I glance across the yard to Mitzi's house. The lights in the kitchen are on, and Detective Briggs has returned to the scene of the crime. She's walking around the backyard with some kind of metal pole, poking at the dirt, taking measurements. I wave hello, and she comes over.

"Mallory Quinn," she says. "I heard you're leaving Spring Brook tomorrow."

"Things didn't work out."

"That's what Caroline said. I was a little surprised you never mentioned it, though."

"It didn't come up."

She waits for me to elaborate, but what does she expect me to say? It's not like I'm proud of being fired. I try to change the subject.

"I just got off the phone with Annie Barrett's grandson. A man named Curtis Campbell. He lives in Akron, Ohio. Claims his Granny Annie lived all the way to age eighty-one."

Briggs grins. "I told you that story was a whopper. My grandfather grew up with Willie. They used to fish together."

Teddy interrupts us, calling from inside the shower stall. "Hey, Mallory?"

"Right here, buddy."

He sounds panicked. "There's a bug on the soap."

"What kind of bug?"

"A big one. A thousand-legger."

"Splash some water on it."

"I can't, I need you to do it."

He unlatches the door and then retreats to the far corner of the stall, getting out of my way. I reach for the bar of Dove soap, expecting some kind of nasty slithering silverfish, but there's nothing.

"Where is it?"

Teddy shakes his head, and I realize the bug was just a ploy, an excuse to make me open the door. He whispers, "Are we getting arrested?"

"Who?"

"The police lady. Is she mad at us?"

I stare at Teddy, bewildered. Nothing about this conversation makes any sense. "No, buddy, everything's fine. No one's getting arrested. Just finish up, okay?"

I close the door and he latches it behind me.

Detective Briggs is still waiting.

"Everything all right?"

"He's fine."

"I mean you, Mallory. You look like you've just seen a ghost."

I sink into a chair to steady my thoughts, and I say I'm still reeling from the phone call. "I'd convinced myself that Annie Barrett was murdered. I can't believe people have been spreading this story for seventy years."

"Well, the truth doesn't reflect well on Spring Brook. If the town had been a little more tolerant, maybe Willie and Annie could have stayed here. Maybe George wouldn't have felt the need to stage a crime scene." Briggs laughs. "You know, there's still guys in my department who think the murder really happened? I tell them the truth, and they act like I'm trying to stir things up, a black woman cop handing out race cards." She shrugs. "Anyhow, I don't want to keep you long. I just had a quick question. We found Mitzi's cell phone in her kitchen. The battery had run down but we found a charger and got it working again. Seems she was in the middle of sending you a text. It doesn't make any sense to me, but maybe it'll mean something to you." She looks down at her notepad, squinting over the tops of her reading glasses. "Here's what it says: 'We need to talk. I was wrong about before. Anya isn't a name, it's'"— Briggs stops and looks to me. "That's as far as she got. Do those words mean anything to you?"

"No."

"How about *Anya*? Is that possibly a typo?"

I nod in the direction of the shower stall. "Anya is the name of Teddy's invisible friend."

"Invisible friend?"

"He's five. He has an active imagination."

"I know she's not real," he calls out. "I know she's just make-believe."

Briggs furrows her brow, puzzled by the cryptic message. Then she flips forward a few pages in her notepad.

"Yesterday I spoke with Caroline Maxwell, and she says she heard Mitzi having an argument on Thursday night. She saw Mitzi leave her house in a nightgown around ten thirty P.M. Did you happen to hear anything?"

"No, but I wasn't here. I was at Adrian's house. Three blocks away. His parents were having a party." At ten thirty Thursday night, I was sitting in the gardens of the Flower Castle, wasting my time with *The Collected Works of Anne C. Barrett*. "Does the coroner know how Mitzi died?"

Briggs lowers her voice so Teddy won't hear. "Unfortunately it appears to be drug-related. Acute lung injury stemming from an overdose. Sometime Thursday night or early Friday morning. But don't go printing that on Facebook. Keep it under your hat for a few days."

"Was it heroin?"

She's surprised. "How did you know?"

"It's just a guess. I saw some things in her house. There were needle caps all over her living room."

"Well, you guessed right," Briggs says. "You don't hear about older people using hard drugs, but the Philly hospitals see them every week. It's more common than you think. Maybe her visitor was a dealer. Maybe they got in an argument. We're still piecing it together." She offers me another business card but I tell her I still have the first one. "If you think of anything else, give me a call, okay?"

After Briggs leaves, Teddy opens the door to the shower stall, squeaky clean and dressed in his fire truck pajamas. I give him a hug and tell him I'll see him in the morning, to say my goodbyes. Then I walk him over to the patio and send him inside the house.

I manage to keep my composure until I'm back inside my cottage and I've locked my door. Then I fall forward onto my bed and bury my face in my pillow. There have been so many bombshell revelations in the last thirty minutes, I can't begin to process them all. It's too overwhelming. The pieces of the puzzle seem more scattered than ever.

But there's one thing I know for sure:

The Maxwells have been lying to me.

26

I wait until dark, until I'm sure Teddy is asleep in bed, before going into the house to speak with Ted and Caroline. They're sitting in the den, at opposite ends of the sofa, surrounded by all my crazy sketches of dark forests, lost children, and winged angels. In one corner of the room, there's a drop cloth and some painting supplies—rollers, dry-wall compound, two gallons of Benjamin Moore Atrium White. Like they're planning to paint in the morning, after Russell takes me away.

Caroline is sipping a glass of wine and there's a bottle of Kendall-Jackson merlot within reach. Ted is holding a mug of hot tea, he's carefully blowing across its surface, and they're listening to some yacht rock radio station on their Alexa speaker. They look happy to see me.

"We were hoping you'd come by," Caroline says. "Are you all packed?"

"Just about."

Ted holds out his mug, encouraging me to smell it. "I just boiled some water. For ginkgo biloba tea. Can I pour you some?"

"No, that's all right."

"I think you'd like it, Mallory. It's good for inflammation. After a long workout. Let me get you some." It's not really a choice anymore.

He darts into the kitchen and I swear I see a flicker of annoyance in Caroline's eyes.

But all she says is, "I hope you enjoyed the dinner?"

"Yes. It was really nice. Thank you."

"I'm glad we could give you a proper sendoff. And I think it was good for Teddy. To give him a sense of closure. It's important for children."

There's an awkward pause. I know the questions I need to ask, but I want to wait until Ted is back, so I can see both of their reactions. I allow my eyes to drift around the room and my gaze lands on two drawings that I'd somehow overlooked—small and fairly close to the floor. It's no wonder Adrian and I missed them. The pictures are near an electrical outlet—in fact, one drawing is composed *around* the outlet, as if the electricity was surging out of the socket and into the picture. The angel is wielding some kind of magic wand, pressing it to Anya's chest—surrounding her in a field of energy, paralyzing her.

"Is that a Vipertek stun gun?"

Caroline smiles over her glass of wine. "I'm sorry?"

"In these drawings. I didn't notice them on Friday. Doesn't her wand look just like your Viper?"

Caroline reaches for the wine bottle and tops off her glass. "If we try to interpret all the symbols in these pictures, it's going to be a long night."

But I know these pictures aren't symbols. They're part of the sequence, they're the missing pieces. Adrian was right about the cryptic black scribbles. *Anya's telling us she's finished*, he'd said. *There are no more drawings. We already have everything we need.*

Ted is back in less than a minute with a steaming mug of gray liquid. It looks like dirty mop water and smells like a pet store. I reach for a coaster and set it down on the coffee table. "It doesn't need to steep," Ted says. "You can drink whenever it's cool enough."

Then he sits next to his wife and fidgets with his laptop, changing Marvin Gaye to Joni Mitchell, that song about rows and flows of angel hair, and ice cream castles in the air.

"I learned something interesting about Mitzi," I tell them. "She was sending me a text right before she died. She wanted me to know that Anya isn't a name. It's something else. Detective Briggs couldn't make sense of it."

"Well, it's definitely a name," Ted says. "It's the Russian diminutive of Anna. It's popular all over Eastern Europe."

"Right, well, I tried putting it into Google Translate. And apparently it's a word in Hungarian. It means 'mommy.' Not mother, but mommy. Like a child would say. Isn't that weird?"

"I don't know," Caroline says. "Is it?"

"The tea's better warm," Ted says. "It thins the mucus in your sinuses."

"You know what else is weird? Teddy says he's never been on an airplane. Even though three months ago, you all flew here from Barce-

lona. And according to American Airlines, that's an eight-hour flight.
I checked. How does a little boy forget about the biggest airplane trip
of his life?"

Caroline starts to answer but Ted quickly talks over her. "That's
actually a funny story. Teddy was nervous about the trip so I decided
to give him a Benadryl. They say it helps kids fall asleep. I just didn't
realize that Caroline had *already* given him a Benadryl. So he got a
double dose. He was out cold for the whole day. Didn't wake up until
we were in our rental car."

"Seriously, Ted? That's your explanation?"

"It's the truth."

"A double dose of Benadryl?"

"What are you implying, Mallory?"

He forces a smile and his eyes are pleading with me to stop asking
questions.

But I can't stop now.

I still have to ask the big one.

The question that will explain everything.

"Why didn't you tell me Teddy is a girl?"

I watch Caroline's reaction very carefully—and if she reveals anything, it's a kind of self-righteous indignation. "Well, for starters
we find the phrasing of your question offensive. Do you understand
why?"

"I saw him in the shower. After swimming. Did you think I'd never
find out?"

"You almost didn't," Ted says sadly.

"It's not a secret," Caroline says. "We're certainly not ashamed of
his identity. We just didn't know if you could handle it. Obviously,
Teddy was born a girl. And for three years we raised him as a girl. But
then he made it clear he identified as a boy. So yes, Mallory, we let him
express his gender with his clothes and hairstyle. And of course we let
him choose a more masculine name. He wanted his daddy's name."

"There is so much interesting research on transgender children," Ted says, and his eyes are still pleading with me to please please *please* shut the fuck up. "I have some books in my office, if you're interested."

And the crazy thing is: I think they honestly expect me to pretend this is all normal. "You're telling me your five-year-old is transgender and somehow *it just never came up?*"

"We knew you'd react this way," Caroline says. "We knew you had strong religious convictions—"

"I don't have any problem with transgender people—"

"Then why are you making such a fuss?"

I've stopped listening to her. My mind is already galloping ahead. Because I'm realizing how all Teddy's quirks and strange behaviors suddenly make sense. His avoidance of the little boys on the playground. His bouts of screaming whenever Ted dragged him to the barbershop. His obsession with wearing the same striped purple T-shirt. It's a very light purple, almost lavender, the most feminine color in his wardrobe.

And all those annoying questions from the school about kindergarten registration . . .

"You don't have vaccination records," I realize. "Maybe you have a birth certificate. I'm sure there's a way to buy a forgery, if you have enough money. But schools in Spring Brook are very serious about vaccines. They want those forms sent directly from a doctor. And you can't get them. That's why the school keeps calling."

Ted shakes his head. "That's not true. We had an excellent pediatrician in Barcelona—"

"Stop saying Barcelona, Ted. You never went to Barcelona. Your Spanish is terrible. You can't even say potato! I don't know where you've been hiding these past three years, but it wasn't Barcelona."

If I weren't so flustered, I might have noticed that Caroline has suddenly become very quiet. She has stopped speaking and now she is just watching and listening.

"You stole someone's little girl. You dressed her as a boy. You raised her into believing she's a boy. And you're getting away with it, because she's five. Because her world is so small. But what happens when she goes to school? When she makes friends? When she's older, when her hormones kick in? How do two people with college diplomas really imagine this could work? You'd have to be—"

And I let the sentence trail off, because the word I want to use is "crazy."

I realize I need to stop talking, I am sharing my conclusions with the wrong people. Did I really expect the Maxwells to agree with me? To come clean and admit everything they've done wrong? I need to leave right now, I need to go find Detective Briggs, and I need to tell her everything.

"I should pack," I tell them, stupidly.

And I stand up, like they're just going to let me walk out of there.

"Ted," Caroline says in a calm voice.

I'm halfway to the door when glass shatters against the side of my head. I fall forward, dropping my phone. Wetness runs down my face and neck. I reach up to stop the bleeding and my hand comes away red. I'm covered in Kendall-Jackson merlot.

Behind me, I can hear the Maxwells bickering.

"It's in the kitchen."

"I checked the kitchen."

"The big drawer. Where I keep the stamps!"

On his way out of the den, Ted steps gingerly over my body, taking great pains not to step on me, even though he's just smashed a bottle over my skull. He walks right past my smartphone, facedown on the carpet. There's an emergency button on my home screen—a single-touch app that will ping the Maxwells' address to an emergency call center. But I'm not close enough to reach it, and I'm too hurt to stand up. The most I can do is plant the toes of my sneakers and push off, inching across the floor on my belly.

"She's crawling," Caroline says. "Or trying to."

"One second," Ted calls back.

I reach for my phone and realize my depth perception is way off. It's no longer inches away from me—suddenly it's halfway down the hall, a distance the length of a football field. I can hear Caroline walking up behind me, I hear her shoes crunching shards of broken glass. I don't recognize her anymore. She is no longer the kind caring mother who welcomed me into her home and encouraged me to believe in myself. She has turned into—something else. Her eyes are cold and calculating. She regards me like I'm a stain on the floor, a blemish that needs to be rubbed out.

"Caroline, please," I tell her, but the words don't come out right; my speech is all slurry. I raise my voice and try again but my lips won't form the proper shapes. I sound like a toy that's running out of battery.

"Shhhh," she says, holding a finger to her lips. "We don't want to wake Teddy."

I roll onto my side and I feel jagged shards of glass pressing into my hip. Caroline is trying to step around me without getting too close, but I'm sprawled across the corridor, blocking her way. I bend my right knee and thank God it moves the way it's supposed to. I draw my right thigh all the way up to my body. And when Caroline finally musters the nerve to step over me, I kick out my leg, connecting the flat of my heel with the front of her shin. There's a loud crack and she comes down hard, collapsing on top of me.

And I know I can take her. I know I am stronger than her and Ted combined. I have spent the last twenty months preparing for this moment. I have been running and swimming and eating right. I've been doing fifty push-ups every other day while Ted and Caroline sit and drink wine and do nothing. So I will not just sit back and give up. Caroline's forearm lands close to my face and I clamp my teeth on it, biting hard. She cries out in surprise, wrests back her arm, and scrambles for my phone. I grab the back of her dress and pull and the soft cotton rips like paper, exposing her neck and shoulders. And in that moment I finally glimpse her much-maligned tattoo from college, the one from her artsy phase, when she was obsessed with John Milton and *Paradise Lost*.

It's a pair of large feathered wings, right between her shoulder blades.

Angel wings.

Ted hurries back from the kitchen. He's got the Viper in his hand and he's shouting at Caroline to get out of his way. I bring back my leg again—I know it's my only hope—if I knock him down, maybe he'll drop the Viper, maybe I can—

27

I blink several times and wake in darkness.

Through the shadows, I can recognize familiar shapes: my bed, my nightstand, a motionless ceiling fan, the thick wood rafters over my head.

I'm inside the cottage.

I'm sitting upright in a hard-backed chair and my sinuses are burning. It feels like they've been rinsed with chlorine.

I try to stand, only to discover that I don't have use of my arms; my wrists are crossed behind my back, twisted at painful angles and bound fast to my chair.

I move my lips to call for help but there's some kind of strap pulled tightly around my head. My mouth has been stuffed with cloth, a wet ball the size of an apple. The pressure on my jaw is excruciating.

My muscles tense and my heartbeat races as I realize all the things I can't do: I can't move, I can't talk, I can't scream, I can't even wipe the hair from my face. Take away fight or flight and there's nothing left but panic. I'm so scared, I nearly throw up—and it's a good thing I don't because I'd probably choke to death.

I close my eyes and say a quick prayer. *Please God help me. Help me figure out what to do.* Then I take a deep sustained breath through my nose, filling my lungs to maximum capacity before letting it out. This is a relaxation exercise I picked up in rehab, and it helps to keep anxiety at bay. It slows my pulse and steadies my nerves.

I repeat the exercise three times.

And then I force myself to think.

I still have options. My legs aren't restrained. There's a chance I can stand up—but if I do, the chair will be bound to my back, like a turtle shell. Walking will be slow and awkward but maybe not completely out of the question.

I can turn my head left and right. I can see just far enough into the kitchen to read the glowing LED clock on the microwave oven: 11:07. Adrian is due back around midnight. He's promised to come see me. But what happens if he knocks on the door of my cottage and no one answers? Is there a chance he'd try to get inside?

No, I don't think so.

Not unless I can signal to him.

I can't reach my pockets but I'm pretty sure they're empty. No cell phone. No keys. No stun gun. But there's a drawerful of knives in my kitchen. If I could somehow reach a knife and cut through the restraints, I would be out of the chair and armed with a weapon.

I plant my feet on the floor and lean forward, trying to stand up, but my center of balance holds me back. I realize my only hope is to throw myself forward with enough momentum to rise up. I'm just afraid that I'll spill forward and topple onto the floor.

I'm still working up the nerve to try when I hear footsteps outside the cottage, climbing the worn wooden stairs. Then the door swings inward, and Caroline switches on the light.

She's dressed in the same scoop neck dress from before but now she's also wearing blue latex gloves. She's carrying one of her pretty supermarket tote bags—the kind you bring to the grocery store, to prevent plastic waste from cluttering up the oceans. She seems surprised to find me awake. She sets the tote bag on my kitchen counter and begins to empty its contents: a BBQ grill wand lighter, a metal teaspoon, a tiny syringe and needle with a plastic orange cap.

All the while I'm pleading with her but I can't form words, only sounds. She's trying to ignore me and focus on her work, but I can tell I'm irritating her. Eventually she reaches behind my head and the strap goes slack; I cough up the wet rag and it rolls down my lap, landing on the floor with a splat.

"No yelling," she says. "Use your inside voice."

"Why are you doing this to me?"

"I tried to give you a nice send-off, Mallory. I made my seafood salad. I hung up streamers. Ted and I even put together a severance package. A month's pay. We were going to surprise you with a check tomorrow morning." She shakes her head sadly, then reaches into the tote for a small polybag filled with white powder.

"What is that?"

"This is the heroin you stole from Mitzi's house. You took it yesterday afternoon, after you snooped around her bedroom."

"That's not true—"

"Of course it is, Mallory. You have a lot of unresolved grief. You've been masquerading as a college student, a track star, and it's generating all this anxiety. And then the pressure of losing your job—losing your paycheck *and* losing your place to live—all those stresses caused you to relapse."

I realize she doesn't actually believe this—she's just rehearsing a story. She continues: "You were desperate for a fix, and you knew Mitzi was using, so you sneaked into her house and you found her stash. Only, you didn't realize her heroin was cut with fentanyl. Two thousand micrograms, enough to bring down a horse. Your opioid receptors flooded and you stopped breathing."

"This is what you'll tell the police?"

"This is what they'll infer. Based on your history. And the autopsy. Tomorrow morning I'll knock on your door to see if you need help packing. When you don't answer, I'll use my key to come inside. I'll find you lying in bed with a needle sticking out of your arm. I'll scream and call for Ted. He'll pound your chest and try to give you CPR. We'll call 911 but the medics will say you've been dead for hours. They'll say there's nothing we could have done. And because we're such good people, we'll make sure you have a proper burial and headstone. Next to your sister. Otherwise Russell would get stuck with the bill, and that doesn't seem fair."

Caroline unseals the polybag and holds it over the spoon, carefully filling it with white powder. She leans over the counter, concentrating on her work, and again I see the tattoo that's just below her neck.

"You're the angel in the drawings. You hit Anya with your Viper and then you strangled her."

"It was self-defense."

"You don't strangle someone in self-defense. You murdered her. You stole her little girl. How old was she? Two? Two and a half?"

The spoon fumbles out of Caroline's fingers and lands on the counter with a clatter. The powder spills everywhere and she shakes her head, irritated.

"Don't pretend like you understand the situation. You have no idea what I've been through."

She reaches for a plastic spatula and slowly drags it across the counter, gathering all the powder into a tiny little mound.

"I know you had Ted's help," I said. "I know he's the man in the pictures. You killed Anya and took her daughter. And then you sent Ted to bury her body. When did this happen, Caroline? Where were you living?"

She shakes her head and laughs. "I know the game you're trying to play. We use it in therapy all the time. You can't talk your way out of this."

"You and Ted were having problems. He said you spent years trying to conceive. Was this the last resort? Stealing a child?"

"I *rescued* that child."

"What does that mean?"

"It doesn't matter. What's done is done and we need to move on. I'm sorry you won't be part of our family anymore."

Caroline carefully pushes the powder back into the spoon and then reaches for the BBQ lighter. She clicks the button several times before it produces a small blue flame, and I see that her hands are trembling.

"Does Teddy remember anything?"

"What do you think, Mallory? Does he seem traumatized? Does he seem sad or unhappy? No, he does not. He remembers nothing. He is a happy, well-adjusted child and I worked very hard to get him to this place. He'll never know how much I've sacrificed for him. And that's fine."

As Caroline speaks, the powder in the spoon smokes and blackens and finally liquefies. East Coast heroin doesn't have much of an odor but I'm struck by a whiff of something chemical—maybe it's the fentanyl, maybe it's some other lethal additive. I remember hearing about a drug dealer in Camden who supposedly cut his product with Ajax cleanser. Caroline sets down the lighter and picks up the syringe. She dips the needle into the bowl of the spoon and then slowly draws back the plunger, filling the syringe with sickly brown sludge.

"He remembers the rabbit," I tell her.

"Excuse me?"

"In Anya's pictures, she shows a little girl chasing after a rabbit. The girl follows a white rabbit down into a valley. Now think back to my job interview, Caroline. The very first day I came here, you had one of Teddy's drawings on your refrigerator. A picture of a white rabbit. Maybe he remembers more than you realize."

"Her pictures are lies. You can't trust them."

"I had a hard time making sense of them. But I think I finally put them in the right order. They're in the folder, on my nightstand. They show exactly what happened."

Caroline reaches in her bag for a length of rubber tourniquet. She stretches it between her hands, like she's ready to tie it around my arm. But then curiosity gets the better of her. She walks over to my nightstand, opens the folder, and starts sifting through the papers. "No, no, see, these drawings are so unfair! This is *her* version of what happened. But if you'd seen my side of things? The big picture? You'd understand better."

"What's the big picture?"

"I'm not saying I don't feel guilty. I *do* feel guilty. I feel remorse. I'm not proud of what happened. But she didn't leave me with a choice."

"Show me what you mean."

"I'm sorry?"

"In the drawer of the nightstand, there's a pad and pencil. Draw what happened. Show me your version of the story."

Because I need all the time I can get.

Time for Adrian to drive home and get here and knock on the door and figure out something is very, very wrong.

And Caroline looks like she wants to do it! She seems eager to tell me her side of the story. But she's smart enough to recognize that she's being manipulated. "You're trying to make me incriminate myself. You want me to draw out a confession, with pictures, so the police will find it and arrest me. Is that the idea?"

"No, Caroline, I'm just trying to understand what happened. Why did Teddy need to be rescued?"

She reaches for the tourniquet and moves behind my chair, but she can't manage to tie it around my arm. Her hands are shaking too much. "Sometimes she gets in my head and it feels like a panic attack. It'll go away in a minute or two." She sits on the edge of my bed and covers her face with her hands. She takes deep breaths, filling her lungs with air. "I don't expect you to have any sympathy but this has been really hard for me. It's like a nightmare that doesn't end."

Her breathing is ragged. She grabs her knees and squeezes hard, as if she can will herself into a state of calm. "Ted and I used to live in Manhattan. Riverside Heights, Upper West Side. I was working for Mount Sinai, thirty-five years old and already burned out. My patients had so many problems. There's just so much pain in the world, so much misery. And Ted, he had some boring IT job that he hated.

"I guess we were two very unhappy people trying to get pregnant, and we were failing, and the failure made us even more unhappy. We tried all the usual tricks: IVI, IVF, Clomid cycles. Do you know about these things?" Caroline shakes her head. "It doesn't matter. Nothing worked. We were both working crazy hours but we didn't even need the money, because my father had left me a fortune. So finally we were like, screw it: Let's leave our jobs and take a one-year sabbatical. We bought a place in upstate New York on Seneca Lake. The theory being that maybe—in a more relaxed state of mind—we would conceive.

"The only problem is, we get up there and we don't have any friends. We don't know a soul. It's just me and Ted alone in this cabin all summer long. Now Ted, he gets really into wine-making. He takes classes with a local vintner. But me, I'm so bored, Mallory. I don't know what to do with myself. I try writing, photography, gardening, breadmaking, none of it sticks. And I have this horrible realization that I am just not a very creative person. Isn't that an awful thing to discover about yourself?"

I try to look sympathetic and encourage her to continue. The way she talks, you'd think we were mother and daughter chatting over coffee and scones at Panera Bread. Not me in a chair with my arms looped behind my back, and Caroline fidgeting with a loaded syringe, anxiously twisting the barrel between her fingers.

"The only thing that gives me any joy is walking. There's a park on Seneca Lake with nice shaded trails, and that's where I first met Margit. That's Anya's real name: Margit Baroth. I'd see her sitting in the shade of a tree, painting landscapes. She was very talented and I guess

I was a little envious. And she always brought her daughter. She had a two-year-old, a little girl named Flora. Margit would just plop her on a blanket and ignore her. For two or three hours at a time. She'd stick a smartphone in the kid's hands and then completely neglect her. And not just once or twice, Mallory. I saw them every weekend! This was their routine! It made me angry every time I walked past them. I mean—here's this perfect child, this beautiful little girl, starved for attention, and the mother's plying her with YouTube videos! Like she's a burden! I've read a lot of research on screen time, Mallory. It's toxic for a child's imagination.

"So after a couple times I decided to intervene. I walked over to the blanket and tried to introduce myself, but Margit had no idea what I was saying. I realized she couldn't speak English. So I tried to panto-mime what I meant—I tried to *show* her she was being an awful mother. And I guess she took that the wrong way. She got angry, I got angry, and pretty soon we were both screaming, me in English and she in Hungarian, until some people finally came over. They had to literally stand between us.

"After that, I tried going to different parks and trails. But I couldn't stop thinking about that little girl. I felt like I failed her, like I had one chance to intervene and I blew it. So one day, maybe two months af-ter the argument, I went back to the lake. It was a Saturday morning, and there was an incredible hot-air balloon festival. They do it every September, thousands of people show up, and the sky is filled with all these big bright colorful shapes. The perfect thing for a child's imag-ination, you know? And Margit is painting one of the balloons but little Flora is just staring at a phone. She's down on the blanket getting sunburn all over her arms and shoulders.

"And as I stood there, getting madder and madder, I notice some-thing. I see this rabbit wriggling out of the ground. It must have been burrowed nearby. It popped out of the grass and shook itself off and Flora saw it. She called, '*Anya, anya!*' and she pointed to the rabbit, laughing, but Margit didn't turn around. She was too caught up in her artwork. She didn't realize that her little girl had stood up and walked away, that Flora was crossing a field and heading down into a valley. Toward a creek, Mallory. So I had to do something, right? I couldn't ignore what was happening. I followed Flora into the valley, and by the time I reached her, she was completely lost. She was bawling, hysterical. I knelt beside her and I told her everything was fine. I said I knew how to find her mommy, and I offered to bring her back. And I really *meant* to, Mallory. I really meant to bring Flora back."

I almost lose the thread of the story because I am remembering the spirit board and its cryptic message and realizing I put too much faith in Google Translate. The message wasn't HELP FLOWER—it was HELP FLORA, help her daughter.

"I just wanted to spend a little time with her," Caroline continues. "Take a short walk and give her some attention. I figured her mother wouldn't mind. She wouldn't even know the girl was missing. There was a little trail nearby, heading into a forest, so that's where we went. Into the woods. Only Margit *did* notice Flora missing. She was looking all over for her. And somehow she found us. She followed us into the woods. And once she recognized me, she was furious. She started screaming and waving her arms like she was ready to hit me. And I always walk with my Viper, I carry it for personal safety, so I used it to defend myself. I only hit her once, just to make her back off. But I guess she had some kind of neurological disorder because she went down and couldn't get up. She started having a seizure. She wet her dress, her muscles were shaking. Poor Flora was terrified. And I knew I should call 911 but I also knew how bad this was going to look. I knew if Margit told her version of things, people would misunderstand.

"So I took Flora and I led her behind a tree. I told her to sit down and close her eyes. So she wouldn't see what happened next. And I don't actually remember the rest, if you want to know the truth. But that's the beauty of the human mind. It blocks out all the bad stuff. You know what I'm talking about, right?"

She waits for me to answer—and when I don't, she keeps talking: "Anyway. I covered her body with leaves. I brought Flora home in my car. I told Ted what had happened and he wanted to call the police, but I convinced him we could make everything right. We were upstate in the middle of nowhere. The woman was an immigrant, she couldn't speak English, I figured she was probably someone's cleaning lady. I figured if we hid her body and kept the child, no one would notice her missing. Or people would just think that she'd run off with her daughter. Women do it all the time. So I sent Ted out to the park. He gathered the easel and the blanket and all of Flora's toys, and he buried everything in the woods. With the body, I mean. He was gone all night. It took him forever. He didn't get back until the sun was up.

"Now it should have ended right there—except Margit's brother is actually a really big deal on Seneca Lake. He owns this stupid goat farm that all the summer people love, and he's sponsored Margit and her husband, József, to move from Hungary to the United States and work for him. And worse, it never occurs to me that Margit must have driven to the lake in a vehicle—a Chevy Tahoe with a child safety seat, it turns out. The police found it in a parking lot and brought out their K9 unit. Within two hours, they'd found her body.

"Suddenly the whole community is looking for a missing two-year-old—the girl I've got screaming and crying in my cabin. So I run out to the Target, I buy her a bunch of boy clothes. Sports jerseys. Shirts with football players. Then I get some clippers and give Flora a buzz cut. And I swear it was like flipping a switch—all I did was change her hair, but you'd swear she was a boy."

There's nothing ragged about Caroline's breathing anymore, and her hands have stopped shaking. The more she talks, the better she looks, as if she's freeing her conscience of some horrible burden.

"Then we got in our car and drove. There wasn't any plan. We just needed to get away, the farther the better. We didn't stop driving until West Virginia, a town called Gilbert. Population four hundred, everybody's retired in wheelchairs. I emailed our friends and said we'd moved to Barcelona, that Ted had an opportunity he couldn't pass up. Then we rented a house on ten acres of land, no neighbors, just a nice quiet place where we could focus on our baby.

"And Mallory, I swear to you, it was the hardest year of my life. For six months, Teddy refused to speak. He was so scared! But I was patient. I worked with him every day. I showed him love and attention and affection. I filled our house with books and toys and healthy foods, and we made progress. He started coming out of his shell. He learned to accept us and trust us and now he loves us, Mallory. The first time he called me Mommy, I started bawling.

"By the end of our first year, we'd made some really amazing progress. We started bringing Teddy out in public. Just little hikes or trips to the grocery store. Normal family outings. And it was picture-perfect. If you hadn't met us, you'd have no idea what we'd been through." And then her voice trails off. As if she's nostalgic for a time when she still had hope.

"What happened?"

"I just never imagined Margit would find us. I've always been an atheist. I've never believed in any kind of spirit world. But after our first year in West Virginia, Teddy started having a visitor. A woman in a white dress. Waiting in his bedroom during naptime."

"You saw her?"

"No, never. She only shows herself to Teddy. But I could feel her, I could sense her presence, I could smell her disgusting rotting stench. We told Teddy she was an imaginary friend. We said she wasn't real, but it was okay to pretend she was real. He was so young, he didn't know any better."

"Did she ever come after you? For revenge?"

"Oh, she'd love to. She'd kill me if she could. But her powers are really limited. I guess she can work a Ouija board and move a pencil but that's about it."

I try to imagine the tedium of being stuck in a lonely house on ten acres of land in the middle of rural West Virginia—with no companions except my husband, a kidnapped child, and a vengeful spirit. I'm not sure how long I would last without losing my mind.

"I knew we couldn't stay in 'Barcelona' forever. We all needed to get on with our lives. I wanted to live in a nice pretty town with good schools, so Teddy could have a normal childhood. So we moved here in April, and by Mother's Day Anya was back in Teddy's bedroom, singing Hungarian lullabies."

"She followed you?"

"Yes. I don't know how. I just know running from her isn't an option. Wherever we go, Anya will follow. So that's when I had my big breakthrough: Bring in a third party. A new playmate to compete with Anya for Teddy's attention. You were the perfect candidate, Mallory. Young, athletic, full of energy. Smart but not too smart. And your history of drug abuse was a big plus. I knew you were insecure. I knew that if you saw some crazy things, you would doubt your own judgment. At least for a little while. I just never counted on those stupid drawings. I never imagined she would find a way to communicate."

Caroline seems exhausted, as if she's just relived the last three years of her life. I steal another look at the clock, and it's only 11:37. I need to keep her talking. "What about Mitzi? What happened to her?"

"The same thing that's happening to you. Last Thursday, a couple hours after your séance, Mitzi came knocking on our door in a panic. She said her spirit board wouldn't turn off. She claimed the planchette was spinning in circles and spelling out the same word over and over: *ovakodik, ovakodik, ovakodik*. Mitzi brought us back to her house and she showed us. She figured out that it meant 'beware.' She said you were right all along, Mallory: Our house was haunted and we needed help. Ted and I went home and argued about the best thing to do, but I finally convinced him to hold Mitzi down while I gave her the overdose. Then he dragged her body out to the woods and I sprinkled all those needle caps around her living room. Left the tourniquet on her end table. Just enough for the police to connect the dots. Then we made up the story about Mitzi having a late-night visitor, so the story wouldn't be too neat."

I check the clock again—only another minute has passed—and this time, Caroline catches me.

"What are you doing? Why are you looking at the time?"

"No reason."

"You're lying. But it doesn't matter." She stands and reaches for the tourniquet. Her hands are steady. She's moving with renewed confidence and control, looping the tourniquet around my arm and knotting it tight. Within moments, my muscles are tingling.

"Please don't do this."

"I'm sorry, Mallory. I wish things worked out differently."

I feel her soft gloved fingers tapping on the crook of my arm, coaxing my veins to swell up and cooperate. I realize she's serious, she intends to go through with this. "You'll feel guilty for the rest of your life," I tell her, and I'm so scared I'm sputtering. "You'll hate yourself. You won't be able to live with yourself."

I don't know why I think I can frighten her into changing her mind. My warning just seems to make her angry. There's a painful pinch as the needle breaks my skin and punctures the vein. "Look at the bright side," she tells me. "Maybe you'll see your sister again."

And then she drops the plunger, injecting me with two thousand micrograms of heroin and fentanyl, enough to bring down a horse. My whole body seizes up as I feel the familiar first chill—like someone's placed an ice cube at the injection site. The last thing I see is Caroline hurrying out the door and turning out the lights. She won't even stay to watch me die. I close my eyes and plead with God to forgive me, please

please forgive me. I feel like I'm falling back in my chair, like my chair and my body have collapsed through the floor and now I'm weightless, suspended in space. Intravenous heroin is lightning-quick and I don't know how I'm still conscious. How am I still breathing? But then I open my eyes and see Margit waiting in the shadows, and I realize I've already OD'd.

28

She's hovering in a kind of mist, a woman in white with long black hair parted in the middle. Her dress is speckled with little bits of leaves and dirt. Her face is obscured by the darkness and her head is tilted at an angle, like she can't hold it up straight. But I'm not frightened anymore. If anything, I'm relieved.

I try to stand up and go to her, but I'm still seated in the chair. My wrists are still bound behind my back.

And then I have a terrifying thought:

Is this my afterlife?

Is this my punishment for the time I've spent on earth? An eternity alone in an empty cottage, bound to a hard-backed wooden chair?

"I don't know what I'm supposed to do," I whisper. "Can you please help me?"

Margit moves closer without actually walking. I'm aware of her scent, that noxious mix of sulphur and ammonia, but it doesn't bother me anymore. I'm so grateful for her presence, the smell is almost comforting. As Margit passes the window, the moonlight illuminates her face and body. And I see that beyond all the scratches and black bruises and broken neck, and all the snags and rips in her dress, she is a shockingly beautiful woman.

"You have to help me, Margit. You're the only one who can help me. Please."

She struggles to raise her head—as if she's trying to listen more carefully—but it just flops back down, like a flower with a broken stem. She rests a hand on my shoulder, but I don't feel any touch or external pressure. Instead, I'm struck with an overwhelming sense of sorrow and guilt. In my mind I see a place I've never actually visited—a field beside a lake, a canvas on an easel, a child on a blanket. I realize I know this place from pictures—from a drawing that Margit left on my porch, and from a stack of Teddy's artwork that Caroline keeps in the den. I can summon both pictures from memory, the same scene from two different artists.

And as I look upon the woman and child, I can feel Margit's grief as plainly as my own: *I should have been paying more attention. I shouldn't have been so distracted. If I had just been a little more careful, everything would still be okay.* Or maybe it's *my* grief, because I also hear Margit saying, *you're not to blame*, *make peace with the past*, *forgive yourself*. I'm not sure if I'm consoling her or she's consoling me, I can't tell where my guilt ends and hers begins. Maybe it's the kind of grief we will never ever shake, not even after we're dead.

Then the door opens and Ted turns on the lights.

He sees my tears streaming and his face falls. "Oh, Jesus," he says. "I'm so sorry, Mallory. Just sit tight."

I look around for Margit but she's vanished.

I am still in my cottage.

I am not in some hazy ethereal afterlife, I am still in Spring Brook, New Jersey, bound to a wooden chair with my feet on the floor, and the clock on the microwave oven says 11:52.

I can still feel an icy chill on the crook of my arm, where Caroline injected the needle—but I am very much alive and not the least bit high.

"She drugged me. Your wife—"

"Baby powder," Ted says. "I switched the heroin with baby powder. You're fine." He moves behind me, tugging at the cloth straps binding my wrists to the chair. "Gosh, she really went overboard with these knots. I need a knife." He goes into the kitchen and starts rummaging through the cutlery drawer.

"What are you doing?"

"Protecting you, Mallory. I've always protected you. Don't you remember your job interview? All those rude and nasty questions about your qualifications? I was trying to scare you away. I tried scaring all the candidates away. But you were persistent. You really wanted to be here. And Caroline thought you were the solution to all our problems."

He carries a serrated blade to my chair and quickly saws through the restraints. My arms fall to my side and I'm free to move them again. Slowly, carefully, I press my fingers to the throbbing lump on my head, and I feel little bits of glass clinging to my scalp.

"I'm sorry I hit you. We'll stop at a gas station and get you some ice." Ted opens the door to my closet and he's delighted to see all the empty clothes hangers. "You're already packed! That's perfect. My bag's in the car, so we're ready to go. I figure we'll drive all night. Find a hotel to catch our breath. Then we'll keep pushing west. I found a gorgeous house on Airbnb. Just to get us settled. You'll love it, Mallory, there's gorgeous views of Puget Sound."

"Ted, slow down. What are you talking about?"

He laughs. "Right, right, I've been planning so long, I forgot we haven't fully discussed it. But I know how you feel about me, Mallory. I feel the same way, and I'm ready to act on those feelings."

"You are?"

"I've cashed in my IRAs, I've got eighty grand in a bank account that Caroline can't touch. That's plenty for us to start over. Build a new life in Washington state. Whidbey Island. But we need to leave right now. Before she comes back to clean up."

"Why are you so afraid of her?"

"She's out of her mind! Don't you realize that by now? She just tried to kill you. She won't hesitate to kill me. And if I tell the police, I'll go to jail. So we have to run. Right now. If we leave the kid, she won't follow us."

"You want to leave Teddy?"

"I'm sorry, Mallory. I know you love him. I love him, too. He's really sweet. But he can't come. I don't need Caroline and Margit chasing us across the country. The kid stays here with his two mommies. They can fight each other, battle each other to the death, I don't care. I can't take this shit anymore. I don't want to be here another minute. This whole nightmare ends tonight, do you understand?"

Outside the cottage, we hear the tiny snap of a twig—and Ted moves to the window, peering outside. Then he shakes his head, assuring me it's a false alarm. "Now, please, I need you to try standing up. Would you like some help?" He offers me his hand, but I wave him away and manage to stand on my own. "There you go, Mallory. That's great. Now do you need to use the bathroom? Because most places won't be open after midnight."

I *do* need to use the bathroom—but only as a quiet place to steady my thoughts. "I'll just be a minute."

"Fast as you can, okay?"

I close the bathroom door, turn on the sink, and splash some cold water on my face. What the hell am I going to do? I pat down my pockets but of course they're empty. I poke through the medicine cabinet and search the shower stall but there's nothing I can use to defend myself. The closest thing to a weapon is a pair of tweezers.

The bathroom has a tiny screened window, just a few inches high, positioned near the ceiling for ventilation. I close the toilet seat and stand on top of it. The window faces south, toward Hayden's Glen, looking toward the shadowy brambles of the forest. I manage to pop out the screen and push it out the window, letting it drop to the floor of the forest. But even if I mustered the strength to pull myself up, there's no way I can fit through.

Ted taps on the door. "Mallory? Almost ready?"

"Almost!"

I have to go with him. I don't have any choice. I'll get in his Prius, I'll smile as he describes Washington state and Whidbey Island, I'll try to sound excited about our new life together.

But the first time we pull over for gas or food or water, I will find a police officer and I will scream like hell.

I turn off the water. Dry my hands on a towel.

Then I open the door.

Ted is standing there, waiting. "Ready?"

"I think so."

"You *think* so?"

His eyes move past me. He looks into the bathroom—and I wonder what he's seeing. Did I leave footprints on top of the toilet seat? Has he noticed the window screen is gone?

I throw my arms around him and rest my head on his chest and I squeeze him as hard as I can. "Thank you, Ted. Thank you for rescuing me. You don't know how much I've wanted this."

He's startled by this outburst of affection. He pulls me even closer, then leans down to kiss my forehead. "I promise you, Mallory, I will never let you down. I will work every day to make you happy."

"Then let's get out of here."

I go to lift my suitcase and my trash bag full of clothes, but Ted insists on carrying them, one in each hand. "You're sure this is everything you need?"

"Ted, that's everything I own."

Again he smiles at me with real love and affection, and he looks like he's about to say something very sweet when there's a loud *POP* and a bullet rips through his left shoulder, knocking him off-balance and spattering my wall with blood. I scream and there are three more *POPs*, and I'm still screaming as Ted slumps onto the suitcase, hands over his chest, blood seeping out between his fingers.

Caroline stands in the open window of the cottage, pointing Mitzi's gun at me. She's telling me to shut up but the words don't register until the fourth or fifth time. She opens the door and with a little flick of the pistol's barrel, she gestures for me to sit back in the chair.

"Were you serious?" she asks. "Were you really going to leave with him?"

I don't even hear the questions. I'm still staring at Ted, down on the floor and struggling to speak, as if he's acquired a stammer. His lips tremble like he's trying to pronounce a difficult word and he's drooling blood, it's running red over his chin and shirt.

"See, I *think* you were lying," Caroline continues. "I think you would probably say anything to get out of here right now. But I can assure you that Ted was completely serious. He's had his eye on you since you first got here." She points across the cottage to the white smoke detector mounted on the kitchen wall. "Did you ever wonder why that fire alarm never went off? Even if you were burning dinner?"

I don't answer and she raps the butt of the pistol on the kitchen counter, three loud bangs. "Mallory, I asked you a question. Did you notice your smoke alarm doesn't work?"

What the hell does she want me to say? She's pointing a gun in my face and I'm too terrified to answer; I'm worried my first incorrect word will cause her to pull the trigger. I have to look down at the floor to muster the courage to speak. "Ted said the cottage had old wiring. He said it was something called knob and tube."

"It's a webcam, dummy. Ted installed it right after your interview. Plus a signal booster so it would reach our Wi-Fi network. He said he wanted to check on you, make sure you weren't using drugs. A 'precautionary measure,' right? But give me a break. I'm not stupid. Some nights he'd stay awake in his office for hours, just praying you would take a shower. I always wondered if you knew, if you felt like you were being watched."

"I thought it was Anya."

"No, mommy stays with her baby at night. It was always Mr. Family Man here. Mr. Father of the Year."

Ted shakes his head, like he wants to contradict her, like he's desperate for me to know the truth. But when he opens his mouth, all that comes out is more blood, running over his chin and chest.

I turn to Caroline and she's still pointing the gun at me.

I want to sink to the floor, cower and beg for mercy.

"Please," I say, raising my hands. "I won't tell anyone."

"I know you won't. You killed Ted, using the gun you stole from Mitzi's house. Then we struggled, but I managed to grab away the pistol. You took a knife from the kitchen drawer so I had to shoot you. It was self-defense." She glances around the cottage, as if she's trying to work out the precise choreography of the sequence. "You know, I'm going to have you stand closer to the refrigerator. Next to the cutlery drawer." She points the gun at me. "Come on, don't make me ask again."

She come closer—the gun comes closer—and I back away from her, moving into the kitchen.

"All right, that's better. Now reach down and open the drawer. Pull it all the way out. There you go." She moves to the opposite side of the kitchen counter, then leans over so she can study the knife block. "I guess you should use the chef's blade. It's the big one, all the way on the end. Reach down and grab the handle. Get a real nice grip on it."

I'm so scared I can scarcely move.

"Caroline, please—"

She shakes her head. "Come on, Mallory. You're almost done. Reach down and grab the knife."

And in my peripheral vision, just over her shoulder, I can still see blood dripping down the wall. But Ted is no longer sitting there. He's vanished.

I reach down. Put my hand on the knife. Wrap my fingers around the grip. It's so hard to do something when you've been told it's the last thing you're ever going to do.

"That's it," she says. "Now hold it up."

Then she screams and falls—Ted has lunged for her legs—and I know this is my moment. Stupidly, I let go of the knife, because I don't want to waste even a second pulling it from the drawer.

I just run.

I throw open the door and behind me there's an explosion—a gunshot, reverberating off the walls of the cabin. I leap off the porch and hit the grass sprinting. For three terrifying seconds I am completely vulnerable, a silhouette moving across the wide-open lawn, and I brace myself for the next explosion.

But it doesn't happen. I dart through the shadows on the side of the big house, past the trash cans and recycling bins. I run across the front lawn and stop at the end of the two-car driveway. All the neighboring houses are dark. Everyone on the block is fast asleep. Nobody walks on Edgewood Street after midnight. And I don't dare knock on a neighbor's door—I have no idea how long it will take someone to come downstairs. Right now my biggest asset is speed—increasing the distance between me and Caroline. If I sprint I can be at the Flower Castle in three minutes, I can bang on the door and scream for Adrian's parents to help me.

But then I glance back at the Maxwells' house and realize Teddy is still sound asleep on the second floor. Oblivious to all the mayhem in his backyard.

What will happen when Caroline realizes I've escaped?

Will she take Teddy, throw him in the car, and flee to West Virginia? Or California? Or Mexico?

How far will she go to protect her secret?

Back at the cottage, there's another gunshot. I want to hope for the best. I want to believe that Ted has somehow wrested the weapon away from his wife. Maybe in his dying moments, he has given me and Teddy a chance to escape.

But if he didn't—well, I still have time to make things right. I'm a fast runner. I used to be the sixth-fastest girl in Pennsylvania. I dart around the side of the house to the backyard and thank you Jesus the sliding glass door to the kitchen is unlocked.

I enter the house and lock the door behind me. The first floor is dark. I hurry through the dining room and take the rear stairwell to the second floor. I crash into Teddy's bedroom but don't turn on the light. I just pull off his blankets and shake him awake. "Get up, Teddy, we have to go." He pushes me away, burying his face in his pillow, but I don't have time to baby him. I pull him off the bed and he grunts in protest, still half-asleep.

"Mallory!"

Caroline is already inside the house, calling to me from the foyer. I hear her climbing the wooden steps. I run the other way, taking the rear stairs back to the kitchen. Teddy can't weigh more than forty pounds but I nearly drop him anyway; I hoist him over my shoulder, steadying my grip, and run outside to the back patio.

Outside, the yard is perfectly still. All I hear is the gentle lap of water in the swimming pool, the occasional trill of a cicada, and my own labored breathing. But I know Caroline is coming. She's either moving through the inside of the house, or advancing around one of the sides. My safest route is forward, toward the Enchanted Forest. It's a long sprint across the yard but I don't think Caroline will shoot at me, not as long as I'm carrying Teddy. And once we make it to the trees, we can make our escape.

Teddy and I have spent the whole summer exploring these woods. We know all the trails and shortcuts and dead ends and there is just enough moonlight to guide our way. I tighten my grip on his body and then throw myself into the brambles, shoving through branches and vines and sticker bushes until we're on the familiar terrain of Yellow Brick Road. The trail runs east-west, moving parallel along all the backyards on Edgewood. We follow it to the large gray Dragon's Egg boulder, and then I veer off onto Dragon Path. I hear footsteps thrashing behind me, but in the darkness I've lost all sense of scale and perspective. I can't tell if Caroline's breathing down my neck or a hundred yards away. I also hear the faint cry of police sirens, all too late. If I had just run to the Flower Castle, I would be safe by now.

But I have Teddy squeezed tight in my arms, and that's what really matters. I will not let anything happen to him.

The Royal River sounds louder in the dark and I'm grateful for its noise, concealing my footsteps. But then we arrive at Mossy Bridge and I don't think I can do it. The log is too narrow and covered with moss and I can't carry Teddy across.

"T-bear, listen to me. I need you to walk."

He shakes his head no and squeezes me tighter. He doesn't know what's happening but he's terrified. I try to set him down but his arms are locked around my neck. There are more and more police sirens wailing in the distance; they must have reached the Maxwells' by now. Most likely a neighbor heard the gunshots and called the police. But they're too far away to help me.

A narrow shaft of white light cuts through the forest. The flashlight beam on Caroline's Viper. I don't know if she's spotted me but I have to keep moving. I tighten my grip around Teddy and take one step onto the bridge, then another. I can see enough to discern the shape of the log, but not its entire surface. I can't tell which parts are rotten or speckled with slippery moss. Below us, the water is rushing swiftly, two or three feet deep. With every step forward I'm certain I'm going to slip off the sides, but somehow I keep my footing. I scramble up the trail to the base of the Giant Beanstalk before my arms give out. I can't carry Teddy another inch. "Buddy, I need you to do this part yourself." I point up to our hideout in the boughs of the tree. "Come on, you need to climb."

He's too petrified to move. Using the last of my strength, I push him onto the tree, and fortunately he grabs a branch to steady himself. Then I push up on his bottom and slowly, haltingly, he starts to move.

The flashlight beam sweeps across the base of the tree—Caroline's at the river, she's getting close. I grab the lowest limb and pull myself up, following Teddy from bough to bough, all the way up to a branch we call Cloud Deck. I wish we could climb even higher but there's no time and I don't dare risk the noise. "This is good," I whisper. I put my arms around his waist, holding him close, and lower my mouth to his ear. "Now we just need to stay very quiet, okay? Are you all right?"

He doesn't say anything. His body is trembling; it's coiled like a spring. He seems to understand that no, we are not all right, something is very very wrong. I stare down at the ground and wish we'd climbed even higher. We're only eight or ten feet above the trail and if Caroline stays on the path she will walk directly underneath us. If Teddy makes so much as a whimper—

I reach into the hollow, fumbling through our arsenal of rocks and tennis balls until I find the broken arrow, the short, splintered shaft with the pyramid blade tip. I know it's a useless weapon but it's comforting to have something—anything—in my grip.

And now I see her coming. Caroline is over the mossy bridge and she's advancing toward us, sweeping the flashlight over the path. I whisper to Teddy that we need to be very quiet. I tell him he's going to see his mommy but he has to promise not to say anything. And fortunately he does not ask any questions because she scrambles up the trail and stops right below our tree. There are voices in the distance, men's voices, shouting. A dog, barking. Caroline looks back in their direction. She seems to understand she's running out of time. I'm so scared, I am holding my breath. And my grip on Teddy is so tight, he can't help but make a little cry of protest.

Caroline looks up. She points her flashlight into the tree and it's so bright I have to shield my eyes. "Oh, Teddy, thank goodness! There you are! Mommy's been looking all over! What are you doing up there?"

I see she's still holding the pistol in her opposite hand, carrying it casually, like it's an iPhone or a water bottle.

"Stay here," I tell Teddy.

"No, Teddy, please, it's not safe up there," Caroline says. "Mallory is wrong. You need to come down and we'll get you back to the house. You should be in bed right now!"

"Don't move," I tell him. "You're okay right here."

But I can feel him moving toward her, instinctively, drawn to the sound of her voice. I tighten my grip around his waist and I'm shocked by the warmth coming off his body. He's burning like he has a fever.

"Teddy, listen to me," Caroline says. "You have to move away from Mallory. She's very sick. She's had what's called a psychotic break.

That's why she drew all over the walls. She stole this gun from Mitzi and she used it to hurt your daddy and now she's trying to keep you all for herself. The police are at our house and they're looking for us right now. So let's get down from there. Let's go tell them what happened. Leave Mallory in the tree and let's go straighten this out."

But there's no way Caroline is leaving me in the tree. She's already told me too much. She's told me the name of Teddy's real mother. Her name was Margit Baroth and she was murdered near Seneca Lake. If the police do even a cursory investigation of my story, they'll realize I'm telling the truth. Caroline has no choice but to kill me. As soon as she gets Teddy down from the tree. And then she'll try to spin the whole thing as self-defense. And I'll never know if she gets away with it, because I'll be dead.

"Come on, sweetie. We need to go. Say bye-bye and come down."

He shakes off my grip and shimmies across the limb.

"Teddy, no!"

And when he looks back, I can see the whites of his eyes. His pupils have rolled back into his head. His right hand reaches out, snatching the arrow from my grip, and then he leaps from the tree. Caroline raises her arms, like she thinks she can actually catch him. Instead she collapses beneath his weight, tumbling backward. The gun and flashlight fly from her hands, disappearing into the bushes. With a sickening thump she lands on her back, holding Teddy close to her chest, protecting him from the fall.

"Are you okay? Teddy, sweetie, are you okay?"

He sits up so his body is straddling Caroline's waist. She's still asking if he's okay when he spears the arrow through the side of her neck. I don't think she realizes she's been stabbed until he pulls it out and stabs her again, three more times, *chop-chop-chop*. By the time she starts screaming she's already lost her voice; all that comes out is a wet gurgling yelp.

I cry out "No!" but Teddy doesn't stop—or rather, Margit doesn't stop. She can't control most of her son's body, just his right hand and his right arm—but surprise has given her the advantage, and Caroline is choking and gagging on her own blood. The dogs bark louder, drawn by the sounds of struggle. The men in the forest are getting closer. They say they're coming to help us, they yell for us to make more noise. I scramble down from the tree and rip Teddy off Caroline's body. His skin is hot to the touch, like a boiling pot on a stove. Caroline lies thrashing on her back, clutching the remains of her neck, and Teddy is soaked with gore. It's in his hair, all over his face, and dripping from his pajamas. And somehow I have the clarity to think clearly, to understand what has happened. I know that Margit just saved my life. And if I don't act very quickly, Teddy will spend the rest of his in an institution.

He's still clutching the arrow in his right hand. I lift him off the ground and pull him close, squeezing hard, so the blood spreads from his clothes onto mine. And then I carry him down the trail to the banks of the Royal River. I step into the water and my foot sinks into the mossy, squelchy mud. I take another step and another, wading deeper and deeper until the water is waist-high and the shock of the cold jolts Teddy awake. His pupils snap back into place; his body goes limp in my arms. He drops the arrow, but I manage to catch it before it hits the water and sinks out of sight.

"Mallory? Where are we?"

Teddy is terrified. Imagine waking from a trance and finding yourself in a dark forest, up to your neck in a cold creek.

"It's okay, T-Bear." I splash water onto his cheeks, scrubbing off the worst of the blood. "We're going to be okay. Everything's going to be fine."

"Are we dreaming?"

"No, buddy, I'm sorry. This is real."

He points to the bank of the river. "Why is there a dog?"

It's a big dog, a black retriever, sniffing furiously and barking like mad. Some men come running out of the woods, dressed in reflective gear and waving flashlights.

"Found 'em!" a man shouts. "Woman and child, down by the creek!"

"Miss, are you hurt? Are you bleeding?"

"Is the child okay?"

"You're safe now, miss."

"Let us help you."

"Come on, buddy, reach out your hand."

But Teddy wraps his arms tighter around my waist, attaching himself to my hip. There are more police officers and more dogs approaching from the far side of the river, closing in on us from all directions.

And then a woman's voice, calling from farther away: "I got another one! Adult female, PNB, multiple knife wounds!"

They've got us surrounded now, a ring of flashlights advancing from every direction. It's not clear who's in charge because everybody's talking at once: It's okay, you're all right, it's safe now, but they see all the blood on our clothes and I can tell they're freaking out. Teddy's freaking out, too. I whisper in his ear: "It's okay, T-Bear. They're here to help us." Then I carry him to the riverbank and gently lower him to the ground.

"She's holding something."

"Miss, what's in your hand?"

"Can you show us please?"

One of the cops grabs Teddy's arm and yanks him to safety, and they all start shouting again. Everyone wants me to step slowly out of the water and lower the arrow to the ground and by the way am I carrying any other weapons? But I've stopped listening because I've noticed another figure in the distance, standing outside the ring of police officers. The moonlight glints off her white dress, and her head lolls crookedly to one side. I raise my left hand, showing everyone the broken arrow.

"It was me," I tell them. "I did it."

Then I hold out my arm and let the arrow drop to the ground. And the next time I look up, Margit is gone.

ONE YEAR LATER

It's been hard to get this story down on paper, and I'm sure it's been even harder for you to read it. Many times I was ready to quit writing, but your father pleaded with me to keep going, while the details were still fresh in my memory. He was convinced that someday in the future, ten or twenty years from now, you'd want to know the truth about what really happened that summer in Spring Brook. And he wanted you to hear the story from me, not some stupid true crime podcast.

Because God knows there have been plenty of podcasts. There have been breaking news stories and clickbait headlines and late-night talk show jokes and memes galore. In the weeks following your rescue, I was approached by *Dateline*, *Good Morning America*, Vox, TMZ, *Frontline*, and dozens of others. I have no idea how all these producers got my cell phone number but they all promised the same thing: To let me tell my side of the story, to defend my actions in my own words, with minimal interference. They also promised big bucks if I would agree to an exclusive interview.

But after a long discussion with your father, we both decided to stay out of the media. We released a joint public statement saying that you were reunited with your family and you needed time to heal, and now we just wanted to be left alone. Then we changed our phone numbers and our email addresses and we hoped people would forget about us. It took a few weeks, but it happened. Eventually, there were bigger stories. A nutcase in San Antonio shot up a grocery store. Sanitation workers in Philly went on strike for eight weeks. A woman in Canada gave birth to octuplets. And the world moved on.

My first few attempts at telling this story went nowhere. I can remember sitting down with a blank pad and totally freezing up. Up until now, the longest thing I'd ever written was a five-page high school term paper on *Romeo and Juliet*. So the idea of writing a book—a real full-length book, like a Harry Potter—it seemed so *epic*. But I mentioned the challenges to Adrian's mother and she gave me some good advice. She said I shouldn't try to write a book, I should just sit down at my laptop and *tell the story*, one sentence at a time, using the same language I'd use to tell a friend over coffee. She said it was okay not to sound like J. K. Rowling. It was fine if I sounded like Mallory Quinn from Philadelphia. And once I got on board with that idea, the words started flowing pretty fast. I can't believe I'm staring at a file with 85,000 of them.

But look at me, getting ahead of myself!

I should probably back up and explain a few things.

Ted Maxwell died from his gunshot injuries on the floor of my cottage. His wife, Caroline, died just a half hour later at the base of the Giant Beanstalk. I confessed to stabbing her in self-defense using the broken arrow (technically, a bolt designed for crossbows) that we'd found in the forest a few weeks earlier. And she might have actually survived, except the tip of the arrowhead ruptured her carotid artery, and by the time the EMTs arrived it was too late.

You and I were brought to the Spring Brook police station. You went into a lunchroom with a bleary-eyed social worker and a basket of stuffed animals, while I went into a windowless cell with a video camera, microphones, and a series of increasingly hostile detectives. To keep you safe, I only told a partial version of my story. I didn't mention any of your mother's drawings. I didn't describe how she supplied me with clues to help me understand what happened. In fact, I never mentioned your mother at all. I pretended that I discovered the Maxwells' secrets all on my own.

Detective Briggs and her partners were skeptical. They could tell I was holding something back, but I held fast to my version of events. As their voices grew louder, as their questions became more and more antagonistic, I kept giving them the same improbable answers. For a few hours, I was pretty convinced I would be charged with a double homicide, that I would be spending the rest of my life in prison.

But by the time the sun came up, it was clear my story contained at least several kernels of truth:

A social worker confirmed that Teddy Maxwell did, in fact, have the anatomy of a five-year-old girl.

A child named Flora Baroth was registered with the National Center for Missing and Exploited Children, and Teddy Maxwell matched all her identifying physical characteristics.

An internet search of property records confirmed that the Maxwells purchased a cabin on Seneca Lake just six months before Flora's disappearance.

A quick flip through Ted's and Caroline's passports (recovered from a dresser in their master bedroom) confirmed they had never been to Spain.

And when reached by telephone, your father, József, confirmed several key details in my story—including the make and model of his wife's Chevy Tahoe, information that was never released to the public.

By seven thirty the next morning, Detective Briggs was going next door to Starbucks to bring me some herbal tea and an egg-and-cheese sandwich. She also invited Adrian to join us in the interrogation room. He had spent the whole night waiting in the lobby on an uncomfortable metal bench. He hugged me so hard, he lifted me off the floor. And after we both stopped crying, I had to tell him the whole story all over again.

"I'm sorry I didn't get there sooner," he said.

It turned out that Adrian was the person who called 911—after arriving at my cottage and finding Ted Maxwell dead on my floor.

"I never should have gone to Ohio," he continued. "If I'd stayed with you in Spring Brook, none of this would have happened."

"Or maybe we'd both be dead. You can't obsess over what-if scenarios, Adrian. You can't blame yourself."

The drive from Seneca Lake to Spring Brook takes about five hours, but that morning your father made the trip in three and a half. I can only imagine what was going through his mind as he barreled down the interstate. Adrian and I were still at the police station, plying ourselves with sugary snacks to stay awake, when your father arrived. I can still remember the precise moment when Detective Briggs led him into the room. He was tall and thin with shaggy hair, an unkempt beard, and deep sunken watery eyes. At first I thought he might be a criminal from a neighboring cell. But he was dressed like a farmer, with work boots and Dickies pants and a button-down flannel shirt. And he knelt down and took my hand and started to cry.

I could write an entire book about everything that happened next, but I'll try to keep things brief. You and your father went back to Seneca Lake, and Adrian moved back to New Brunswick to finish his last year at Rutgers. He invited me to come with him, to live rent-free in his apartment while I figured out the next stage of my life. But my whole world had turned upside down, and I was afraid of making big commitments in a moment of weakness. So I moved to my sponsor's guest bedroom in Norristown.

You might not think of a sixty-eight-year-old man as the ideal roommate, but Russell was quiet and clean and he kept our pantries stocked with countless varieties of protein powder. I took a job at a running shoe store, just to get some money rolling in. The other employees had a little informal running club and I started going out with them, two or three mornings a week. I found a good church with plenty of twenty- and thirty-something parishioners. I started attending NA meetings again, sharing my stories and experiences with the goal of helping others.

I wanted to visit you in October, for your sixth birthday, but your doctors advised against it. They said you were still too fragile and vulnerable, that you were still "assembling" your true identity. We were allowed to speak on the phone, but only if you initiated the conversation, and you never showed any interest in speaking to me.

Still, your father called once or twice a month to update me on your progress, and we exchanged a lot of emails. I learned that you and your father were sharing a big farmhouse with your aunt and uncle and cousins, and instead of starting kindergarten, you participated in a slew of therapy programs: art therapy, talk therapy, music therapy, puppets and role-playing, the works. Your doctors were astonished by the fact that you had no memory of being roused from bed, dragged into the woods, and pushed up into a tree. They concluded that your brain had repressed these memories as a response to the trauma.

Your father was the only person who knew what really happened in the forest that night. I told him the whole story, and of course it sounds crazy, but once I sent copies of your mother's drawings, in her inimitable style, he had no doubt I was telling the truth.

Your doctors gave you a very abridged version of the facts. You learned that you were born a girl named Flora and your real parents were József and Margit. You learned that Ted and Caroline were very sick people who made a lot of mistakes, and their biggest mistake was taking you away from your parents. Their second-biggest mistake was dressing you in boy clothes and changing your name from Flora to Teddy. Going forward, the doctors explained, you could choose to be called Flora or Teddy or Some Brand-New Name, and you could choose to dress as a boy or a girl or a little bit of both. No one pressured you to make any quick decisions. You were encouraged to take your time and do whatever felt right. The doctors warned that you would likely spend years grappling with your gender identity, but the doctors were wrong. Within eight weeks you were borrowing your cousin's dresses and braiding your hair and answering to "Flora," so there really wasn't much confusion. Deep down inside, I think you always knew you were a girl.

A few days before Halloween, I answered the phone and was shocked to hear my mother's voice. She said my name and immediately burst into tears. Apparently she'd been following our story on the news and she'd spent weeks trying to reach me—but with all my efforts to avoid the media, I'd made myself impossible to find. She said she was proud of me for getting sober, and she missed me and would I please consider coming home for dinner? I kept my composure just long enough to ask "When?" and she said, "What are you doing right now?"

My mother had finally quit smoking and she looked great, and I was surprised to learn that she'd remarried. Her new husband, Tony—the man I'd glimpsed on the ladder, clearing leaves from the gutters—was a gem. They had met in a support group after Tony lost his son to methamphetamines. He had a good job managing a Sherwin-Williams store and he channeled all his excess energy into home improvement projects. He'd painted every room in the house and repointed all the bricks out front. The bathroom was completely renovated, with a new shower and tub, and my old bedroom had been converted into a fitness room with an exercise bike and a treadmill. The biggest surprise was learning that my mother had started running! All through high school, Beth and I could never drag her off the couch, but now she was pacing nine-minute miles. Now she had Lycra shorts and a Fitbit and everything.

My mother and I sat in the kitchen and talked all afternoon and late into the night. I was prepared to tell her the whole story of the Maxwells, but she already knew most of the details. She had a giant folder stuffed with printouts of stories she'd read on the Internet. She'd clipped every article from the *Inquirer* and pasted them into a scrapbook. She said she'd become a minor-league celebrity, that all my old neighbors were so proud of me. She'd kept a list of all the people who'd called the house hoping to reconnect with me—friends from high school, old teammates and coaches, my housemates at Safe Harbor. Mom had dutifully recorded all their names and numbers. "You should call these people, Mallory. Let them know how you're doing. Oh! And I nearly forgot the strangest one!" She crossed the kitchen to her refrigerator and lifted a magnet to retrieve a business card: Dr. Susan Lowenthal at the University of Pennsylvania Perelman School of Medicine. "This woman actually knocked on my door! She says she met you in some kind of research project? And she's spent years trying to track you down. What the heck is she talking about?"

I told her I wasn't really sure and then I put the card in my wallet and changed the subject. I still haven't mustered the nerve to call the phone number. I'm not sure I want to hear what Dr. Lowenthal has to tell me. I definitely don't want any more public attention or celebrity.

Right now, I just want life to be normal.

By late July—a full year since we left Spring Brook—I was getting ready to move into a sober-living dormitory at Drexel University. I was thirty months clean and feeling great about my recovery. After a year of deliberating next steps, I'd settled on going to college and studying to become a teacher. I wanted to work in elementary education, preferably in a kindergarten classroom. I reached out to your father for the hundredth time and asked if a summer visit might be possible. And this time, miraculously, your doctors said okay. They felt you were adapting well to your new life and agreed it could be healthy for us to reconnect.

Adrian suggested we turn the visit into a vacation—our first big trip together. We'd kept in touch all through the year as he finished his classes at Rutgers. He graduated in May and got a job at Comcast, in one of the big skyscrapers in Center City Philadelphia. Adrian proposed that we visit you in upstate New York, then continue north to Niagara Falls and Toronto. He packed a big cooler full of snacks and made a playlist of driving songs and I brought a bag of gifts to share with you.

You lived west of Seneca Lake in a town called Deer Run and your new neighborhood was nothing like Spring Brook. There were no Starbucks or strip malls or big-box stores—just long stretches of forests and farmland, with houses few and far between. The last mile of our trip was down a winding gravel road that led to the gates of Baroth Farms. Your father and uncle raised goats and chickens, and your aunt sold milk, eggs, and cheese to wealthy tourists on the Finger Lakes. Your new home was a sprawling two-story log home with a green shingled roof. Goats were grazing in a nearby pen, and I could hear chickens clucking in the barn. The whole place felt oddly familiar to me, even though I was certain I'd never been anywhere like it.

"Are you ready?" Adrian asked.

I was too nervous to answer. I just grabbed my bag of gifts, walked up the steps to your front door, and rang the bell. I took a deep breath, bracing myself for the shock of seeing you as a little girl. I was afraid of having a weird reaction, something that might embarrass you or me or both of us.

But your father answered. He stepped outside onto the porch and welcomed me with a hug. He'd put on some weight, thank goodness.

Maybe fifteen or twenty pounds. He was dressed in crisp denim jeans, a soft flannel shirt, and black boots. He started to shake Adrian's hand—but then he hugged him, too.

"Come in, come in," he said, laughing. "It's good you are here."

Inside, the house was all warm woods and rustic furniture, with big windows overlooking bright green pastures. Your father led us into the Great Room, a sort of living-room-kitchen-dining-room with a massive stone fireplace and stairs winding up to the second floor. There were playing cards and jigsaw puzzle pieces scattered all over the furniture. Your father apologized for the clutter; he said your aunt and uncle had been called away on a business emergency, and they'd left him with all the children. I could hear everyone playing upstairs, shrieking and laughing, five young voices talking at the same time. Your father seemed exasperated, but I assured him it was fine. I said it was great to know that you had friends.

"I will call Flora soon," he said. "First, let's just relax." He brought out coffee for Adrian and a mug of herbal tea for me. He also set out a platter of tiny pastries stuffed with apricot. "These are kolache," he said. "Please, take."

His English had improved tremendously over the past year. He still had an unmistakable accent—"these" sounded like "deese" and "we'll" came out "vill"—but for someone who'd only been in the country for a few years, I thought he was doing remarkably well. I noticed a large painting hanging over the fireplace, a still lake on a placid sunny day. I asked if it was your mother's work and your father said yes, and then he walked us around the Great Room, showing off her other paint-ings. They were hanging in the kitchen, in the dining room, in the stairwell—all over the house, really. Your mother was very talented, and your father was so proud of her.

I asked if you were still drawing, if you were still interested in art, and your father said no. "The doctors talk about Teddy's World and

Flora's World. And there is not much overlap. Teddy's world had swimming pools. Flora's world has Finger Lakes. Teddy's world had lots of drawing. Flora's world has lots of cousins who help raise animals."

I was a little afraid to ask my next question, but I knew I'd have regrets if I didn't.

"What about Anya? Is she part of Flora's world?"

Your father shook his head. "No, Flora does not see her *anya* anymore." Just for a moment, I think he sounds disappointed. "But it is better this way, of course. This is how things ought to be."

I couldn't really think of how to respond, so I looked outside to a half-dozen goats grazing in the grass. I could still hear your cousins playing upstairs, and suddenly I recognized the pitch and cadence of your voice. You sounded just like I remembered. Your cousins were acting out scenes from *The Wizard of Oz*. You were Dorothy, and one of your cousins was the mayor of Munchkinland, and she was inhaling helium from a balloon to make her voice sound funny. "Go see the Wizard!" she croaked, and you all exploded with giggles and laughter.

Then all five of you came marching downstairs singing "We're Off to See the Wizard." Your oldest cousin was twelve or thirteen and the youngest girl was a toddler and the rest were somewhere in between. And even though your hair was longer and you were wearing a bright blue dress, I recognized you immediately. Your face was exactly the same. Everything surrounding your face was different—but all the soft sweet features were still there. You were carrying a drum major's baton and waving it high over your head.

"Flora, Flora, wait!" your father called. "There are guests. Mallory and Adrian. From New Jersey, remember?"

The other children stopped and gaped at us, but you didn't make eye contact.

"We're going outside," the oldest explained. "We're going to the Emerald City and she's Dorothy."

"Flora can stay," József said. "Someone else can be Dorothy."

They all started protesting, listing all the reasons why this was un-fair and impractical, but József chased them out the door. "Flora stays. The rest of you come back later. Half hour. Go play outside."

You sat beside your father on the couch but still wouldn't look at me. It was really remarkable how a blue dress and slightly longer hair shifted my entire perception of you. Just a few subtle cues and my brain did the rest of the work, flipping all the switches. You used to be a boy. Now, you were a girl.

"Flora, you look beautiful," I said.

"*Muy bonita*," Adrian said. "You remember me, too, right?"

You nodded but kept your eyes on the floor. It reminded me of meeting you for the first time, during my job interview. You were drawing on your sketch pad, refusing to make eye contact. And I had to work a little bit to coax you into a conversation. It felt like we were two strangers again, like we were starting over.

"I heard you're starting first grade next month. Are you excited?"

You just shrugged.

"I'm starting school, too. I'm going to be a freshman in college. At Drexel University. I'm going to study education and become a kinder-garten teacher."

Your father seemed genuinely happy for me. He said, "That's good news!" and he spoke for several minutes about studying agriculture back in Hungary, at the University of Kaposvár. And I felt like he was overcompensating, trying to talk over all the awkward silences.

So I tried a different approach.

"I brought presents." I passed my shopping bag across the room, and I swear I've never seen a child look so afraid to receive gifts. You actually backed away from the bag, like you thought it might be full of snakes.

"Flora, this is good," your father said. "Open the bag, please."

You pulled the wrapping paper off the first package—a box of water-color pencils in a spectrum of colors. I explained that they worked like regular pencils, but if you added a drop of water you could brush the color around, and the effect was a bit like painting. "The lady at the art store said they're really fun. In case you want to try drawing again."

"And beautiful colors," your father said. "What a nice, thoughtful gift!"

You smiled and said "thank you" and then ripped the wrapping paper off the next gift—six waxy yellow fruits nestled in a box of white tissue paper.

You just stared at me, waiting for an explanation.

"Don't you remember, Flora? They're star fruits. From the grocery store. Remember the day we bought a star fruit?" I turned to your father. "Some days we would walk to the supermarket for Morning Activity, and I would let Flora buy anything she wanted. Any one food item, but it had to be a food we'd never tried before, and it had to cost less than five dollars. So one day she picked out a star fruit. And we thought it was incredible! It was the best thing we'd ever tasted!"

Only then did you finally start nodding, like the story sounded familiar, but I wasn't sure if you really remembered. And by this point I felt embarrassed. I wanted to take back the tote bag—I really didn't want you to open the last gift—but it was too late. You yanked off the paper and revealed a small booklet called MALLORY'S RECIPES that I printed up at a copy shop. I had typed up the ingredients and instructions for all the desserts we'd made together—the cupcakes and the cream cheese brownies, the magic cookie bars and the homemade chocolate pudding. "In case you ever want to have them again. In case you want to try any of our old favorites."

And you said thank you, very politely, but I could tell the book would be put away on a shelf and never touched.

Suddenly, it was painfully clear to me why your doctors didn't want me to visit—it was because *you* didn't want me to visit. You were trying to forget me. You didn't really know what happened in Spring Brook—but you knew it was bad, you knew the subject made grown-ups uncomfortable, you knew people were happier discussing other things. So you were moving on, you were adapting to your new life. And with a stunning shock of clarity, I realized I would never be part of it.

The front door swung open and your cousins came marching back into the house, triumphantly singing "Ding-Dong! The Witch Is Dead!" as they stomped upstairs to the second floor. You turned to your father with a pleading expression and his face turned pink. He was mortified. "This is very rude," he whispered. "Mallory and Adrian drove a long way to see us. They brought you very generous gifts."

But I decided to let you off the hook.

"It's fine," I said. "I don't mind. I'm glad you have so many friends, Flora. It makes me really happy. You should go upstairs and play with them. And good luck in first grade, okay?"

You smiled and said, "Thanks."

And I would have appreciated a hug, too, but I had to settle for a quick wave from across the room. Then you bounded upstairs after your cousins and I could hear you gleefully joining them for the final lyric, shouting over all their voices: "Ding-dong, the wicked witch is deeeeeeead!" And then you all exploded with shrieks and laughter while your father stared at his boots.

He offered us more tea and coffee and said he hoped we would still stay for lunch. He explained that your aunt Zoe had made *paprikas*, a kind of goat stew served with egg noodles. But I said we should probably get going. I explained that we were driving to Canada, that we were visiting Niagara Falls and Toronto. Adrian and I lingered just long enough to be polite, and then we gathered our things.

Your father could tell I was disappointed. "We can try again in a few years," he promised. "After she gets older. After she knows the whole story. I know she will have questions, Mallory."

I thanked him for allowing me to visit. Then I kissed him on the cheek and wished him good luck.

Once we were outside, Adrian put his arm around my waist.

"It's okay," I told him. "I'm fine."

"She seems great, Mallory. She looks happy. She's on a beautiful farm with family and nature. It's gorgeous here."

And I knew this was all true, but still.

I guess I'd hoped for something different.

We followed the winding gravel driveway back to Adrian's truck. He walked around to the driver's side and unlocked the doors. And I was reaching for the handle when I heard soft footsteps running up behind me and I felt the full force of your body slamming into my hips. I turned around and you wrapped your arms around my waist, burying your face in my belly. You didn't say anything but you didn't need to. And I've never been more grateful for a hug.

Then you broke away and ran back to your house, but not before pushing a folded sheet of paper into my hands—one last drawing to say goodbye. And that was the last time I ever saw you.

But I know your father is right.

Some day in the future, ten or twenty years from now, you will become curious about your past. You will read the Wikipedia article about your abduction, you will discover all the rumors surrounding your case, you may even spot one or two inconsistencies in the official police report. You might wonder how the Maxwells fooled so many people for so long, or how a twenty-one-year-old addict pieced together the whole puzzle. You're going to have questions about what really happened in Spring Brook.

And when that day comes, this book will be waiting.

I'll be waiting, too.

ACKNOWLEDGMENTS

I'm so glad Will Staehle and Doogie Horner agreed to draw the pictures in this book—long before I had a contract, or a manuscript, or even a clear idea of what the pictures might be. Thanks, guys, for your faith in this project, for the terrific artwork, and for keeping me company during the lockdown.

Dr. Jill Warrington shared valuable insights on addiction, recovery, and prescription painkillers, and her daughter Grace alerted me to some embarrassing first-draft mistakes. Rick Chillot and Steve Hockensmith gave me close reads and good ideas. Nick Okrent helped with fairy tale research. Deirdre Smerillo helped with legal questions. Jane Morley gave me information about distance running. And Ed Milano shared additional perspective on addiction and recovery.

Doug Stewart is a great guy and a fantastic literary agent. He introduced me to Zack Wagman, a terrific editor who suggested many smart ways to improve this book. Thanks also to: Maxine Charles, Keith Hayes, Shelly Perron, Molly Bloom, Donna Noetzel, and everyone at Flatiron Books; Darcy Nicholson at Little Brown UK; Brad Wood and the rest of the Macmillan sales force; Szilvia Molnar, Danielle Bukowski, and Maria Bell at Sterling Lord Literistic; Rich Green and Ellen Goldsmith-Vein at the Gotham Group; Caspian Dennis at Abner

Stein; Dylan Clark, Brian Williams, and Lauren Foster at Dylan Clark Productions; and Mandy Beckner and Liya Gao at Netflix.

Above all I am grateful to my family, especially my mother (who worked as a nanny), my son Sam (a cross-country runner), and my daughter Anna (who has been drawing since she could hold a pencil). I couldn't have written this book without them. Or without my wife, Julie Scott, who has this book's dedication and all my love. XOXOXO.

The Art of
HIDDEN
PICTURES

An interview with Will Staehle and Doogie Horner

By Jason Rekulak

Back at the start of 2020, I called my good friends Will Staehle and Doogie Horner with an unusual proposition: "I want to write an illustrated mystery, and I want you guys to draw the pictures. What do you say?"

They both said yes, which was a miracle, because at the time I had little idea what my illustrated mystery might be. All I had were a few simple parameters: I wanted the pictures to contain clues, so they rewarded careful attention. I wanted the art to change or evolve throughout the book, so the images remained fresh and surprising. And I knew (for practical purposes) the illustrations would need to be black-and-white, because publishers would balk at printing a full-color novel.

So I knew a lot about the form of *Hidden Pictures*, even if I didn't know the actual story. I must have brainstormed a dozen different concepts before landing on the idea of a five-year-old drawing creepy pictures. I've always loved horror movies, and kids drawing creepy pictures is such a classic horror movie trope. I realized I could model my story after *The Turn of the Screw*, and I started drafting pages.

I didn't have a contract with a publisher or a deal or even the promise of a deal. But as I stumbled through my first draft, Will and Doogie started drawing pictures. We were all determined to submit a complete manuscript to editors, with every illustrated clue in place. And there is no way I ever would have finished *Hidden Pictures* if these two guys hadn't been willing to go along for the ride.

The three of us spent close to a year working on the novel; I wrote all of the words, Doogie drew all of the pictures created by Teddy, and Will drew all of the (more mature, sophisticated) pictures created by

"Anya." The final book has fifty-four images, but to arrive at those perfect fifty-four, the illustrators created close to three hundred (or probably more; I'm sure there were drafts they never shared with me). Many of the rejected illustrations are perfectly chilling in their own right, and the three of us recently sat down to discuss them.

Jason Rekulak: Doogie, you've worked for many years as an art director and professional illustrator. How did you unlearn all of your good habits and start drawing like a five-year-old?
Doogie Horner: I'm right-handed, so I drew with my left hand. This eliminated a lot of my motor learning. Also, my son Kirby was five years old at the time, so that helped.

So Kirby inspired you?
DH: All the time. You look at art by real kids, and it's all good. It's all interesting. Same thing with dancing; every kid is a good dancer. So yes, I observed my son's art and analyzed what makes it good. One thing is confidence. Every line is laid down with assertion. Secondly, the art is made without any judgment or expectations. A kid isn't afraid of making bad art, and they're not hoping to make good art. They create without fear or hope.

That's the mindset you need when trying to draw like a kid. I tried to mimic the small, specific choices almost all kids make: They treat the bottom of the page like the top of the ground. They draw hair as individual strands; same with grass. And they don't draw what they see, they draw what they think. I don't know if that makes sense, but they don't draw from observation is what I mean. They draw from their own understanding of what things are.

With the character of Anya, you had an opportunity to design the novel's signature monster. How did you arrive at her look?

DH: I knew that if we could nail this design, the whole book would work. The challenge was that kids draw very simply. So the design needed to be simple, but still specific and powerful. I tried to make the shading on her face look accidental, like random scribbles. I drew lots and lots of versions.

What was the hardest illustration to draw?

DH: The one where Anya is being strangled by an unseen murderer [in Chapter 8]. For this illustration to read clearly, the hands needed to be drawn in a gripping position that a kid would never draw. Kids always draw hands flat, a circle with lines radiating from it. I must've done fifty versions of this drawing.

Do you have a favorite illustration in the book?

DH: The grave digger [in Chapter 7]. It's so creepy. While I was drawing it, I tried to induce a trance state by staying up very late, drawing
lots of pictures quickly, without thinking, and listening to the Stooges'
song "I Wanna Be Your Dog" over and over and over. The practice took
me to a strange place. The pictures really got inside my head. I didn't
feel normal for a while, but I think I'm better now.

**I'm not so sure! But let's shift gears. Will, you've designed book
jackets for dozens of bestselling authors—everyone from
Stephen King and Michael Crichton to Madeline Miller and
V. E. Schwab. Is it a big pivot to go from cover design to drawing
interior illustrations?**

Will Staehle: Yes, totally. Doing the interior art for *Hidden Pictures*
was a really different experience for me. When I'm working on cover
designs, the goal is to give a small taste of the book in an interesting package for those quick in-store glances—so the work tends to be
iconic and simplified. But with interior art, the goal is to help along
the narrative, which is very detail-oriented. So this allowed me to
work some different muscles!

You were responsible for what we started calling the "Murder Sequence"—the twenty-one-illustration cycle that tells the story of Flora's abduction and Margit's murder. How did you approach the style?

WS: Initially, I tried to attack the problem logically, and I wondered what the work of a possessed five-year-old might look like. I imagined something on the level of a talented high school artist.

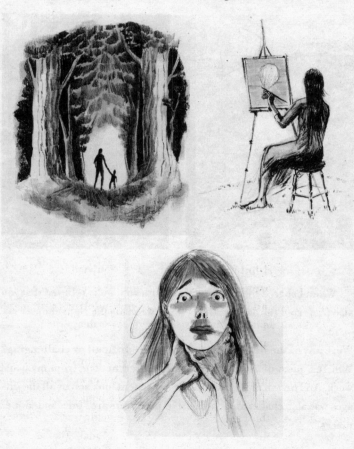

But as these early pieces came together, they felt a little flat and cartoonish. So I tried some other options. I wanted to push the art into a more moody and cinematic direction, and I leaned into a more layered, macabre, and collaged technique. This new look was closer in style to the black-and-white artwork of the great Dave McKean.

When I shared the two directions with you, I was relieved that you also preferred the darker style. I think we made the right choice!

Were any of the illustrations particularly difficult or challenging?
WS: Yes, most of them! It was such a different style from my usual work. And on top of that, keeping a consistent look across all the images was also challenging, as most of my covers are "one-and-done" pieces.

Do you have a favorite illustration in the sequence?

WS: I have two. The long-shot silhouette of Ted Maxwell in the woods [in Chapter 15] is one of them. I love how iconic that image is. My other favorite is Ted dragging the dead body through the woods [in Chapter 11]. That was a really challenging pose to lay out and execute, but I think the gestures and the shading worked really well.

You've done so many of my favorite book covers—so I was thrilled when Flatiron agreed to let you take a swing at the cover for *Hidden Pictures*. Can you tell people how you approached the job? And maybe share some alternate versions?

WS: It's always a little stressful when taking on a cover project for an author you know personally. You obviously want to do your best work for them. So for *Hidden Pictures* I tried a variety of visual approaches. Initially, I played with some optical illusions to lean into the "hidden pictures" concept. One of these comps was *almost* the final cover.

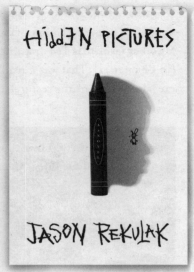

I also tried some covers with silhouettes of Teddy, an all-type cover, and finally the cover you are holding in your hands right now. I like the childlike icons in the title, juxtaposed against the moody and realistic background image. I've also always liked the crayon-drawn trees in the forest. A subtle wink, but a nice detail for those who spotted them.

DH: I spotted them!

We all spotted them! I love those trees. And thank you, guys, I never could have done this without you.